THE
TATTERED
COVER

Also by Ellery Adams:

The Secret, Book, and Scone Society Mysteries:
The Secret, Book & Scone Society
The Whispered Word
The Book of Candlelight
Ink and Shadows
The Vanishing Type
Paper Cuts
The Little Lost Library
The Tattered Cover

Book Retreat Mysteries:
Murder in the Mystery Suite
Murder in the Paperback Parlor
Murder in the Secret Garden
Murder in the Locked Library
Murder in the Reading Room
Murder in the Storybook Cottage
Murder in the Cookbook Nook
Murder on the Poet's Walk
Murder in the Book Lover's Loft

THE TATTERED COVER

ELLERY ADAMS

KENSINGTON PUBLISHING CORP.
kensingtonbooks.com

This book is a work of fiction. Names, characters, businesses, organizations, places, events, and incidents either are the product of the author's imagination or are used fictitiously. Any resemblance to actual persons, living or dead, events, or locales is entirely coincidental.

To the extent that the image or images on the cover of this book depict a person or persons, such person or persons are merely models, and are not intended to portray any character or characters featured in the book.

KENSINGTON BOOKS are published by

Kensington Publishing Corp.
900 Third Avenue
New York, NY 10022

Copyright © 2025 by Ellery Adams

All rights reserved. No part of this book may be reproduced in any form or by any means without the prior written consent of the Publisher, excepting brief quotes used in reviews.

Without limiting the author's and publisher's exclusive rights, any unauthorized use of this publication to train generative artificial intelligence (AI) technologies is expressly prohibited.

All Kensington titles, imprints and distributed lines are available at special quantity discounts for bulk purchases for sales promotion, premiums, fund-raising, educational or institutional use.

Special book excerpts or customized printings can also be created to fit specific needs. For details, write or phone the office of the Kensington Special Sales Manager: Kensington Publishing Corp., 900 Third Avenue, New York, NY, 10022. Attn. Special Sales Department. Phone: 1-800-221-2647.

Library of Congress Card Catalog Number: 2025937905

KENSINGTON and the KENSINGTON COZIES teapot logo Reg. U.S. Pat. & TM Off.

ISBN-13: 978-1-4967-4382-4
First Kensington Hardcover Edition: November 2025

ISBN-13: 978-1-4967-4384-8 (ebook)

10 9 8 7 6 5 4 3 2 1

Printed in the United States of America

The authorized representative in the EU for product safety and compliance is eucomply OU, Parnu mnt 139b-14, Apt 123
Tallinn, Berlin 11317, hello@eucompliancepartner.com

This book is for all the Barnes and Noble booksellers. Thank you for recommending my books, placing them on your "staff picks" shelf, or putting them into readers' hands. This former Barnes and Noble bookseller is very grateful.

Come back! Even as a shadow, even as a dream.
—Euripides

The Secret, Book, and Scone Society Members

Nora Pennington, owner of Miracle Books
Hester Winthrop, owner of the Gingerbread House Bakery
Estella Sadler, owner of Magnolia Salon and Spa
June Dixon, Guest Experience Manager, Miracle Springs Lodge

Relevant Miracle Springs Residents

Sheriff Grant McCabe
Deputy Jasper Andrews
K9 handler Paula Hollowell
Sheldon Vega, Nora's friend and bookstore employee
Charlie Kim, part-time bookstore employee
Jack Nakamura, proprietor of the Pink Lady Grill
Gus Sadler, Estella's biological father

Those Present at the Psychic Reading

Lara Luz, medium
Enzo Russo, Lara's partner
Allie Kennedy, mystery author
Grace Kim, Charlie's mom and urgent care nurse
Terry Rowe, pharmacist

Chapter 1

Dear Sir or Madam, will you read my book?
It took me years to write, will you take a look?
—The Beatles

Nora Pennington had never seen so many people inside Miracle Books at once. Her heart swelled as she gazed around, taking in the glorious sight.

Customers stood in the aisles, milled around the stacks, and occupied the folding chairs arranged in tight rows in the Readers' Circle.

Earlier that day, Nora's new employee, Charlie Kim, had loaded the old and well-loved upholstered chairs onto a furniture dolly and wheeled them into the stockroom. After clearing away the coffee table, he'd stood back and examined the space.

"It's gonna be a tight squeeze," he'd said.

Nora hadn't shared his concerns. "We probably won't have a very big crowd. It's our first time trying this type of event, so I'm keeping my expectations low."

The event had come together at the last minute. Allie Kennedy, a cozy mystery author, planned to be in the area visiting her in-laws and thought Miracle Books would be the perfect place to promote her new release, *The Dry Bar Murders*. After receiving a call from Allie's publicist, Nora had agreed to host the event. Then she'd immediately called Charlie.

Making no effort to suppress her panic, she'd said, "I'm sorry to bother you on a Sunday, but this is an emergency. We're about to have our first author event. Ever."

"Ever?"

Charlie had every right to be surprised. After all, Miracle Books had been in business for over a decade.

"I know, it's crazy that we haven't had one before, but we really don't have the space for a big audience. I can't cram an author into the children's section while their audience sits on the alphabet rug like a bunch of preschoolers. And until you came along, I didn't have the staff to manage an author signing. That might change now. I got an email from another publicist this morning, asking for a last-minute booking on Halloween, and I'm going to say yes."

"This is so cool, Ms. P. How many days do I have to promote the event?"

"Er, Allie Kennedy is coming next Saturday."

Charlie had let out a low whistle. "I'll do what I can, but we're gonna need help spreading the word."

Nora's friends had been happy to oblige. Estella Sadler hung a flyer at her salon, June Dixon added the event to the activities calendar placed in every guest room of the massive hotel where she worked as Guest Services Manager, and Hester Winthrop had immediately offered to bake treats for the occasion.

Nora's next move had been to run a Google search on mocktail recipes. Allie Kennedy's cozy mystery series featured an amateur sleuth who'd opened a bar serving nonalcoholic beverages in a small town known for its cocktail lounges and microbrewery pubs. It was a clever premise, and when Nora read reviews of the latest release in the series, it was clear that many readers wanted to visit a dry bar like the one Allie Kennedy had invented.

Allie's publicist promised to FedEx copies of *The Dry Bar Murders* as well as the other five books in the series, but Nora hoped Allie's readers wouldn't limit their purchases to cozy mysteries, so she ordered a dozen mocktail recipe books, easy appetizer cookbooks, and a few books on entertaining at home.

The orders required expedited shipping, which was expensive. As Nora placed the order, she prayed the event would be a rousing success.

"If I let her down, she might kill a bookstore proprietor in her next book," she'd murmured, feeling anxious about the whole affair. "What if no one comes?"

After pouring herself a glass of wine, Nora had sat in her partner's living room, wondering if it had been a mistake to agree to the event.

When Nora first bought the town's old train station building, she'd dreamed of opening a bookstore that would become a social hub for the residents of Miracle Springs and an unforgettable destination for visitors. Though she'd succeeded in both of these endeavors, she wanted more. She wanted the shop to be a mecca for readers *and* writers of every genre, and fantasized about Miracle Books becoming a fixture on promotional tours.

However, staying open past six in the evening required staff.

Until recently, Nora had worked nine hours a day for six days a week. Her part-time employee, Sheldon Vega, worked from ten to three. With Charlie joining their team, it was possible to host more after-hours events.

Charlie showed up after school three days a week and worked until closing. He also worked Saturdays. The high school senior was bursting with ideas for special displays, storytime activities, and new menu items. He was naturally shy, but he'd been coming out of his shell more and more.

"Second best thing you ever did, hiring that kid," Sheldon had said as he opened another folding chair in preparation for Allie Kennedy's signing. The event was scheduled to kick off at six thirty, but attendees were arriving early to claim a seat.

"The best thing was investing in these chairs, right?" Nora had teased.

Sheldon had thrown a scowl her way. "*I'm* the smartest decision you ever made. If I quit, who'd make the perfect latte? What would happen to the singles who come to mingle at my book club? Who'd use silly voices and throw glitter like a stripper during story time? Who'd charm the money right out of people's wallets?"

"You know I couldn't survive without you. You're as much a part of this store as"—Nora had looked around—"that throw pillow."

The throw pillow in question was embroidered with the text IF YOU DON'T HAVE ANYTHING NICE TO SAY, COME SIT BY ME.

Sheldon's face had split into a wide grin. "I bet we sell that by the end of the event. Cozy mystery readers like their tea and cats. Their crocheting and cupcakes. But they also love a flawed protagonist, a juicy murder, and a bit of snark. Allie Kennedy gives them all of that and more. *Esta noche va a ser asombrosa.* Tonight's going to be amazing."

Two hours after this declaration, Nora was behind the checkout desk, sliding the needlepoint pillow into a bag along with four Allie Kennedy paperbacks.

"Thank you for coming," she said, handing the receipt to a woman in a pumpkin-orange coat.

"Thank *you*. I haven't had this much fun in years! My friend, Doris, had to twist my arm to get me out of the house. I mean, it's October! It's dark by six. And it's cold. From now until April, I spend my nights the same way. I fix myself a drink and read by the fire. Then I watch something on Acorn or BritBox before going to bed. But Doris wouldn't let me stay home."

Doris put a hand on her friend's shoulder. "Betty, Nora won't get out of here until midnight if we don't let her be."

Swiveling, Betty paled at the sight of the long line. "Oh, I'm sorry!" Turning back to Nora, she said, "Quick question. Will you be having more events like this?"

"Yes. In fact, we're having another one this month. We're celebrating Halloween with a Fun and Fright Night. We're going to have activities for young readers, a reading from a horror writer, and a talk and demonstration by a psychic medium named Lara Luz."

"A medium?" Betty cried. "Count me in! What about you, Doris?"

Doris looked a little frightened. "I don't know. I don't read horror—it gives me nightmares—so I think the medium might be too scary for me. The only place I want to talk to my dead relatives is at the cemetery."

Nora handed Doris her bag of books. "The readings are a separate ticketed event, but Lara's talk will focus on her childhood. She's going to explain how she suddenly became sensitive to other presences and how that changed her life." Raising her voice so that everyone waiting in line could hear her, Nora gestured at the display table to the right of the checkout desk. "If you're interested in Lara's memoir, we have plenty of copies."

A man stepped out of line to pick up one of the blue books with a white birdcage on the cover. The door of the antique-style metal cage was ajar, and little white birds flew toward a pair of cupped hands. Some of the birds looked like doves, while others had straggly feathers and sharp beaks. Nora believed the cover designers were trying to convey the message that not all of the medium's encounters were positive. Several people purchased copies of Lara's memoir and told Nora how much they were looking forward to meeting the medium.

"Do you believe in this stuff?" a man asked Nora. "Spirits talking through people or whatever it is she does."

"I've never met a medium before, so I don't know what to expect," Nora admitted. "However, I started reading her book last night, and Ms. Luz has some fascinating stories. I have no doubt that her event is going to be *very* entertaining."

The man thought this over. "Maybe, but I hope folks don't get upset. There's a reason why we say people have passed on. If we accept the idea that they've gone on to another place, we can move forward with our lives. Trying to reach that other place? It doesn't seem right."

The woman standing next to him plunked a copy of *Too Many Voices: Memoir of an Empath* on the counter. "I'm buying this, hon, but you don't have to read it." She gave her husband a pat on the arm and then smiled at Nora. "Can I bring the book back when Ms. Luz is here? I want her to sign it."

Nora swiped the woman's credit card. "Of course."

It was almost nine by the time the last customer left. Nora was exhausted but elated because it had been a banner evening for sales. Not only had all but one of Allie Kennedy's books sold, but at least ten customers had bought Lara Luz's memoir as well.

Nora locked the front door and turned the corner of the fiction section. She heard her best friends—Hester, Estella, and June—moving around in the ticket agent's booth. Once upon a time, a clerk had sat on one side of the pass-through window, distributing train tickets to travelers. Now the narrow space was the bookstore's kitchen. It was a tight squeeze for two people, let alone three.

Peering around the doorway, Nora said, "I hope you're not cleaning."

June shoved something in the fridge and closed the door. "Just putting the extra food away so it doesn't spoil. Estella's wiping the counters. Sheldon was serving mocktails as fast as he could, so everything's super-sticky."

"Even the money." Estella put a pile of cash on the window ledge. "The tip jar was overflowing. Looks like these bills took a bath in lime juice."

"I wiped chocolate buttercream off a few too," Hester said, raising her voice to be heard over the splash of sink water. "Someone's cupcake got decapitated on that counter." She held up the knife she'd just washed and flashed Nora a maniacal grin. "It was a case of cupcake murder!"

June pointed at the knife. "I bet the baker is the killer in Allie's latest book. We should read it for book club and find out."

"I'll order more copies," Nora said. "Now, I love you gals, but you need to get out of this kitchen. Go home and put your feet up." She pointed at Estella. "Especially you."

The corners of Estella's red lips turned down. "Ever since I started showing, people treat me like I'm fragile. Just because I'm pregnant doesn't mean I'm weak."

"You're a steel magnolia, but you've been on your feet all day taking care of clients." Nora studied her friend. Despite her flawless makeup, Estella looked tired.

"No need to worry, because we're done," June said, propelling Estella out of the ticket agent's booth. "If you're looking for Ms. Kennedy, she was browsing the cookbook section."

Nora gave each of her friends a hug, wished them a good night, and headed past the mystery and romance sections. She paused to switch off lamps in the horror and science fiction nooks before continuing on to the cookbook and gardening shelves. As she walked, her eyes scanned the familiar lines and angles of her store. She wanted to add a display of signed books but could see there wasn't a square inch to spare.

Her eyes roved over the colorful spines marching along the polished wood shelves. On the end of every row, more books filled endcap displays. Waterfall shelves and tables stuffed with books were scattered throughout the store. Every space was being used. There was no room for a new display.

"I'll just hang them from the ceiling," she muttered under her breath.

Turning the corner of nonfiction, she arrived at Young Adult, which was a dead end surrounded by bookshelves on all sides. This was a popular hangout spot for Miracle Springs teens. They loved to sit on the floor with their backs pressed to the shelves and a rainbow of books spread around them. They'd read cover blurbs, scroll through social media on their phones, or do homework. They drank hot chocolate and scooped up new releases from their favorite authors on pub day. They were some of Nora's best customers.

Because this section was in the far corner of the store, the teens rarely disturbed other shoppers. As a rule, they weren't loud, but a large group of teenage girls could produce a cacophony of sound that wasn't always in keeping with the bookstore's calm vibe.

However, the sound Nora heard as she approached Allie Kennedy's turned back wasn't a happy one. It was sniffling.

Allie Kennedy was crying.

"She was here! At my event!" Allie whispered into her phone. "I won't let her ruin everything. Never again. *Never!*"

Nora retreated as quickly and quietly as she could and helped Charlie reposition one of the bulky upholstered chairs that made up the Readers' Circle.

When they were done, he pointed at the front of the store. "We still have a customer. He just wants to look at the new release table before he goes. I didn't even know he was in the store. Bro just popped out of the bathroom while Sheldon and I were pushing the cartload of folding chairs. You should've seen Sheldon. I thought he was going to need an adult diaper."

Nora wagged a finger at Charlie. "One day, your body will age, and you'll be sorry you ever made fun of your elders."

"Sheldon's not old. He's only in his sixties."

Nora nodded in approval. "Better."

Catching movement out of the corner of her eye, Nora turned to see Allie approaching. The mystery author looked completely composed. Her eyes were dry, and she'd applied a fresh coat of lipstick. Glancing between Nora and Charlie, she put a hand on her chest and said, "I'm *so* sorry! Am I keeping you from closing?"

"Not at all," Nora assured her. "We still have a customer up front. I'm going to see if he needs any help. When you're ready to head out, I can unlock the door for you."

"If it's okay, I'd like to grab a mocktail book before I go."

Nora led Allie to the front to find a man in a gray coat and newsboy cap standing by the display of Lara Luz's books. He held a copy in his hands and was so engrossed that he didn't look up until Nora was almost on top of him. He seemed embarrassed to be caught reading the memoir and hastily put the book down on the table.

"I hope I haven't overstayed my welcome," he said. "I'll settle up now and be on my way."

As Nora walked behind the checkout counter, she noticed the abrupt shift in Allie's demeanor. The light had leached from her face, and her eyes looked haunted. She stared at the table of memoirs as if hypnotized.

Hoping to distract her, Nora smiled at the man in the cap. "When I was in college, I always stayed at the library until they kicked me out. There's just something about being in the company of books. But it's about to get noisy because Charlie's plugging in the vacuum."

The man tapped his temple. "I should do that before my wife gets home. She's out of town, visiting her sister." He turned to Allie. "She'll be devastated when she hears you were in Miracle Springs and she missed meeting you. But she won't suffer for long. Next Wednesday's her birthday. She's going to be so surprised when I give her a stack of your books."

Allie smiled sweetly. "You're a gold-star husband—sitting through this entire event just to get books for your wife."

"I enjoyed it," the man enthused. "I had no idea how much research goes into writing a mystery novel, and I love the idea of a dry bar. Even though I come from a long line of folks who were far too fond of alcohol, I never got the hankering for it. Which of these mocktail recipe books do you recommend? I'd like to get one for my wife."

Allie picked up a white book with a ginger-colored drink on the cover. "I've heard great things about this one."

The man read the title out loud. "*Zero Proof: 90 Non-Alcoholic Recipes for Mindful Drinking.*" He flipped through the pages. "I have no idea what mindful drinking means, but the pictures are very pretty. I'll take it."

The man gestured for Allie to proceed him to the checkout counter. When Nora tried to make a present of the mocktail book to thank the mystery author for such a successful event, Allie refused.

"You bent over backwards to arrange everything at the midnight hour. I'm not used to showing up to a signing to find food, drinks, and a packed house. When my publicist hears how amazing it was, she's going to want to add Miracle Books to all of her authors' tour stops."

This was exactly what Nora wanted to hear. "Sounds good to me," she said as she shook Allie's outstretched hand.

Allie stepped aside, and the man placed his books on the counter. "My wife and I might come back to see the psychic lady. Maybe she can reach out to my granddaddy and ask him where he hid those Civil War coins he showed us when we were kids."

Nora accepted the man's credit card, glancing at his name before swiping it. "Ms. Luz offered to host a special session after her talk and book signing. It's limited to six people, so if you're really interested, you can sign up using the link on our website." She passed over his card and his bag of books. "Thank you, Mr. Gentry."

While Allie waited for Nora to complete the transaction, she opened the cover of one of Lara Luz's books to read the info on the dust jacket flap. Whatever she saw there unnerved her, and the book slipped right out of her hand.

It fell to the floor, landing in a pool of shadow under the display table. The darkness distorted the images of the birds on the cover until they no longer resembled songbirds. The blue background became more of an ashen gray and the black shapes looked like a cauldron of bats.

Mr. Gentry bent over to retrieve the book. As he put it back on the table, he gazed at Allie in concern. "You're white as a ghost. Did something in that book scare you?"

Allie waved off the idea. "I was just worried that I damaged the book."

Nora didn't believe her, and she could tell that Mr. Gentry didn't either.

"It's okay if you got spooked," he said kindly. "I was joking when I mentioned talking to my granddaddy. The dead should be left in peace. Even if we could communicate with them, nothing good could come from reaching across the void. Such things go against nature. Against God."

Hoping to put an end to the discussion, Nora came out from behind the counter and opened the front door. The movement caused the sleigh bells hanging on the back of the door to clang loudly, shattering the tranquil atmosphere.

As Nora put a hand over the bells to subdue the noise, a cold wind swept into the shop, depositing a scattering of dried leaves on the carpet.

"'Wind from the North, do not go forth,'" said Mr. Gentry. "That's what Granddaddy used to tell us. He was a fisherman, and he had sayings about every which way the wind blew."

Pale-faced and wild-eyed, Allie shouted, "Goodnight!" and hurried out of the store.

Mr. Gentry shot a nervous glance at the table of Lara Luz books. "Maybe the dead are always speaking. Maybe only some of us can hear them."

He stepped outside, holding onto his cap to keep the wind from carrying it off. Hunching his shoulders against the bite in the night air, he scuttled up the street. The lamps lit his way until he turned into an alley and disappeared.

As soon as he was out of sight, Nora's fingers closed around the skeleton key in the door. She heard the satisfying click as the lock engaged.

Turning aroumd, she saw that one of Lara Luz's books was on the floor, splayed open to a chapter called "Voices from Beyond."

Nora scooped up the book and closed it with a firm snap. The knife-sharp air seemed to follow her to the back of the store, sinking in her bones with a dampness that felt very much like dread.

Chapter 2

Nothing haunts us like the antiques we didn't buy.
—Anonymous

Nora woke to one of those October mornings that had social media influencers quoting Lucy Maud Montgomery. Spent leaves drifted down from the trees and the mountains were draped in gowns of gold and crimson. There was a Jackson Pollock wildness to the splashes of bright colors. Wispy clouds spiraled across the vivid blue sky.

"Good morning, beautiful," said a low, gravelly voice from the bedroom doorway. "I have coffee."

Nora smiled at her partner, Sheriff Grant McCabe. "You're even better-looking than this view, and that's saying something."

McCabe laughed. "Are you talking about me or the coffee?"

"Both."

Raising the mug to his lips, McCabe whispered, "She's into us right now, but as soon as she sees her breakfast, we'll be yesterday's news." He passed her a very full mug. "You'd better take a sip. I don't care about the carpet, but you're wearing my favorite Cat Dad T-shirt."

Nora did as he asked. The coffee was rich and creamy. She felt more awake after a single taste. "Where are my feline alarm clocks?"

"Sharing a square of sunlight in the living room. They woke me up hours ago, so I fed them and closed the door to keep them from getting to you. I tried making eggs in a basket again, and I think I nailed it this time."

Following him into the kitchen, Nora saw two plates with perfectly browned pieces of rye toast. In the middle of each piece of toast was a fried egg, topped with a sprinkling of salt and pepper.

"You really know how to spoil a girl," Nora said.

McCabe carried the plates to the dining table. "To be completely transparent, this is an apology breakfast. I have to miss our hike today."

"Something come up at work?"

"The complaints we've been getting about illegal dumping near the AT trailheads? We got another one, so I'm meeting with the park ranger today to come up with a plan."

The Appalachian Trail attracted thousands of visitors to the area every year, and Nora always found it ironic that some of the same people who hiked the trail to commune with nature saw nothing wrong with depositing their garbage in the woods.

Miracle Springs had a large group of volunteers who spent hours picking up trash from the local trails. McCabe told Nora how the head of this group had asked the sheriff's department to track down the person or persons responsible for dumping construction debris, including pieces of drywall and roofing shingles, in the woods.

"Once is bad enough," the man had said to Deputy Jasper Andrews. "But it's happened three or four times now, and never at the same trailhead. The last time, the crap was right near the river. A bunch of drywall ended up in the water. I'd like to find this guy and throw *him* in the river. Better yet, I'd like to smear his body with honey and drop him in the middle of the forest—see how he feels about getting lots of attention from our bear population."

McCabe had been passing by the interview room when he heard the man's comment and stopped to ask for more detail. He repeated the conversation to Nora.

"The man was happy to elaborate. He said, 'I've already talked to Ranger Nick. His department has a few trail cameras here and there, but Bob the Builder hasn't shown up on any of them'."

The reference to the children's show character had elicited a laugh from Andrews but not McCabe. Like so many small, picturesque towns across the state, Miracle Springs was experiencing a building boom. The surge of new homes and businesses was great for the economy, but it also caused plenty of headaches. In Miracle Springs, those headaches were inevitably brought to McCabe's attention.

"Where did the latest incident take place?" Nora asked.

"Around sunset yesterday, two women coming down the western mountain path saw a cargo van pull into the parking lot. The ladies had heard about the Midnight Dumper from another hiker, which is why they decided to hang out in their car and keep an eye on the van. The park closes at dusk, so they thought it was pretty suspicious that someone driving a van had arrived minutes before the light was gone."

Nora put her fork down. "This story's making me nervous."

"Don't worry, the ladies are fine. Anyway, someone got out of the van and opened the back door. The ladies saw a bunch of black garbage bags and a pile of wood planks inside the van. But the driver suddenly shut the doors and started walking toward their car. That's when they hightailed it out of there."

"Good for them. I mean, amateur sleuthing is fine for cozy mysteries, but in real life, it can get you killed."

McCabe gave her a knowing look. "I'm glad you recognize the hazards. However, these ladies may have given us our first lead. On their way out of the parking lot, they noticed a Porky Pig sticker on the van's left rear window. There was a decal on the other window, too, but they couldn't see it clearly. Either way, that pig might help us find the culprit."

"Are you calling him the Midnight Dumper because he's throwing his trash in the woods after dark?"

McCabe swallowed his last bite of food before answering. "Midnight dumper is a generic term for people who toss environmentally hazardous waste everywhere but the landfill or recycling center. It's illegal, and when we catch this guy—the ladies are positive the van driver was a man—he *will* be arrested and charged with a crime."

"What would motivate someone to do this? Laziness? A desire to get revenge against poison ivy?"

McCabe gave her a wry grin. "As someone who gets a rash just by looking at the stuff, I wouldn't mind if it disappeared off the face of the earth, but my guess is the dumping's about money. The guy probably doesn't want to pay the county fees."

Nora fetched the coffeepot from the kitchen and refilled their cups. "Why go through all the trouble to dump it in the woods? Why not wait until it's dark and then toss it in a bin behind a business? Or leave it in an alley? It doesn't make sense."

"People break the law for all kinds of reasons, and it never fails to amaze me how illogical some of those reasons are," McCabe replied. "I should get a move on. After I fill the ranger in on our possible lead, I'm going van hunting."

"And I'm going treasure hunting," said Nora. "I'll do a sweep of the flea market parking lot before I go inside. If I see Porky Pig, I'll call you." She pointed at his plate. "Leave that. I'll clean up."

After McCabe headed out, Nora perused the classifieds, hoping to find a promising yard sale.

There weren't nearly as many listings as there were in the summer, and most of the ads mentioned furniture, children's toys, and electronics. No books.

Nora's phone pinged. She smiled as she read the text from

Bea, a flea market vendor who came from a big family of antiques dealers, pickers, and auctioneers.

Bea was Nora's best supplier of shelf enhancers—Nora's made-up term for knickknacks that added interest to any bookshelf. Over the years, the two women had become friends. **The collection of bookends I told you about is in my truck. Come into the barn and get my keys. When you're done looking through the boxes, you can tell me how great I am.**

The text was all the motivation Nora needed to finish her coffee and get dressed.

McCabe's cats, Magnum and Higgins, didn't even crack an eye as she gave them a quick pat before leaving.

She climbed into her truck, which was arguably the most recognized vehicle in town. The truck had lived several lives, starting as a mail truck in 1973 before becoming an ice cream truck in the nineties. After that, it was the work vehicle for a local mason, who'd invested in a new engine and tires before suddenly deciding to retire.

Nora fell in love with the truck at first sight. As soon as it was hers, she paid for a custom paint job. Now, colorful books danced over a canary-yellow background. The shop's name, done in bold cobalt letters on both side panels, was impossible to miss.

Seeing the truck for the first time, Sheldon had said, "It looks like a big banana."

A customer had overheard the comment and repeated it to a friend. And just like that, everyone in town started calling Nora's yellow truck the Banana Van.

Nora drove to the big red barn and circled the parking lot. She saw only two vans and neither had a Porky Pig sticker on the rear window.

Then she remembered the designated vendor lot behind the barn. Most of these vehicles were vans or trucks because the vendors had to haul items to the flea market every Sunday.

Bea's truck would be there too, which gave Nora an excuse to walk around the lot, examining rear windows.

By the time Nora parked and walked to the barn's massive front doors, the flea market had officially opened.

Miracle Springs was a sleepy place on Sundays. Despite the hundreds of visitors who traveled to their little valley in western North Carolina, most of the local businesses were closed on Sundays. For the locals, this was a day of worship or family gatherings. A day to enjoy the natural beauty of the blue mountains and pristine forests surrounding their town.

On October Sundays, the orchards and pumpkin patches could expect large crowds, but the farmers wouldn't open their gates until after noon. Until then, people would bide their time browsing the flea market. They'd meander up and down the aisles, sipping hot cider, socializing, and buying small trinkets they probably didn't need.

Once inside the big red barn, Nora picked up her pace. She shopped the flea market like she was in a grocery store at the start of the apocalypse. She strode directly to her favorite booths, engaged in a round or two of good-natured haggling with the vendors, and moved on.

Having seen an announcement in the paper, Nora knew that the flea market was "going pink" in honor of Breast Cancer Awareness Month. There would be pink balloons for the kids, pink lemonade and cotton candy at the snack bar, and all the vendors would be donating fifteen percent of their profits to support local women battling the disease.

Skirting around a family entranced by a display of Barbie dolls, Nora headed to a booth in the middle of the barn. After examining the vendor's offerings, she bought a vintage copper creamer and pitcher, a pottery vase with an ochre glaze, and a cloisonné dresser mirror. The mirror glass was covered with spots, but she believed that baking soda or toothpaste could remove them. If she restored the glass, she could charge double what she'd just paid for the lovely little mirror.

She browsed her other favorite booths, but their items were either too expensive or too big to sit on a bookshelf. She was very tempted by a display of vintage Halloween noisemakers, but the vendor couldn't give her the discount she needed to turn a profit.

"Sorry, hon. You know I'd take off more if I could," the vendor said.

"I know you would. And I bet you'll sell those before the hour is up. The tambourine with the black cat is so cute."

The vendor shrugged. "People can be funny about black cats. I've got two of them—sweetest animals you've ever seen—but I keep 'em inside on Halloween. Some suspicions die hard."

The vendor turned to help another customer, and Nora continued on to Bea's booth.

"I see you're giving money to my competition again," Bea groused, eyeing the bags in Nora's hands. "My truck keys are by the register. Poke around the boxes while I take care of these fine folks."

The fine folks in question were a pair of smartly dressed tourists. Nora didn't usually notice people's jewelry, but it was hard to miss the man's flashy gold wristwatch or the ring on the woman's finger, which had a diamond the size of a hummingbird egg.

The woman was clearly interested in an antique teapot with pink cabbage roses. Seeing the sparkle in her eyes, Nora knew the woman would be leaving the flea market with that teapot and several other items from Bea's Bounty. Bea was the best salesperson Nora had ever met.

"I can sell a cape to Superman," Bea liked to boast.

Bea was a petite woman with stringy blond hair, pale blue eyes, and skin that had seen plenty of sun without a drop of sunscreen. Bea had no interest in books unless she could sell them, but she was one of the few people who'd been kind to Nora when she first moved to Miracle Springs.

Others had seen the burn scars swimming from Nora's right hand all the way up to her temple and shied away. Those who didn't immediately shun her whispered about her behind her back.

Not Bea. She'd treated Nora just like any other customer from the start. Her gaze didn't linger on Nora's scars, and she never asked Nora why she was missing half of her pinkie. She didn't dig for details about the car accident that caused the scars, nor did she judge Nora when she told the story of how she'd caused the accident that had nearly killed a young mother and her toddler. Of how she'd had too much to drink and ended up on the wrong side of the road. How she'd pulled the mother and child from their burning car and, after spending months in a burn unit, ran away from her old life to start a new one in Miracle Springs.

Even after Bea learned Nora's darkest secret, she treated her the same. She haggled with gusto and sent word to her family members that the owner of Miracle Books was looking for vintage shelf enhancers. From that point on, Bea always set special items aside for Nora.

Their casual friendship had recently become something more meaningful. In September, the two women had worked together to appraise a book collection belonging to an octogenarian hoarder. When the old woman's death turned into a murder investigation, Nora had leaned on Bea for support.

September had been a hard month for Nora. A longtime customer had been killed, and Nora had been the victim of arson. Someone had thrown a Molotov cocktail through the bedroom window of her tiny house, and the damage had been substantial. Nora loved Caboose Cottage, which was what the locals called her converted train car parked on a grassy knoll behind the bookstore, and she was devastated to see flames shooting out of the window and smoke billowing through a hole in the blackened roof.

She was grateful to McCabe for sharing his house with her, but she missed her sunny little kitchen and her cozy little living room. She missed having coffee on her pint-sized deck and hearing the train rumble over the tracks behind her house.

With any luck, the repairs would take two or three months. Until then, Nora would live with McCabe and his cats.

Exiting the barn through the vendor's door, Nora circled the parking lot until she was satisfied that none of the vans had a Porky Pig sticker. Returning to Bea's truck, an old blue Ford with a bed cab, Nora unlocked the tailgate and raised the window.

There were six boxes labeled BOOKENDS.

Nora reached into the first box, unwrapped a pair of bronze owls, and grinned.

"You'll fly off the shelf. Ha, ha. What? You don't like puns?"

After admiring the owls for a few more seconds, Nora unwrapped a pair of art deco dogs, windmills, flower baskets, Dutch girls, and anchors. The next box contained pirates, kittens, eagles, lions, and Abraham Lincoln.

There was no need to unwrap the rest. Bea had said the entire collection was good, and Nora trusted her completely.

Back inside the barn, Nora found Bea arranging a group of silver serving pieces on the table. It was the exact place where the teapot had been moments before.

"I knew you'd sell that teapot. What else did that couple buy?"

"Oh, just some bits and bobs." Bea's eyes held an impish gleam. "The husband didn't want to take fragile items on the plane, but when I generously offered to cushion everything in bubble wrap, the wife was happy to add the creamer and sugar bowl to the ticket."

A man approached the booth and picked up a silver bowl with a scalloped edge. "My mama had one just like this," he said. "I sure wish we'd kept more of her things, but we just don't have the room."

"Happens to the best of us, hon," Bea said. "But you don't need a silver bowl to remind you of your mama. You thought of her just now when you saw this one. I bet you see things that make you think of her all the time."

"I sure do." The man jerked a thumb toward the center of the barn. "A lady at the candle booth was talking about hummingbird cake. That was my mama's favorite. Her birthday's coming up, and I'd love to make it for my brothers and sisters, but I'm useless in the kitchen."

Bea scribbled a name and number on a piece of paper and handed it to the man. "Give my cousin a call. She'll make you a hummingbird cake that'll make your mama smile down on you from heaven."

"That's mighty kind, thank you." The man was about to walk away when he turned back and asked Bea if she had a business card. "My older sister is downsizing, and she's got a bunch of Victorian art pottery and Depression glass to sell. I'd feel good about her selling it to you."

"That's what it's all about," Nora said as the man walked off. "Those connections."

Bea smirked. "You'd be surprised how many folks bring up dead relatives in hopes that I'll give them a discount. They get all teary-eyed while they're telling me about dear so-and-so. I might take off a few bucks if their performance is good, but that's it."

An image of Lucille, the old woman who'd died in September, rose in Nora's mind. As she gazed at all the items in Bea's booth, she thought about all the artifacts of Lucille's life. Soon they'd be sold to strangers.

"Hey." Bea touched her arm. "How've you been doing?"

Nora wrote out a check as she answered. "I still think about Lucille and everything that happened more than I want to."

"Give yourself a little time." Bea put the check inside her cash box. "By the way, I really like your window display. It's got Halloween vibes but in the cutest way."

The storefront window was a point of pride for Nora and Sheldon. They changed it every month, and an area of the stockroom was devoted to decorations from windows past. They even had mannequins, which Sheldon kept in the attic of the house he shared with June because they gave Nora the creeps.

For the October window, Sheldon had suggested they opt for cute and colorful over creepy.

"The skeletons we've used in years past can stay in their damned closets," he'd said. "I have an idea, and I want it to be a surprise. Charlie can help me set it up."

Nora had gone home for the night and returned to the shop the next morning to find a round table in the middle of the display window. The table was draped in purple velvet and a crystal ball sat in the center. A plush owl wearing a midnight-blue turban touched the tips of his wings to the crystal ball. Silver letters pinned to an indigo background said, I SEE BOOKS IN YOUR FUTURE.

Instead of traditional Halloween reads, Sheldon had filled the window with new releases from every genre. There was a stack on the table next to the crystal ball, and the rest were arranged in clear acrylic floating shelves, their covers facing the street.

The owl's crystal ball was actually a disco ball they'd purchased for a previous display. As it spun around, it threw slivers of light onto all the books. The effect was magical.

Nora was about to thank Bea for the compliment when she let out a gasp of horror. "Oh, God. The window."

"What's wrong with it?"

"A psychic is coming to the store on Halloween to promote her book. She might be offended by our display."

Bea smiled at a woman showing interest in a pair of botanical prints before moving closer to Nora. "A psychic? Have you done this sort of thing before?"

"No. Yesterday was our very first author signing, and it was a hit. That event happened by chance, and the one we have planned for Halloween came together almost overnight. After getting an email from the psychic's publicist, I reached out to a bookseller friend in Raleigh to see if they knew of any North Carolina authors with fall- or Halloween-themed books who'd be willing to come here for a signing. I figured having authors from different genres would get more customers in the door."

"Aren't these events planned months in advance?"

"For bigtime authors, yes, but small press and self-published authors often get the short end of the stick when it comes to publicity. The psychic we invited? Her memoir was published by a small press, so she was thrilled to be included in our Halloween event."

Bea put a hand to her heart. "I want to come! How does this work? Do you sell tickets?"

"You only need a ticket if you want to attend her reading. That event, which is limited to six people, will take place after the author talk and signing."

"What kind of reading?"

The woman who'd been examining the botanical prints said, "Excuse me. Is this your best price?"

Nora gave Bea's car keys a shake. "Go help her. I need to load the bookends into my truck anyway."

By the time she made the transfer, Bea had sold the prints and was busy convincing a young man that vintage barware was incredibly trendy.

Nora waited for the man to choose between a set of brass bar tools in a wooden box and a crystal cocktail shaker with a silver top. Bea offered him a deal for both, but in the end, he settled for the box of tools.

"Tell me quick," she said when he was out of earshot.

"What kind of reading? Tarot cards? Palm? Auras? What's she gonna do?"

"Lara refers to herself as a conduit. When she touches certain people, she hears messages that are meant for them. It doesn't work for everyone. Less than half of the people she touches, actually. There's no guarantee she'll have a message for you."

Grabbing the cash box, Bea jerked the lid open and pointed at a stack of bills. "I'll take my chances. How much is a ticket?"

A couple pushing a stroller stopped to admire a vintage toy car. The car, a red tin convertible, was driven by a man in a suit. His dog sat in the passenger seat.

"Oh, my gosh!" the woman cried in delight. "This dog looks just like Rex."

The man's face broke into a grin. "He really does. How much is it?"

While the couple examined the car, their curly-haired toddler reached for the pink balloon tied to his wrist and reeled it in closer. The balloon snagged on the propeller of a vintage toy plane and popped.

The sudden bang ricocheted off the concrete floor, startling everyone in the vicinity. Across the aisle, someone shrieked, and Nora heard the high, tinkling sound of breaking glass.

The toddler in the stroller began to wail. As the mother bent down to comfort her son, her purse slipped off her shoulder. The crocheted strap caught the edge of the toy car, knocking it off the table.

The car struck the floor, dislodging the dog and sending it skittering into the aisle where it was crushed under a large black boot.

Staring at the debris of the broken toy, Bea snapped the cash box shut. Then she turned to Nora and said, "Bad things come in threes. I don't need a crystal ball to know a sign when I see one. I'm not going within a mile of that psychic, and you shouldn't either."

Nora was surprised by Bea's vehemence. "Why not? I don't believe in that stuff, so it doesn't scare me."

Bea's fingertips brushed the burn scar on the back of Nora's right hand. "Ever since your accident, you've been a magnet for violence." Her voice was taut with urgency as she gripped Nora's wrist. "It doesn't matter what you believe. If this psychic deals in death, you *should* be scared."

Chapter 3

Why was the wind always trying to tell me something? Something I didn't want to hear!
—V. C. Andrews

Halloween arrived, and with it, an abrupt change in the weather.

For most of October, the air had been crisp but not too cold. When the sun was shining, it gilded the trees with a soft, golden light. On windy days, leaves danced in the streets and the scent of woodsmoke wafted through the air. Even the rainstorms had been gentle. They'd moved in slowly from the west, soaking into the thirsty soil and stringing silver beads onto every cobweb.

On this last morning of the month, early risers had pulled back their curtains to discover dark skies and frost-kissed lawns. Residents who jogged or walked their dogs were startled by the slap of frigid air on their faces.

When Nora looked out the window and saw one of McCabe's neighbors bundled up in a down jacket, she immediately checked the forecast on her phone.

"It's going to be a high-volume coffee day," she told McCabe over breakfast.

"At the station too," McCabe said. "It's a good thing I

bought two extra machines last month. I wish they tasted like the bookstore's coffee. That brew is special."

Nora smiled. "It's all Sheldon. If I made you a latte, it would be just fine. But if Sheldon made you a latte, it would be absolutely delicious."

McCabe pointed at the window. "I feel bad for the kids. They'll have to wear coats over their costumes tonight and really hustle if they want to get a bagful of candy before they turn into ice cubes. According to the paper, a polar vortex has dipped into our region, and it's just sitting there, pushing cold air at us. Maybe our Midnight Dumper will stay inside this weekend."

"Did he strike again?"

McCabe grunted. "Last night. I forgot to tell you because we started watching that Agatha Christie remake and I got totally caught up in whodunit."

"I wish Poirot could help you find the litterer. Did he dump construction debris again?"

"Yes, but he didn't park in a public lot this time. He carted the trash to the woods near the RV campground. The campground manager is livid, and I don't blame him." McCabe expelled a sharp, frustrated breath. "I thought we'd have this guy by now. I hate the idea of park rangers and volunteers spending so much time cleaning up after this jackass." He put a hand over Nora's and gave it a squeeze. "Maybe you could ask the psychic when he'll strike next."

"Sorry, but you didn't buy a ticket for the reading. The event has sold out."

McCabe turned Nora's hand over and kissed her palm. "I thought I had an in with the woman who owns the bookstore."

"You don't want the residents of Miracle Springs thinking you're susceptible to bribery."

"Good point. So, who are the lucky ticket holders?"

Nora thought about the list sitting next to the register at the bookstore. "Most are from Miracle Springs. There's Hester, Estella, and Grace Kim. Grace is Charlie's mom. She bought two tickets, so she must be bringing a friend. Charlie thinks it's probably another nurse from the urgent care office where she works. The fifth person is a woman I've never heard of, and the sixth person is Terry Rowe."

"The pharmacist?"

"Yes. He lost his wife last year, so he might be looking for comfort—for a way to deal with his grief. And I'm not saying he needs to deal with it. A year is a drop in the bucket when the person you love most dies."

McCabe's expression turned somber. "You can tell he's had a rough time. He's lost a bunch of weight, and he's gotten very quiet. Before his wife passed, he was jollier than Santa. I couldn't pick up a prescription without hearing one of his cheesy cop jokes."

"He told me a book-related joke whenever I went in too—and never the same one twice. He prepared material for his customers like an actor getting ready for the opening night of a play."

"Maybe it *was* an act—something he did to convince the world he was okay while his wife's health deteriorated."

Nora's heart constricted at the thought. "Terry and Deanna didn't have kids. Now he's all alone. Do you ever worry about that? I mean, it's just you and me? If something happened to one of us, the person left behind could end up just like Terry."

McCabe gestured to where Higgins and Magnum were curled up together in the cat bed. "We'd have our fur babies."

"I'm serious."

"I am too," said McCabe. "We talked about this. We're child-free for many reasons, and pets can keep us company in our old age. Does Terry have a pet?"

"I don't know. Maybe Lara will tell him to get one."

McCabe glanced at his cats, his eyes softening with affection. "I never wanted a pet, but here I am, surrounded by cat furniture, toys, treat jars, and litter boxes. I know how to get cat puke out of the carpet. I can trim their claws without needing a trip to the ER. And I sleep better with their little warm bodies on the bed. We're a family, the four of us." He looked at Nora. "One day, they'll pass on, and I'll be a mess. But another animal will need rescuing, and as long as you're on board, I'll keep bringing them home."

"If people knew what a softie you really are—"

"My authority would be seriously undermined. You're the only one I trust with my cat dad identity. Now, go to work, sell a ton of books, and I'll see you tonight." After leaving the table, he dropped a handful of treats into the cat bed. "You guys are so spoiled. You don't even have to say trick-or-treat."

He was almost out the door when Nora shouted, "Don't forget the candy for the station!"

McCabe smacked his forehead. "What would I do without you?" Retrieving the bags from the pantry, he examined the selection of fun-sized candy Nora had picked up from the grocery store a few days ago. She wondered if he'd notice that the assortments were all nut-free. When she'd asked what kind of candy his staff liked best, he'd rattled off several kinds. Upon hearing that Deputy Paula Hollowell loved candy bars with nuts, Nora made a mental note to buy the exact opposite.

Nora and the truculent K9 handler had disliked each other from the moment they'd first met, and now that Hollowell was dating Hester's ex, Deputy Andrews, Nora's aversion had grown even stronger.

The feeling was clearly reciprocal. Hollowell went out of her way to make life difficult for Nora and her friends. She'd pull them over for not coming to a complete stop, driving four miles over the speed limit, or having an expired inspection sticker. She paraded Rambo, her huge black German Shepherd, outside their businesses. The dog intimidated their customers, and when Nora complained to McCabe that many of the young kids visiting her shop were scared of Rambo, he promised to speak with his deputy.

When he raised the subject with Hollowell, she acted surprised and insisted that she and her partner patrolled the area around the bookstore as part of her regular duties. That was all.

"What a load of horseshit," Nora had said upon hearing Hollowell's reply. "You don't see the side of her that other women see. She acts like a different person around you and the male officers. She's chummy with all the guys—a real team player—but she'd cut off any woman at the knees."

"She seems to get along with her female colleagues just fine."

Nora had tried to suppress her annoyance and failed. "You didn't think she had designs on Andrews, either. And now they're together."

"What Hollowell and Andrews do outside of work is none of my business," McCabe had snapped. "They're two consenting adults who happen to like each other. If Hester is okay with it, then why are *you* upset?"

"Hester doesn't like it any more than I do. Not because she wants to get back together with Andrews, but she just doesn't want him to get hurt," Nora had retorted.

McCabe had shrugged. "As long as their relationship doesn't impact their work, I don't give it any thought. Maybe you should try thinking about Hollowell a little less."

It was good advice, but the K9 handler was like a fly banging against the inside of the window glass—too irritating to ignore.

Nora knew she was being petty when she didn't buy the candy Hollowell preferred, but she didn't care. She'd sat across the table from the woman—a suspect in a murder investigation—and seen the glee in Hollowell's eyes. The deputy had done everything in her power to prove Nora's guilt, including twisting the truth to suit her own narrative.

"Stop letting her walk around in your head," Nora told herself as she dressed in a black sweater and skirt with a pink spiderweb design. She braided a fabric spiderweb into her hair and admired the result in the mirror. Then she grabbed her coat and drove to the bookshop.

After switching on the lights, she put on the Halloween playlist Charlie had created. She sang along to "Zombie" as she brewed coffee and tidied the shelves and display tables.

"Hester is a kitchen witch!" Sheldon shouted when he breezed in at quarter to ten. "Look at these muffins!"

He opened the lid of a large bakery box with a flourish, revealing a dozen green muffins with monster faces.

"They're vegan monster muffins." He put the box aside and opened another. "These cuties are mummy muffins. The bandages are made of cream cheese frosting. And *these* are my favorite."

The final box held chocolate muffins. On the dome of each muffin, Hester had piped the letters R.I.P. in vanilla icing.

"They're called Death by Chocolate. Watch this." Sheldon plated a muffin and then cut it in half. A small pool of red liquid oozed out onto the plate. "Raspberry puree blood. *Muy lista.*"

Sheldon popped a piece in his mouth and gestured for Nora to help herself.

The muffin was soft, rich, and sweet. "If this is what she made for the daytime crowd, I can't wait to see what she'll bring tonight."

"She's using the same flavors for bite-sized cupcakes. No wrappers. No mess. See what I mean? *Muy lista.*"

Fridays were always busy at the bookstore, but a cold and blustery Friday meant even more customers. Visitors from the Lodge practically ran from the trolley stop, eager to escape the weather. As soon as they entered Miracle Books, they lined up for coffee or claimed one of the soft reading chairs.

"This feels like a hug," an elderly man told Nora, patting the arm of the mustard-colored chair.

An hour later, he was still there, contentedly sipping a cappuccino while paging through Henry Winkler's memoir. When Nora walked by, he said, "I came in with my wife, but I may never see her again. The two things she can't live without are antiques and books. I never thought I'd give up the ghost on Halloween, but when she shows me everything she wants to buy, it might just be the end of me."

His wife appeared at the checkout counter fifteen minutes later balancing a stack of books, two candles, and a pair of bookends shaped like wirehaired fox terriers.

"Can you wrap the bookends so my husband can't tell what they are?" she asked Nora. "I'm going to give them to him for Christmas. Our dog looks exactly like these bookends. Her name is Pippa, and she's the love of my husband's life."

When the couple finally departed, they were holding hands.

Watching them through the window, Nora thought about Terry Rowe, and how he no longer had someone's hand to hold. Standing there, looking out at the gray sky, she was in danger of succumbing to gloomy ruminations. Luckily, a woman looking for not-so-scary Halloween picture books distracted her.

"I'm the cool aunt, and I'm watching my sister's kids tonight. We're going to make indoor s'mores and read books out loud around our tiny tabletop fire pit."

Nora grinned at her. "You *are* the cool aunt. Let's find you some equally cool books."

The rest of the day passed quickly. At three, Sheldon went home for a brief siesta, and Charlie took his place in the ticket agent's booth.

At five, Nora closed the shop.

She and Charlie placed card tables in different areas of the store and stacked copies of the guest authors' books on each table. The author of the children's book, a woman named Maeve Sullivan who bore a close resemblance to Ms. Frizzle, would kick off the evening with a reading of her book, *The Pumpkin Patch Pact*.

Nora had already sold a dozen copies of the charming story about an unlikely friendship between a scarecrow and a white crow, and she expected to sell more after Maeve's reading.

She was in the middle of setting up the horror novelist's table when he called to say that he wouldn't be there after all.

"I'm so sorry! I drive an EV and my battery died. I'm waiting on a tow truck, but I'll never make it in time."

After wishing him luck with his car situation, Nora pocketed her phone and went to find Charlie.

"We've lost our horror writer to car trouble, but I think we'll still have a packed house."

At five thirty, Hester and Estella appeared at the delivery door, their arms laden with pink bakery boxes. June showed up a few minutes later.

"The ghouls are all here," she said, hugging Nora, Hester, and Estella in turn.

Hester offered her a cupcake. "I didn't think you were coming tonight."

"I'm skipping the reading because my faith isn't down with fortune-telling, but there's nothing wrong with listening to Lara's story," June explained before turning to Nora. "How can I help?"

Nora asked her to supervise Charlie and Sheldon, who were arranging the folding chairs into wobbly rows, and headed to the front. She'd just finished tidying the display table when someone knocked on the door.

Night had fallen. The sky was a deep indigo. Shadows darkened the trees and hovered in the alleyways. The light above the bookstore entrance shone down on a woman with white-blond hair.

Nora opened the door and invited Lara Luz and her male companion inside.

Lara was a short, round, pale-faced woman in her late fifties. Freckles danced over the bridge of her nose, and she had pronounced furrows on her forehead. She was bundled in a lavender puffy coat, and her hat and scarf were a darker shade of purple.

She looks like a tea cozy, Nora thought.

She smiled and introduced herself.

"This is my boyfriend, Enzo Russo," Lara said with a sniffle. She dug a tissue from her coat pocket and pressed it to her nose. Her gray eyes were red-rimmed and watery. "I've been fighting a cold all week, and I'm losing. But I'll make it through tonight."

Enzo placed a meaty hand on Lara's shoulder. "You just need some tea, babe."

Nora gave him the once-over. Though he wasn't much taller than Lara, he was powerfully built with thinning black hair combed back off his forehead. Whenever he moved, his gelled hair reflected the light like an oil slick. He wore a leather jacket that amplified his broad shoulders, black pants, and V-neck gray sweater. Strands of black chest hair curled over the neck of his white undershirt, reminding Nora of fuzzy spider legs.

"Let's go to the back," she said to Lara. "I can get you a cup of tea or coffee—whatever you'd like."

Very few book lovers could wander through Miracle Books for the first time without going starry-eyed or sighing in delight. Their gazes would move from shelf to shelf, taking in all the genres and sub-genres and special displays. They'd touch book spines, pick up vintage knickknacks, and smell the scented candles.

Lara and Enzo didn't seem very interested in their surroundings until they reached the Readers' Circle and Lara spied the table featuring her memoir.

"How nice," she said before coughing into her hand.

The cough sounded like a seal bark, and when Sheldon heard it, he retreated into the ticket agent's booth, eager to put distance between himself and the guest author.

Enzo also moved, but in the opposite direction. He walked right up to the food table and said, "Cupcakes! Are these for us?"

"They're for everyone." Nora handed him a small paper plate. "What can I get you to drink?"

"Espresso for me. Herbal tea for Lara," Enzo mumbled around a mouthful of cupcake.

While Sheldon got started on their orders, Nora introduced Lara to her friends.

Estella hung back, eyeing Lara's red nose and watery eyes with apprehension. She put a protective hand over her baby bump while giving Lara a friendly wave.

Sheldon served the drinks, and Enzo downed his espresso in two gulps. The temperature didn't seem to bother him at all. While Lara sipped her tea, he devoured three more cupcakes and regaled them with stories of Halloweens from his childhood. He chattered nonstop, only pausing to see if Lara needed tissues or a lozenge.

"No, honey, I'm fine." She moved her hand to her throat and gave Nora a plaintive look. "Would it be okay if my talk is more like fifteen minutes instead of thirty? I want to be sure I have enough energy for the readings."

Nora agreed as affably as she could, but inside, she felt a stirring of uneasiness. She'd already lost her horror author to car trouble, and now her second author was sick. Was the night destined to be a disaster?

"You're catastrophizing," Sheldon singsonged in her ear. "I can tell. Have a cupcake before Enzo eats them all. Is it me, or does he remind you of a very hairy Shrek?"

Nora let out a snort of laughter and returned to the front to unlock the door.

Maeve, the children's book author, was the first person to enter. She gave Nora a big hug and gazed around in delight. "What a fabulous store! Where do you want me?"

Nora led Maeve to the Children's Corner. When she checked on her ten minutes later, Maeve was warming up her audience by asking them about their best friends. There were only a handful of children present, but those who listened to Maeve's story loved it so much that they begged her to read it a second time.

She happily complied, signed copies for her new fans, and then joined the audience waiting to hear Lara speak.

From his place in the ticket agent's booth, Sheldon gave Nora a thumbs-up, and she faced the crowd.

"Happy Halloween, everyone," she began. "I want to thank Maeve Sullivan for enchanting us with her charming story of friendship. We still have a few copies of *The Pumpkin Patch Pact*, so grab yours while you can. And now, I'd like to introduce Lara Luz, the author of *Too Many Voices: Memoir of an Empath*. Lara is joining us from Greensboro, where she lives and works as a psychic medium."

In the front of the store, the sleigh bells jingled. Charlie was manning the checkout desk, and the shop was so quiet that Nora could hear his muffled greeting. A moment later, Deputy Hollowell appeared in the Readers' Circle. She threw a frown at Nora before sitting in one of the few available chairs.

What the hell is she doing here?

Focusing on friendlier faces, Nora continued speaking. "Lara is a bit under the weather tonight, so I'm going to share a few fascinating facts from her memoir before turning the program over to her."

Though the sleigh bells rang again, Nora kept talking.

"Lara's childhood in rural Michigan was rather unremarkable. That is, until one summer day when she and her dad went fishing. They loved to fish together and would often spend hours out on the lake. But one Saturday, when Lara was eleven, they got caught in a storm. Their boat was aluminum, and the air was filled with thunderclaps. Lara's dad raced to get them to shore as quickly as possible."

A woman entered the Readers' Circle. Nora was surprised to see that it was Allie Kennedy, the cozy mystery author who'd been at Miracle Books for her own talk and signing two weeks ago.

What is going on tonight? Nora wondered, acknowledging Allie with a nod. *Is it a full moon?*

Allie didn't notice Nora at all. She was laser-focused on Lara. Her eyes radiated hostility, though Nora couldn't understand why.

Someone in the first row shifted, and Nora realized her pause had gone on too long. Abashed, she murmured a quick "sorry," before resuming the narrative.

"When the boat drew near the shore, Lara's father hopped out and began dragging it onto the sand. By this time, the thunder was deafening, and forks of lightning split the sky. Lara's dad managed to beach the boat. Then he held his hand out to his daughter. In that second before she could take his hand, lightning struck the boat. It swept over the metal and through Lara's body. She collapsed, falling to the bottom of the boat. She wasn't breathing, and her father couldn't find a pulse." Nora waited for a moment, letting the suspense build. "He performed CPR, and miraculously, he was able to bring her back."

As if responding to the story, the overhead lights flickered. From somewhere farther back in the stacks, a light bulb popped.

Someone in the audience let out a soft cry. A woman clapped her hand over her mouth, her eyes wide with fright.

Nora remembered what Bea said at the flea market two weeks ago.

Bad things come in threes.

"And now," she continued, her voice clear and calm. "Lara will tell you what happened next."

Lara got shakily to her feet and placed a hand on Nora's arm for support. The moment her fingers made contact with Nora's bare skin, the space above Nora's missing pinkie tingled wildly.

This phantom sensation had always been a bad portent. A warning.

Nora knew she should be afraid, but her store was full of customers and her guest author was about to speak, so she sat down and listened.

Lara's gaze moved over the crowd. Her voice was little more than a dry rasp as she said, "The day I was struck by lightning, I died. My father brought me back to life, but the girl I used to be was gone. The girl who came back looked like me. She sounded like me. But she was different. And she wasn't alone."

Chapter 4

It seemed incredible that this day, a day without warnings or omens, might be that of my implacable death.

—Jorge Luis Borges

The ghost tingle in Nora's finger refused to subside, so she covered her right hand with her left and squeezed, hoping a bit of pressure would diminish the sensation.

"I didn't hear voices right away," Lara said. "That happened a few months later, on the first day of school. Our homeroom teacher was out in the hall, shaking hands with all the students as they entered the classroom. When it was my turn, she introduced herself and took my hand. She waited for me to say my name, but I couldn't. A voice was whispering to me—a man's voice I'd never heard before. It said, 'be free, little bird,' over and over. I tried to ignore it, but it got louder and louder inside my head."

While Lara paused for a sip of water, Nora scanned the audience. No one moved. No one whispered to their neighbor. Their expressions ranged between curiosity and genuine wonder.

The only exception was Allie Kennedy. Her hostile stare was gone, but the open distrust in her face did nothing to reassure Nora that all was well.

Allie's demeanor combined with the pins and needles feeling

in her finger had Nora on edge. Still, there was nothing she could do but watch and listen.

"The voice in my head got so loud that I couldn't hear the teacher speak to me. Later, my friends said that I looked like I was sleepwalking. My eyes were open, but I was far away. In that moment, I'd become a mouthpiece for another soul. Someone who'd crossed over." Lara drew in a raspy breath and let out a slow and ragged exhalation. "This man had a message for my teacher."

"Oh, my," murmured a woman in the front row.

Lara wiped her nose with a tissue and continued. "This was the only time I heard what a voice from beyond had to say. When they speak to me now, they speak *through* me, and I can't hear them." She reached for another tissue. "When I gave my teacher the message, she dropped my hand like she'd been burned."

"What did the message mean?" asked a man in the third row.

Lara grinned at him. "I don't need to be a psychic to know that you don't like to be kept waiting."

The audience laughed.

Nora's phantom tingle was gone. She lowered her shoulders and took a breath.

"I didn't find out what the message meant until my parents came to school for a conference," Lara said. "My teacher told them that her father had called her his little bird. Before he died, he begged her to leave her husband. The man was a drunk. He'd never been violent, but the danger signs were there. My message was a warning, but it took a broken arm for my teacher to believe that her father had been speaking through me."

A woman in a red coat covered her mouth in shock.

Lara coughed twice before continuing. "In the end, my teacher did file for divorce. Two years later, she remarried and had a daughter. She named her Bridget, but everyone called her Birdie or Little Bird."

This elicited smiles and titters from the audience, but Lara wasn't done yet.

"That was the first time a soul used me as a conduit. I don't know if there's an official term for my gift. I haven't researched it or tried to make sense of it. Some things are beyond explanation." She held out her hands as if beseeching the crowd. "I have to touch a person for my gift to be activated, but if I touched every person in this room, only a few of you would receive a message. When I'm unable to provide a message, I use my empathy and intuition to help people. I've steered many clients away from bad situations and set them on the right road."

Lara was clearly flagging, so Nora motioned for her to sit down while she addressed the audience.

"Does anyone have questions for Lara?"

A man near the back stood up and said, "Do you meet all of your clients in person? I mean, if you have to touch them, I assume online sessions don't work."

"Not for messages, no," Lara agreed. "But I provide online coaching for clients looking for direction."

A young woman in an oversized cardigan said, "Can people get more than one message?"

Lara blew her nose before responding. "No. Once their loved ones have spoken, they're no longer reachable. However, after I've delivered a message, I have a connection with that person and can see what's going on in their lives more clearly than they can."

Nora pointed at an elderly man sitting in the second row. "Last question, please."

"Are all the messages good? Or do the spirits pass on warnings too?" His voice turned tremulous. "Do they tell you if they're in pain? Or being punished for their sins?"

As soon as the words left his mouth, the atmosphere in the room changed. The air grew heavy, and the audience members went very still. Their anxiety was almost palpable.

"Negative entities do make contact, but very rarely," Lara said. "Love is what opens the channel between me and the souls who've crossed over. But sometimes, a person's residual anger is strong enough to bridge the divide. These encounters don't last long because my body senses the threat and jerks me out of my trance. This is why it's crucial for mediums to have someone watching over them. Enzo watches over me."

The couple exchanged tender glances, effectively restoring the equilibrium.

Nora pointed at the table stacked with Lara's memoir and said, "What you've heard tonight is just the tip of the iceberg. Every chapter of Ms. Luz's book is more fascinating than the last. Please purchase your copy before joining the signing line. Thank you for coming, and Happy Halloween."

Enzo got Lara settled at the signing table, brought her a fresh mug of tea, and then stood behind her like a bodyguard.

"He takes such good care of her," June whispered to Nora.

"I'm glad he's here. She looks like she might keel over any second."

For the next thirty minutes, Nora opened Lara's memoir to the title page so that Lara could quickly add her signature before moving on to the next customer.

"Do people ever touch you without your permission?" the woman asked.

"When my book first came out, I did a talk at a local library. Several people tried to grab my hand after I signed their book. A few got a bit aggressive. Luckily, Enzo was there, and he made sure no one else touched me. I bring gloves to all my events now, but I don't think I'll need them tonight. You're all very polite."

The woman with the oversized cardigan was next in line.

"I tried to buy tickets for tonight's reading, but they sold out too fast!" she complained. "I don't necessarily need to talk to someone from the other side, but I need help deciding if I should move across the country with my boyfriend. I'd have to leave everything to go with him. My family. My friends. My job. I don't know what to do."

Lara smiled at her. "If you're willing to drive to Greensboro, I'd be happy to help you. I have online booking, and I have a few open spaces in November. My website is on my card."

The business cards, which were stacked on the corner of the table, were very simple. They included Lara's name, her website URL, and a silhouette of a bird in flight—no doubt inspired by Lara's first experience receiving a message when she was a young girl.

It was obvious to everyone that Lara wasn't feeling well, and Nora's customers kept their interactions to a minimum. The signing line moved quickly, and it wasn't long before the shop began to clear out.

When there were only a handful of customers left, Nora took Charlie's place behind the checkout counter. While he worked on putting the folding chairs away, June offered to bag books for Nora.

In between sales, she whispered, "Why is Hollowell here? She didn't buy Lara's book, and she's acting all chummy with Charlie's mama."

Nora rang up the next customer and wished her a happy Halloween before answering. "Wait a minute. Grace bought two tickets for the reading. You don't think the second ticket was for Hollowell, do you?"

June looked shocked. "No way they're friends. I don't see that viper hanging out with anyone we know, let alone a hardworking single mom in her forties."

"I guess we'll find out in a few minutes," Nora said.

When the last customer left, Nora hung the CLOSED sign in the window.

"I'm gonna head out," June said. "Tyson and I are watching a scary movie. He has to settle for me because Jasmine's on call tonight. I wish he'd hurry up and propose to that girl. I'm ready for grandbabies. With my insomnia, I could knit so many booties that their baby could wear a different pair every day of the year."

"Don't take one of your midnight walks tonight, okay?"

June cocked her head. "Why not? Did you get one of your feelings?"

Nora nodded.

"Are you going to ask Lara about it?"

"No. I'm just here to facilitate. I do *not* need messages from the dead, even if they're totally made up." June was about to leave when Nora grabbed her arm. "Lara touched me. That's when my finger started tingling."

June glanced at the puckered skin of Nora's pinkie knuckle and shuddered. Not because she was disgusted by her friend's injury, but because she was frightened. "Can't you call this off? Lara's sick as a dog, and Estella's not going to stay. She doesn't want to be within a mile of that woman's germs. You could just refund everyone's money. It's only five people. They'd understand."

But Nora had seen how Terry Rowe had hung on Lara's every word, his eyes shining with hope. He hadn't been this animated in ages.

"I can't cancel now. We'll have to power through."

Nora followed June to the back where Charlie and Sheldon were busy restoring the Readers' Circle to its usual setup.

Sheldon shifted the purple velvet armchair a few inches to the left and winced. When he put a hand to his lower back, Nora saw that his knuckles were swollen.

"You're having a flare," she said.

Leaning against the chair, he groaned. "I was fine all day. But I only made three drinks tonight when my joints started protesting."

"Stubborn goat! You never tell me when you're hurting." Nora took his hand gently in hers. "You're going home. June's leaving now too. Ask her to bring you your heating pad and some peppermint tea while you catch up on *Real Housewives*."

Sheldon huffed in disgust. "They're so 2014. I'm watching the new season of *Love Is Blind* like the rest of the cool kids."

"June, will you take this cool kid home? His knuckles are the size of golf balls."

June took one look at Sheldon's hands and bundled him out the door.

"I'm going too. I'm worn out," Estella said as Lara sat down in the purple chair.

Nora told her to grab a copy of *The Pumpkin Patch Pact* from the stockroom. "For your baby's library."

"You're already spoiling this kid," Estella scolded. She gave Hester a hug and walked away.

Hester looked like she wanted to leave too.

"I don't know if I want to have a reading in front of Hollowell," she said. "You know she's here for some nefarious purpose. If she wasn't, why else would she ask Charlie's mom to buy her a ticket? Maybe she's going to drug us, boil us in a cauldron, and eat us for breakfast."

Nora patted the mustard-yellow chair. "If you bow out now because of her, then she wins. I'm going to treat her like any other customer, so she can't bitch about my rudeness to Mc-Cabe."

Hester sat down. Terry took the chair to Lara's left, and Grace took the chair to her right. Hollowell sat between Terry and an empty folding chair. When Nora spotted Allie Kennedy heading for the chair, she hurried over to her. "May I have a word?"

Nora led Allie into the romance section. "I wasn't sure if you realized that this is a ticketed event."

"I bought a ticket using my real name. Allie is a pen name." She pressed her hands together as if in prayer. "Please don't tell anyone. Privacy is really important to me."

Nora said, "Of course. But . . . do you know Lara?"

"I've heard of her, but I've never been to one of her events."

Nora knew she risked alienating Allie with her next question, but after the warning tingle in her finger, she had to ask. "Forgive me for being blunt, but I saw your face during Lara's talk. You looked pretty angry."

Allie shook her head. "I'm going to include a psychic in my next book. I'm here for research. During the talk, I was imagining how I'd write my psychic. She's going to be very unlikeable."

"Ah, I see. Is she the villain?"

"The victim," Allie said. "And no one will be sorry when she's dead."

Nora wasn't sure if she believed Allie. She seemed like a different woman than the upbeat, cheerful writer who'd entertained a roomful of readers two weeks ago.

"I can't pretend to understand how a writer's mind works, but try to remember that Ms. Luz is not a fictional character. Please don't glare at her." Nora smiled to soften her words and waved toward the Readers' Circle. "Let's join the group. I think Lara's ready to start."

While Allie took her seat, Enzo caught Charlie's eye and pointed at the overhead lights, signaling that he wanted them turned off. Lara had made this request via email earlier in the week, which was why Charlie had already positioned a floor lamp behind Lara's chair. Other than the lamp, the only light would come from the sailboat lamp in the Children's Corner.

"Now that we're all settled, we're going to turn off the main lights," Nora told the small group.

As she glanced around the circle, she saw a wide range of expressions. Hester and Grace Kim looked apprehensive. Hollowell seemed mildly curious. Allie crossed her arms and studied Lara like she was an insect under glass. Terry Rowe sat forward in his chair, eager to begin.

Lara blew her nose with a loud honk, and Charlie switched off the lights, plunging most of the bookstore into darkness.

Enzo pulled several objects from Lara's purse and placed them on the coffee table. There was a fresh packet of tissues, a bottle of hand sanitizer, a bottle of nasal spray, and a string of mala beads. Most of the beads were purple, but a few were pale pink or white.

Picking up the beads, Lara said, "Purple is for insight and tranquility. White is for intuition. Pink is for compassion—for opening the heart. I will hold my prayer beads when I take your hands, and you'll feel my fingers moving over the beads. This helps me focus on the energy surrounding you. Not everyone here will receive a message from beyond. Most of you will receive a reading based on my intuition. If I suddenly release your hand, don't be alarmed. I can still speak to you, but I can get overwhelmed by feelings and may need to create a little space."

Enzo tucked Lara's bag under her chair and then stood in a sentry position behind her.

"I'm going to close my eyes and open myself up to the energy that connects our world and the world beyond. Please be as quiet as possible while I do this. I'd also like all of you to focus on what you'd like to discover here tonight. Narrow your thoughts down to the most important question and let it repeat on a loop in your head."

Nora glanced over to where Charlie leaned against the wall near the floor lamp. Dressed in dark jeans and a black shirt, he nearly faded into the shadows. Nora wanted to be equally unobtrusive, so she edged closer to the stacks. She always felt steadier with a row of books behind her.

The silence stretched on as Lara took deep breaths through her mouth. As her shoulders rose and fell, her beads slowly moved through her fingers.

The bookstore was very quiet. The only sounds were the hum

of the refrigerator and a nearly imperceptible buzz from the floor lamp. But outside, the wind rattled the windows and hurdled over the roof. The gusts had been increasing in force all day.

It was eerie to hear the shriek of wind without the accompaniment of rain. It was as if the wind had sprinted ahead of the rest of the storm, determined to wreak havoc on its own.

As the wind let out another howl, Lara opened her eyes and said, "I'm ready."

She reached for Hester's hands first. Hester hesitated, then placed her palms on Lara's palms. Lara closed her eyes and winced. Seconds later, she broke the connection.

"Your people hurt you when they were alive and would continue hurting you if they could. I will not give them the satisfaction of repeating their cruel words. The sooner you reject their memory, the sooner you'll find the happiness you deserve. You must let go of the past to claim ownership of your future."

"Thank you," Hester whispered. "I'll try."

Lara smiled at her. After sanitizing her hands, she offered them to Terry. His hands dwarfed hers, but she gave him a reassuring squeeze and closed her eyes.

When she spoke next, her voice sounded lighter and higher. "Don't be sad, Terry Berry. I'm not in pain anymore. You were my life, and I'll always love you, but it's time to let me go. Be brave, Terry Berry. Be happy again. Joy is waiting."

Lara opened her eyes and blinked several times. She looked genuinely confused.

"*No!*" Terry shouted. "Deanna, wait!"

"I'm sorry, but the connection is broken," Lara said.

Terry began to cry. He hid his face in his hands as his grief spilled out, his sobs thunderous in the quiet store. "I can't let her go," he wailed. "She was my whole world!"

"Look at me," Lara commanded. When he obeyed, she passed him a wad of tissues and said, "Tell me about Deanna."

Terry began to talk about his wife. He spoke for five minutes or so, and when he paused to catch his breath, Lara asked him what Deanna would want him to do with his life.

"She'd want me to keep smiling. To tell my stupid jokes and go out with my friends. She'd tell me to work on my golf game. To get a dog. To sign up for one of those dating apps. But I *can't.*"

"Which one of those things *can* you do?"

Terry thought about it.

"I'm not ready to tell jokes. I could hang out with friends, but I'd probably just bring them down." Terry shrugged. "And the dog? I love dogs, but I'm not home very often. It doesn't seem right to leave an animal alone."

"Can you bring a dog to work?" Lara asked.

Terry was about to say no, but Hollowell piped up before he could.

"You own the pharmacy, right?"

Terry nodded.

"As long as your dog is friendly, doesn't trigger allergies, bark all the time, and is kept in the back, I don't see a problem," she said as if the decision was hers to make. "I read an article about a pharmacist who kept her dog at work. Her customers volunteered to walk it, which was great for everyone. The dog got tons of social interaction, and the customers got fresh air and exercise."

"I like that idea." Terry's face brightened a little. "A dog. I could adopt one from the shelter."

"You'll rescue the dog, and the dog will rescue you," said Lara.

Terry's reading had ended on a high note, and the positivity affected the entire group. Allie was the only one who sat, silently radiating disapproval, as Lara cleaned her hands and reached for Grace Kim.

"I want to hear from my husband," Grace said, clutching the cross pendant at the end of a delicate gold chain.

Lara nodded, and Grace released the pendant and placed her hands on top of Lara's. Both women closed their eyes, and in the silence, the wind reasserted its presence. It banged on the windows and sent shivers through the sleigh bells hanging from the front door.

Nora tried to ignore the sensation that someone was trying to force their way into the bookstore.

It's just the wind. It's not a ghost or a spirit. Just wind.

After a few minutes, Lara said, "The connection isn't strong enough for a long message, but this is what your husband wants you to hear. Grace, you are doing your best, and your best *is* enough. Your husband is proud of you. Your parents are proud of you. Your children are proof of your hard work and success. I see a possible promotion in your future. It will mean more money, but it will also be more demanding. Before you say yes, make sure you can maintain your balance. Look into grants for college. There is money waiting for Charlie."

"Ohhhhh," Grace breathed. In the soft lamplight, her face glowed like a full moon. "That's good news!"

Lara smiled. "Let's take a short break. I need to use the restroom and drink a little tea."

"Let me heat that up for you." Nora carried Lara's mug into the ticket agent's booth and turned on the light. Behind her, in the Readers' Circle, she heard the murmur of voices and the creak of chairs as people stood up to stretch or move around.

Hester followed Nora into the kitchen. "I didn't know what to expect, but this feels . . . real. I don't think I'll ever forget tonight."

Nora dropped a fresh teabag into a clean mug. She'd just finished filling the mug with hot water when the lights went out.

Someone—a woman—let out a shriek.

"It's okay, friends." Nora spoke with forced calm. "The

wind probably knocked out the power. Use the flashlight function on your phones to get back to your seat."

"Lara?" Enzo called out.

"I'm here, honey." Lara's voice sounded small and weary.

When Nora returned to the Readers' Circle with the tea, she found Lara in the purple chair. Her hand was pressed to the back of her neck, and she looked alarmingly pale.

Deathly pale.

"Friends, I think we should give Lara a little space," she said. "Charlie, would you take everyone to the front for a few minutes?"

Charlie took his mother by the elbow and waved at the rest of the guests to follow him. Nora watched the lights from their cell phones disappear around the corner of the fiction section.

Enzo sat down next to Lara and said, "Honey, we need to call this off. You don't look too good."

"I feel really bad. I felt this sharp pain, and now . . . something's not right." Lara grabbed the material of her shirt over her left breast and balled it in her fist. "My heart . . ."

"I'm calling for help." Nora pressed the emergency call button on her home screen. As soon as the operator answered, she asked for an ambulance and rattled off the address.

When the dispatcher asked for more details about Lara's condition, Nora passed the phone to Enzo.

"She has a heart condition!" he bellowed into the phone. "You gotta get here *now*! She can't breathe!"

It was true. Lara was gasping for air. Her hands clutched the collar of her shirt. Her eyes bulged with fear.

Enzo tossed the phone aside and pushed Lara's damp hair off her forehead. "Babe? Can you hear me? *Lara!*"

Nora had no medical training, but she could see that the situation was dire.

"Grace!" she shouted. "Hollowell! Help!"

She heard the muffled pounding of feet and saw a light coming toward her like the headlamp of an oncoming train. Hollowell rounded the corner of the stacks first. Dropping to her knees next to Lara, she shone her light on Lara's face.

Nora shrank away from the sight.

Lara's mouth hung open. A line of drool ran down her chin. Her gaze was lifted, as if she'd seen something in the darkness above the Readers' Circle. Her eyes were glassy.

She wasn't blinking.

She wasn't moving at all.

And when Hollowell placed two fingers on Lara's neck in search of a pulse, Enzo began to scream.

Chapter 5

Survivors look back and see omens, messages they missed.

— Joan Didion

Nora was still trying to process what she was seeing when Hollowell started barking orders at her.

"Help me get her to the floor! I'm going to try to resuscitate her."

Nora pushed the chairs away as Hollowell slid her arms behind Lara's back and lowered her to the floor.

Enzo clung to Lara's hand, begging her not to leave him. The way he held on impeded Hollowell's ability to start CPR.

"Grace! Can you deal with him?"

Grace hurried forward and guided Enzo to a chair. He collapsed into it, his face slack with shock.

Hollowell began chest compressions. As she pushed down on Lara's chest, she shot a glance at Nora. "Get me some light."

Nora bolted to her feet and ran into the ticket agent's office. She grabbed the battery-powered lantern and heavy-duty flashlight stored under the sink. She put the lantern on the coffee table and aimed the flashlight beam at Lara's face. The concentrated illumination made her look even paler than before. Her body shifted and jiggled under Hollowell's hands, but the movements were involuntary. Her eyes stared into a world only she could see.

"Bring her back!" Enzo shrieked. "You have to bring her back!"

Ignoring him, Hollowell focused all of her energy on keeping Lara's blood flowing and filling her lungs with air.

"Don't go, Lara!" Enzo howled, sinking to the floor next to Hollowell.

Grace tried to coax him away. "Please, Enzo. Give the deputy room."

When he refused to budge, Nora took hold of his arm and pulled. It was like tugging on a boulder.

"She needs me!" he screamed, shoving Nora with both hands. She crashed into the coffee table, her head colliding with the wood edge. Pain exploded inside her skull. She slumped sideways and the room tilted like a capsizing boat. Suddenly, she was on the floor, aware of nothing beyond the throbbing in her head and the tickle of liquid running into her left eye. Her thoughts turned fuzzy. Then everything went black.

When she opened her eyes again, the overhead lights burned like a dozen suns. It hurt to look at them, so she let her lids droop. Before her eyes were fully closed, she glimpsed a face framed by a corona of blonde curls.

"Thank God," Hester whispered. "Just stay still, okay? You're hurt."

Nora slitted her eyes against the light. Tentatively, she reached up to touch her temple. She felt Hester's fingers holding a soft cloth.

"You have a cut, and it's bleeding," Hester explained. "You're going to need stitches."

When Nora tried to raise her shoulders off the ground, the room wobbled. The lights expanded into tiny supernovas. There was a ringing in her ears, and nausea roiled in her stomach.

She croaked, "I'm going to be sick."

"Charlie! Grab a bucket from the kitchen!"

Hester supported Nora's head as she vomited. When her stomach was empty, she collapsed against Hester and tried to breathe through her nose. She heard voices. And from somewhere outside, the wail of sirens.

"The cavalry's here," Hester whispered. "They're going to take care of you."

Nora wanted to escape the noise, to drift away on waves of sleep. Maybe then, she'd wake to find that this was nothing but a dream.

But it was no dream. It was a nightmare.

Lara was dead.

She'd died in the bookstore. In June's favorite purple chair.

"Can you help me sit up?" she asked Hester.

"The paramedics are coming. I'll help you up if they say it's okay." Hester's voice was taut with concern. "You were out cold, Nora. I was really scared. Are you still dizzy?"

The room had stopped rocking like a boat in choppy seas. Nora was able to focus on Hester's face. "Not anymore. I need to sit up, or I'm afraid I'll puke again."

Hester guided Nora's left hand to the cloth pressed to the side of her head. "Keep applying pressure. I'm going to shift you a little. Just so your back is against the chair."

After years of working with dough, Hester's upper-body strength was formidable. She eased Nora upright just as the first responders began streaming into the room.

Nora let her dull gaze rest on Lara's body. Hollowell was still performing CPR, but one of the paramedics asked her to stop while he checked Lara's vitals.

He confirmed the obvious. Lara wasn't breathing. She had no pulse. The skin on her face was chalk white. Her lips were the color of crushed blueberries, and the spark in her eyes was nothing more than the reflection of the ceiling lights.

"Her partner said she had a bad heart," Hollowell told the paramedics.

Nora glanced at the other chairs in the circle. They were all empty.

"Where's Enzo?" she asked Hester.

"After he pushed you, Terry took him to the stockroom. I don't think he meant to hurt you."

Nora started to shake her head, but the motion made her queasy. "He didn't. He was just lashing out."

"Poor guy. Everyone's pretty shaken, and we didn't even know Lara. I can't imagine what Enzo's going through right now."

The first paramedic, a man named Jamie who frequented the bookstore one or two times a month in search of his next Nordic Noir read, squatted down next to Nora.

"I heard you got in a fight with the coffee table. How are you doing?"

"Okay."

Jamie began asking her questions about her symptoms. While he peeked under the cloth she held against her temple, he asked if she was experiencing any dizziness, confusion, ringing in her ears, double vision, or nausea.

As he listened to her answers, he shone a penlight in her eyes. She winced in discomfort.

"Sensitivity to light?" he asked.

"Yes. And I feel wobbly."

Jamie smiled. "Well, you won't be running any marathons tonight. You'll be riding in style in the back of my rig."

Nora didn't like the sound of that at all. "Can't Hester take me?"

"No, ma'am. The hospital is forty-five minutes away, and I need to monitor your condition the whole time."

Nora knew it was useless to argue. "Can you help me into a chair?"

Together, Jamie and Hester lifted Nora off the floor and

eased her into the chair. The movement made her dizzy again, so she closed her eyes and focused on her breath sounds.

Jamie asked if she wanted smelling salts. When she refused, he patted her shoulder. "We're going to move our other patient. Then I'll be back for you."

"I'm not going out on a stretcher," Nora warned.

Hester clicked her tongue in disapproval. "You need to do what the man says."

"Listen to your friend," Jamie said. "She's pretty *and* smart."

Nora opened her eyes in time to see Hester's cheeks turn pink. "Should I tell the others to go home?" she asked.

"Yes. Except for Charlie. He has to lock up."

The first paramedic headed for the delivery exit and returned a few minutes later pushing a gurney. Hollowell asked the men to wait a minute while she snapped photos with her phone. Not only did she capture images of the Readers' Circle, but she photographed Lara's body as well.

"What are you doing?" Nora hissed.

Hollowell didn't even glance her way. "Documenting the scene. Just in case."

"In case of what? Didn't she have a heart attack?"

The paramedic pulled a face. "We don't determine cause of death, ma'am."

Hollowell stared at Lara's body. "She had a cold. She went to the bathroom right before we lost power. Maybe she took the wrong medicine or was accidentally given the wrong medicine."

Nora replayed the moments leading up to Lara's death. She'd been sniffling and blowing her nose all night, which is probably why Enzo put a bottle of nasal spray on the coffee table.

"Where's the nasal spray?"

Hollowell reached behind a chair. When she straightened, she was holding a brown coffee filter. The nasal spray sat in the middle of the filter like an egg in a nest.

"What are you going to do with that?"

Hollowell arched her pencil-drawn brows. "You must've taken one helluva hit. Your brain is not working right." She pointed down at the nasal spray. "I'm going to have it analyzed. Check it for prints. You know, all that cop stuff you people love to see on TV."

"Who are 'you people'?" asked Jamie.

"Civilians," said Hollowell.

The paramedics wheeled Lara down the hall and out the delivery door. A gut-wrenching sob floated back to the Readers' Circle, and Nora pinned Hollowell with a glare. "Are you going to let him ride with her, or are you going to interview him in my stockroom?"

Hollowell ran a hand through her short hair. Once, Estella had suggested she try an alternative color, but Hollowell continued to dye it a dark, black cherry shade that clashed with her skin tone. She refreshed the color and cut—an angled bob with blunt bangs—every six weeks.

Estella had been delighted when Hollowell left her for another stylist.

Nora wished Hollowell would leave the bookstore and never return. Instead, the deputy curled her lip and said, "I detained that man because he pushed you into the table. I thought you might want to press charges, considering you need stitches and probably have a concussion."

Unbelievable, Nora thought. She'd never met someone with such a complete and utter lack of empathy.

"I'm not going to press charges. The woman he loved died in front of him. He didn't know what he was doing."

Hollowell shrugged. "Have it your way. I'll tell him he's free to go."

Nora heard the sleigh bells ring. Her guests were hurrying out into the windy night. What had promised to be another successful author event had ended in tragedy. All Nora wanted to do was crawl into bed and sleep for a week.

Hester reappeared in the Readers' Circle, and she wasn't alone.

McCabe rushed to Nora's side. "Hey, sweetheart. How are you feeling?"

"Like I'm getting too much attention considering a woman died here tonight."

"I'm so sorry." McCabe turned to Hester. "I'm really glad you were here. Not just to take care of Nora, but to look after her customers too. She's lucky to have a friend who can stay calm during a crisis."

"I didn't do much," Hester said, turning shy. "Hollowell took charge."

McCabe took Nora's hand and rubbed the pad of his thumb over her skin. "Are you in any pain?"

"A little, but I'm more concerned about Lara's partner, Enzo. He doesn't know anyone in the area, and the woman he loves just died. He shouldn't have to go through this alone."

"I'll call the hospital and see if the chaplain on call can meet the ambulance. If not, I'll do it."

Nora responded with a grateful smile.

McCabe gave her a butterfly kiss on the cheek and then strode down the hall toward the stockroom.

As soon as he was gone, Hester whispered, "What the hell, Nora? What's with the photos Hollowell took? Does she think one of us did something to Lara?"

"I don't know, but I have a bad feeling about this. About all of it."

"Me too. That shrew would do anything to make us miserable. And the way she had Charlie's mom buy her a ticket so she could attend the event without your knowing is shady. Why did she do that? Why not just buy the ticket herself?"

At that moment, Charlie poked his head around the corner

of the stacks to tell Nora that everyone was gone. She thanked him for being such a trooper and then asked if his mom was okay.

"She's a little spooked. She wants me to come home." Charlie ducked his head in embarrassment. "I ran a sales report and shut down the computer. Lights are off in front, and the door's locked."

"Charlie, please don't post anything about Lara on social media. The authorities need to contact her family, and we want to respect their privacy at this time." She gazed at the purple velvet chair. It was surreal to think that Lara had been sitting there less than an hour ago, holding people's hands and offering them insight and compassion.

Before Charlie could walk away, Hester said, "One more thing. Can you ask your mom why she bought Deputy Hollowell's ticket? And can you text Nora when you find out?"

Though clearly baffled by the request, Charlie said that he would.

McCabe returned to the Readers' Circle and gave the area a once-over. "Everyone's cleared out. The paramedics didn't want Enzo riding in the ambulance—he's too keyed up—so Terry's going to drive him to the hospital. Hester and the paramedics are okay with my driving Nora, so I'm going to carry her to my car. Can you follow behind and switch off the lights in the back hallway?"

Using the chair for support, Nora pushed herself to her feet. "Can I try walking on my own?"

McCabe slipped an arm around her waist and supported her as they slowly proceeded to the back door.

Nora's stomach lurched in protest, but by concentrating on the feel of McCabe's arm and the scent of peppermint clinging to his shirt, she was able to make it outside.

"What did Hollowell tell you?" she asked, shivering a little as the night air curled around her shoulders.

"She said that Ms. Luz had collapsed in her chair and didn't appear to be breathing. She moved Ms. Luz to the floor, intending to start CPR, but Ms. Luz's partner hampered her attempts. Grace tried to get him to back away but couldn't. Then you tried. That's when he pushed you."

Hester fished Nora's keys out of her purse and locked the delivery door. The wind whipped her hair as she returned the keys and opened the passenger door of McCabe's truck.

Nora waited until she was settled in her seat and McCabe was fastening his seat belt before saying, "Why did she take photos of Lara's dead body? Or collect evidence?"

"I haven't had time to talk to her yet, but I'm sure she had her reasons."

Nora and Hester exchanged worried glances. Then Hester squeezed Nora's hand and said, "Call me tomorrow. Love you."

"Love you too."

As soon as McCabe started driving, all Nora wanted to do was close her eyes. Her head felt so heavy, like sleep was trying to pull her into its arms. She wanted to surrender to it but knew she needed to stay awake. The only way she could fight the temptation was to tell McCabe everything she could remember about the evening.

McCabe listened closely. Other than an occasional noise of encouragement, he never interrupted her narrative.

"Sounds like Ms. Luz's cold was pretty bad," he said when she was done. "Maybe it was more than a cold. Did you see her take any medicine?"

"No. It was all tea and tissues until Enzo took out the nasal spray. I saw it on the coffee table, but I never saw Lara use it."

They drove in silence for a while. Nora raised her gaze, searching for stars, but there was nothing to see beyond the pewter-colored clouds.

Straight ahead, the sky was much darker. It felt like they were driving directly toward a black hole.

As Nora stared at the ink-black horizon, a tongue of lightning licked the sky.

"Must be a big storm to have sent such a strong wind ahead of it."

McCabe glanced at his speedometer. "I want to beat it to the hospital if I can. I caught a glimpse at the power outage map earlier tonight. This system has already made a mess in Tennessee, so we're in for it."

The lightning made Nora think of a little girl in an aluminum boat. She imagined an expanse of gray water reflecting an expanse of gray sky. Of rain piercing the lake's skin like bullets. She could almost hear a cannon boom of thunder as the girl reached for her father's hand. And then, a blinding flash as the lightning struck her small body.

Lara Luz had died once before. Long ago, in the middle of another storm, her father had brought her back.

Tonight, the storm had been miles away when Lara died for a second time. This time, the man she was with couldn't bring her back.

He hadn't even tried.

Hollowell had done her best, but her efforts hadn't been driven by a desperate desire to save someone she loved. Perhaps it was love that brought Lara back from death when she was a child. Or something far more mysterious. Something no one was meant to understand.

"Penny for your thoughts," McCabe said as the first drops of rain careened into his windshield.

"I was thinking about electricity. Like, if I'd had a defibrillator in the store—for emergencies—could we have saved Lara?"

"It's hard to say without knowing what kind of heart condition she had. Sometimes, the heart is just too damaged to keep working."

Nora thought of a heart covered in scar tissue like those on her hand and arm.

McCabe squeezed Nora's thigh. "Hey. This isn't your fault."

"I know. I was just thinking that if electricity stopped her heart when she was a kid, maybe it could've started it again."

The rain increased in tempo and lightning veined the sky, its proximity startling Nora.

McCabe exited the highway and followed the signs for the hospital's emergency entrance. He parked in front of the doors and helped Nora to a chair in the waiting room. Then he strode up to the check-in desk and explained the nature of Nora's injuries.

Whatever he said had the woman behind the glass partition smiling and nodding. When he was done, she handed him a clipboard and picked up her phone.

Nora glanced around the waiting room. There were only a few people sitting in the molded plastic chairs, including an old woman reading a magazine, a teenage boy in a zombie costume with an arm in a makeshift sling, and a young couple with a toddler. The toddler, who wore Paw Patrol pajamas, had her arms crossed over her belly and kept whining about how much her tummy hurt. Her mother tried to distract her by showing her something on her phone.

Watching her, Nora remembered that Hester had asked Charlie to speak to his mom about Hollowell. That had been an hour ago, so she pulled her phone out of her bag and checked for new messages. Hester, June, and Estella had all written to see how she was feeling.

Charlie had also sent a text. It said:

I asked my mom about Deputy Hollowell. She ran into DH at the grocery store on Tuesday. DH said she didn't want you to know she was coming to the reading because she had a surprise for you. That's why she asked my mom to buy her ticket. My mom thought it was weird, but she wasn't going to say no to someone in uniform. She hopes she didn't do anything wrong.

The sliding doors leading outside opened, and a blast of cold air accompanied a man in blue hospital scrubs. He tucked a pack of cigarettes in his shirt pocket and waved at the registration nurse before passing through the automated doors into the ER's inner sanctum.

The outer doors had closed, but Nora still felt chilled. It was as if the wind that had been haunting her all night had come to roost in her rib cage.

She hugged herself for warmth, but it didn't help. As soon as McCabe sat down next to her, she leaned into him, seeking comfort from the cold and the storm of unsettling thoughts swirling inside her head.

McCabe put an arm around her and told her everything would be okay. She didn't believe him, but at that moment she was grateful for the lie.

Chapter 6

Wounds heal. Love lasts. We remain.
—Kristin Hannah

A night in the hospital left Nora feeling irritable and sleep deprived.

If it had been yet another nurse coming in to check her vitals for what seemed like the hundredth time since she'd been admitted, she would've shouted, "Leave me alone!"

But she was glad to see Tyson's girlfriend, an ICU nurse with a mellifluous voice and radiant smile. Jasmine looked different with her box braids tucked into a blue scrub cap, but her familiar face put Nora at ease.

"Good morning, Ms. Nora. My shift starts in fifteen, but I had to pop in and see you before I head up to the third floor."

"I'm just relieved that I get to leave this place. I'm exhausted," Nora croaked.

Jasmine let out a tinkling laugh. "The Four Seasons we are not. And our coffee tastes like it was brewed in a bedpan, which is why I brought you some of Wawa's finest."

From behind her back, she produced a take-out cup and a paper bag. "Tyson's mama said that you'd feel much better if you had a skinny latte. She called me at six this morning to ask if I'd swing by her place to pick up your breakfast and then grab you a latte on my way in. Seeing as she might be my mother-in-law one day, I wasn't about to say no."

"You're an angel."

Jasmine waved off Nora's compliment. "This is a win-win. I get to make you feel better *and* rack up brownie points with Mama June. Now, let's raise the bed so you can feast like a queen."

Once Nora was sitting up, Jasmine put the coffee on the bedside tray and spread out a paper napkin. Then she opened the brown bag and removed an item wrapped in wax paper.

The scent of buttery toast wafted over Nora. "I'd know that smell anywhere. Sheldon's Cuban bread."

"Mama June says she and Sheldon poured a whole lot of love into this sandwich. It's been in an insulated bag, so it's still warm. I'm supposed to report back after you've had every last crumb, but I'm not gonna pressure you. You eat what you want to eat."

Nora peeled back the wax paper to reveal a toasted egg and cheese sandwich. She didn't think she was hungry, but the sight of the golden-brown bread and melted cheese stirred her appetite.

"Ms. Dixon and the rest of your friends will be here as soon as visiting hours start, so if you need another hit of caffeine, they're willing to bring you some."

The latte couldn't hold a candle to Sheldon's, but it did the trick. After a few sips, Nora felt less irritable.

"Thank you, Jasmine. This was so sweet of you." Nora gestured at the wall clock. "I know you need to get to the ICU, but I'd really like to know about another woman who was brought here last night. Her name's Lara Luz. She collapsed in my store and . . . she died."

Jasmine gave her a sympathetic gaze. "I'm sorry."

"Me too. It was really sudden. I think there was something wrong with her heart, but I'd really like to know exactly how she died. I won't be able to stop thinking about her until I know."

Jasmine shook her head. "Even if I knew, I couldn't tell you. She's still a patient of this hospital, and we take patient privacy very seriously. Any findings will be reported directly to her family, but that won't happen right away. The coroner doesn't usually get called in after-hours unless someone from law enforcement makes a request."

"I understand. It's just that I feel responsible for this woman because she died in my bookstore. Not only that, but I'm worried about her partner too. He completely fell apart last night."

"That's really sad." Jasmine gave Nora's hand a squeeze. "I see it all the time—folks who've been together for ages, and then one of them is suddenly gone. The person left behind always looks so lost. I don't think I'll ever get used to it, but I console myself by thinking that it's better to have someone to lose than to be alone."

Nora smiled. "You're very wise for your years."

After tossing Nora's empty cup and sandwich wrapper in the trash, Jasmine bounced to her feet and headed for the door. "Rest up and drink lots of water. It'll help your body heal."

"I will," Nora promised, reaching for the water cup on her nightstand. McCabe had left her phone there as well, so she checked for new messages.

McCabe had sent a text late last night, saying that he loved her and would call in the morning. The rest of the texts were from Hester, June, Estella, and Sheldon. They all hoped she was feeling better and wanted to know if she needed anything.

As always, Nora's thoughts turned to the store. She messaged Sheldon to ask if he'd be willing to handle the week's flea market shopping. Even though it was barely past seven in the morning, he replied immediately.

I thought you'd never ask! June says I can use her car, so I'll have plenty of trunk room. Don't worry, I know I need to buy low

so we can sell high. If I have any doubts, I'll ask Bea for advice. Take care of yourself, *mi amor*.

A nurse bustled into the room to see if Nora was ready for breakfast.

"I already ate, thank you. I'd like to know when I can go home."

"Doctor Rafferty will let you know. He's about to start his rounds. Let's make sure you're comfortable until then. On a scale from one to ten, what's your pain level?"

Nora had a headache, but it was nothing compared to the discomfort she'd felt last night. "Maybe a three?"

"I'll get you some Tylenol."

The nurse left, and Nora got out of bed and shuffled to the bathroom. Seeing her reflection in the mirror, she winced. Her skin looked sallow, which was only partially due to the yellowish lighting, and her eyes were bloodshot. A rectangle of white gauze, held in place with strips of medical tape, stretched from her right brow to her temple. The bandage sat on top of a bump the size of her fist. She'd been told the swelling would go down in a few days, but the bruising, which was the color of plum skin, would haunt her face for weeks.

I'm the Bride of Frankenstein.

She stuck out her tongue at her reflection. She refused to feel sorry for herself because she knew she was lucky. She would be able to walk out of the hospital today. Eventually, her injury would heal. There were plenty of other patients who'd spend a long time in this place. Others would never leave.

Nora's bathroom was equipped with a shower, so she slipped on a disposable shower cap and washed the previous night away as best she could. Then she dressed in yesterday's clothes and settled into a chair to wait for the doctor.

Twenty minutes later, a baby-faced young man rapped on her open door with his knuckles.

"Looks like you're raring to go," he said after introducing himself as Dr. Rafferty.

Nora nodded. "I feel more like myself this morning."

He studied his iPad screen for a moment and then set it aside. "My colleague wanted you to spend the night because you were experiencing periods of dizziness and nausea. There were signs of confusion as well. Are you feeling any dizziness or nausea now?"

When Nora said no, he gave her the same assessment she'd been given the night before.

"Very good. Last night you couldn't provide your home address or phone number."

Nora was stunned. "I don't remember that at all."

Because she passed the concussion test, Dr. Rafferty promised to sign her discharge paperwork. "I'm going to send some post-concussion care instructions with you. You'll need to take it easy for the next week—maybe more. Pay attention to your body. If you get dizzy, or your headaches increase in intensity, or you have vision changes, seek medical help right away."

As soon as he left the room, Nora called June.

"Don't drive here because I'm going home soon. Can we meet at McCabe's house instead?"

"You tell us when you're ready for company, and we'll be there."

Nora's next call was to McCabe.

"I'm on my way up to your room," he said.

She saw the flowers first. McCabe stood in the doorway, holding a bouquet of persimmon-colored roses. "Good morning, sunshine."

Nora opened her arms for a hug. McCabe laid the flowers on the bed tray and embraced her as if she were made of glass.

"It's safe to hug me," she said, moving her fingers through his soft hair. "It looks worse than it is."

McCabe kissed her cheek and whispered, "You're beautiful."

Nora snorted and told McCabe to get his vision checked while he was at the hospital. Then she gave his uniform shirt a tug. "I thought you were off today."

"I'm covering for Hollowell. She hung around here until God-knows-when last night. She needs to catch up on sleep."

It seemed like he was about to say more but decided against it. He smoothed her hair, taking pains to avoid her injury.

"Where's Enzo?" she asked.

"Terry Rowe took him back to his place. He said he knew what Enzo was going through and didn't want him to be alone. Enzo spoke with the hospital chaplain for a long time. After that, Terry bundled him into his car and persuaded him to lie down in his guest room for a few hours. Terry's off today, and he promised to do whatever he could for Enzo."

Nora put a hand to her heart. "He's such a good guy."

McCabe pointed at the chair, signaling that he wanted Nora to sit down. "I debated over whether to tell you this first thing, but I know you'll be upset with me if I don't, so here goes. The nasal spray Hollowell bagged wasn't the over-the-counter medicine Lara bought from Rowe's Pharmacy yesterday. It's a nasal spray, but we don't know which medicine it contained because someone altered the bottle. Parts of the original bottle were cut off, and all identifying labels or marks were scratched off."

"*What?*"

"Did you see her use a nasal spray last night?"

Nora gave a tiny shake of her head.

"Hey." McCabe put a hand on her shoulder. "We're not jumping to any conclusions. That bottle may be totally unrelated to Lara's death."

"You don't believe that, and neither do I."

McCabe was saved by the arrival of the nurse. She had Nora's discharge forms and, after reviewing her post-treatment instructions, wished her a happy, healthy November.

"November," Nora murmured in surprise.

It was a new month. That meant lots of changes at the bookstore. A new window display. New shelf displays featuring books about food and family. Different shelf enhancers.

Nora was glad to have tasks waiting for her. She wanted to focus on something other than Lara's death, but once she was in McCabe's truck, heading back to Miracle Springs, it was all she could think about.

"Were you able to contact Lara's family?"

"Her sister lives in Virginia. Just outside Charlottesville. According to Enzo, the sisters weren't close. He said he was the only person who truly cared about Lara."

"That's sad," Nora said.

When McCabe didn't elaborate, Nora stared out the window. Last night's storm had passed, and the sky was a cloudless blue. No fog clung to the mountain ridges, and ribbons of golden light wound through the trees. The autumnal foliage covering the mountainsides was as brilliant as a sunset. Coming on the heels of Lara's death, the beauty was almost too much to take in.

Turning to McCabe, Nora said, "I felt like something bad was about to happen last night, and then it did."

"Maybe Lara's reading had an effect on you? Hollowell told me that almost all of the lights were off. And that it was so quiet inside the bookstore that she could hear the wind howling. I know you lost power before Lara could finish her session. The dim lighting, the storm, and the nature of these readings must've made for one helluva spooky atmosphere."

As much as Nora wanted to dismiss the idea that she'd been influenced by outside forces, McCabe had a point. "I'm sure those things were a factor, but my sense of foreboding was pretty strong right from the beginning. I was surprised to see Allie Kennedy at the event, and even more surprised to find that she'd bought tickets for the reading using her real name.

She asked me to keep it to myself, which isn't unusual. What *was* unusual is how she seemed to wear her Allie Kennedy identity like a mask. I saw it slip last night, Grant. I saw the person behind that sweet, personable cozy mystery author. That person didn't like Lara."

McCabe's brows twitched in surprise. "Did they know each other?"

"I asked her the same question. She said she knew *of* Lara and came to the event to do research for her next mystery novel. She plans to kill a psychic in her new book."

"That's not what I want to hear."

Nora said, "Allie wasn't the only one acting strange. I need you to listen with an open mind because this is about Hollowell. I need you to forget she's a deputy for just a minute. Can you do that?"

He shot her a wary glance and said, "I'll try."

"You know that there's no love lost between me and Hollowell," Nora began. "I avoid her when I can, and she only comes near Miracle Books to exert her authority. She's never been a customer. You could've knocked me over with a feather when she showed up last night and sat in the audience."

McCabe shrugged. "She told me she was interested in Lara's story."

"Then she stayed for the reading—the one reserved for six people."

"I see where you're going with this. The other day, when I asked you who was going, you didn't mention Hollowell's name."

Nora's voice tightened with irritation. "That's because Hollowell asked Grace Kim to buy her ticket. When Grace bought two tickets, I assumed she was bringing a friend from work. She and Hollowell barely know each other, but Grace is a sweet person and was probably happy to do a favor for Hollowell."

"Did Lara do a reading for her?"

"She did readings for Grace, Terry, and Hester, but she died before she could get to Hollowell." Nora tried to block out the memory of Lara's body on the floor. "I didn't have the chance to ask Hollowell why she didn't buy a ticket for herself, but Charlie asked his mom about it. Grace said that Hollowell didn't want me to know she was coming because she had a surprise for me."

McCabe's face creased in puzzlement. "What was it?"

"I have no idea. Why was Hollowell really there? To mess with me?"

"Next time I see her, I'll ask."

Nora put a hand on McCabe's arm. "No, Grant. I have to do it. I need to look in her eyes—to see how far she's willing to go to score a point."

The rest of the ride passed in silence.

When McCabe turned onto his street, Nora saw June's car parked at the curb. June, Hester, and Estella sat huddled together on McCabe's front steps. When he pulled into the driveway, they rushed over to his truck to greet Nora.

"How long have you been sitting out here?" she asked her friends.

"Long enough to witness a UFC-level rumble between two squirrels." Hester pointed at the massive maple tree in the front yard.

Nora heard high-pitched barks and whistles from the canopy of scarlet leaves.

Taking Nora by the elbow, June said, "Are you up for company? Because we'll understand if you don't feel like talking."

"I definitely want company."

McCabe carried in the flowers he'd bought Nora yesterday, dropped them in a vase, and returned to the front door. "Ladies, I'm leaving my lovely lady in your hands. Call me at work if she needs anything."

He blew Nora a kiss and headed back out to his car.

Estella gave Nora a searching look. "You two okay?"

"He's just chewing over something I told him in the car." Nora waved toward the living room. "Sit down. I'll tell you about it."

June insisted on fussing over Nora first. She got her a glass of water and draped a blanket over her lap. "We've already filled Estella in on everything that happened after she left."

Estella nodded. "But what happened to Lara? Was it her heart?"

"There's no word on her cause of death yet."

"Hollowell was acting like she was the lead detective on *CSI: Miracle Springs*," Hester muttered.

"Because she saw something the rest of us didn't see."

Nora told her friends about the bottle of nasal spray and then filled them in on Allie Kennedy's claim that she'd come to the event in the name of research.

June made a time-out gesture. "Wait. She's planning to kill a psychic in her next book, and the psychic she was researching suddenly keels over and dies? That's shady as hell."

Next, Nora told them about Hollowell.

"A surprise for you? She probably baked her dog's poop into a pie, like Minny did in *The Help*," Hester said.

Estella grimaced. "Or she was going to fine you for having too many people in the bookstore or not getting a permit for visitors from the other side."

"I'm going to ask her, but right now, I'm more interested in the nasal spray. I want to know if anyone besides me saw Enzo put it on the coffee table."

"I did," said Hester. "He put it next to her teacup. I thought it was sweet—how he fussed over Lara. He looks tough and dresses like Danny Zuko, but he loved that woman."

Nora asked Hester if she'd seen Lara use the nasal spray.

"No, but she might have after the lights went out," said Hester. "Why? Was the bottle tampered with?"

"I think it was swapped for a totally different medicine," said Nora. "No one would've gone through the trouble of cutting the bottle and removing the label unless they were trying to hide what was really inside."

Estella put a protective hand over her bump. "So, someone wanted to hurt Lara?"

"That's the impression I got from Grant."

The four women fell silent, each lost in thoughts of the previous night.

Nora drank some water and then looked at June. "Back when you worked at the assisted living facility, do you remember seeing the residents use nasal spray for anything besides cold or allergy symptoms?"

"I don't."

Estella pulled up a website on her phone and started to read the names of various medications. "Most are antihistamines or steroids, but here's an antidepressant that looks pretty powerful. It's not a prescription you can take home, though. It's administered at the doctor's office only. Same goes for this oral fentanyl used as pain relief for cancer patients."

Hester, who was also studying her phone screen, said, "You can get addicted to over-the-counter nasal sprays. According to this article, it's more like a rebound effect than addiction. People use a spray to get rid of congestion, but after a few days, the medicine stops being effective. Then people need more and more to deal with their congestion because it keeps coming back."

"Can overuse be fatal?" asked June.

"According to this hospital website, some decongestants can interact negatively with blood pressure medications. People with certain types of heart disease have to be careful of the ingredients in some of these nasal sprays." She glanced up from her phone. "Do you think Lara was overusing a nasal decongestant?"

Nora recalled how frequently Lara had sniffled. "Her nose was running all night. I saw her use plenty of tissues, but no nasal spray. She could've taken it to the bathroom or had it in hand when the lights went out. I just don't know."

Estella waved her hands in the air. "Let's forget about the spray for a sec and ask ourselves *why* someone would want to hurt Lara. Other than Enzo, no one knew her, right? We didn't. Sheldon didn't. Charlie and his mom? Highly doubtful. That leaves Terry, Allie, and Hollowell."

"I think Allie knew Lara," said Nora. "I think she was lying when she said that she only knew *of* her. There's history between those two women, I'm sure of it."

A buzzing came from inside Nora's purse. She hesitated for a moment, wondering if she felt like talking to anyone outside this room, but then she reached into her purse and grabbed the phone.

"It's Grant," she said before answering the call.

He asked her two quick questions. She replied "no" twice, and that was the extent of their conversation.

Nora lowered her phone to her lap, slack-jawed with astonishment.

"What did he say?" Estella demanded.

"He asked if I knew where Allie was staying. I don't. Then he asked if I had any idea that Allie and Lara were related."

"Related?" Hester twirled a strand of hair around her finger. "How?"

Nora rubbed her eyes as if the motion could clear the confusion in her head and said, "Allie is Lara's daughter."

Chapter 7

Wherever a man commits a crime, God finds a witness. Every secret crime has its reporter.
—Ralph Waldo Emerson

"Where's your laptop?" June demanded as the rest of the group sat in stunned silence.

"At the bookstore."

June pursed her lips. "Right. You probably weren't thinking about your stuff while you were bleeding from a head wound."

Hester mimed a mind-blown gesture. "I can't believe that Lara is Allie's mama. They don't look alike at all."

Estella held up a finger. "Wait. Allie said she was at the event to do research for her next book, but why would she need to research her own mom? And, more importantly, why would she want to murder a fictional character based on her mother?"

Nora wanted answers to these questions as well, so she asked June to see if McCabe's laptop was in his office.

"I'm going to make coffee. I think we're going to need it," Hester announced and turned to Estella. "Do you want herbal tea?"

Estella looked at Nora. "Do you have any?"

"My whole supply is here."

While Hester called out the names of flavors of various tea

blends, Nora thought about Allie's request to keep her true identity private.

If Lara didn't die of natural causes, it's going to come out. All of Allie's secrets will be on full display.

When June reappeared carrying McCabe's laptop, Nora told her to google Aubrey Koch, Allie's real name.

"Don't start without me!" Hester protested over the gurgling coffee machine and the rumble of the teapot.

"Okay, so Aubrey lives in Knoxville, Tennessee," June said once everyone had their drinks. "She's thirty-seven and shares a residence with three other people. Leon Koch, age thirty-nine, Kayla Koch, age thirteen, and Kimberly Koch, age eleven."

"Try searching Aubrey Luz instead of Aubrey Koch."

June pecked at the keyboard. "Here's an Aubrey Luz from Grand Haven, Michigan. Her name comes up in an article from 2007 about a group of Michigan State bio majors. The timing fits, right? Allie/Aubrey would've been twenty in 2007."

"Is there a photo?" asked Estella.

"No. It's just a little blurb about these pre-med students who started a club to drive people without transportation to the hospital or area doctor's offices."

Nora wasn't convinced this was the same Aubrey. "If it is, I guess she wasn't planning a career as a mystery writer."

"It's not unusual to have a bunch of different jobs," said June. "I spent fifteen years working for assisted living facilities. Now I'm working for a five-star resort with a multimillion-dollar budget. When I was younger, I thought I'd do one job for my whole life because that's how it was with my folks, but now people change careers all the time."

"Guess I'm old-school," said Hester.

"Me too," agreed Estella. "But JoJo, my new aesthetician, has been a server, car salesperson, dog groomer, and the manager of a wedding-gown boutique. She went to night school to get her aesthetician license and raised three kids. Her previous jobs are a huge asset because she can handle all kinds of people. She makes even my prickliest and most anxious clients feel comfortable."

Nora pointed at the laptop. "Does Aubrey have a social media presence?"

June's brow furrowed as she scanned the results. "This could be her Facebook account, but it's private, so I can't tell."

Estella leaned closer to June. "What about her husband? Leon?"

"Let's see."

While June ran a new search, Nora sipped her coffee and silently wondered how Sheldon had made out at the flea market.

"What are you smiling about?" Hester asked.

"I'm picturing Sheldon darting around the flea market like a pinball. A pinball with a credit card."

June glanced up from the computer. "Honey, he was there before the doors opened. By this point, he's hit up two tag sales and is on his way to the antiques store in Asheville. He's having the time of his life."

"Who wouldn't want to shop with someone else's money?" Estella rubbed her belly. "I'm sure this little peanut will do plenty of damage to my checking account balance."

June grunted. "You know that's right. I told Tyson I'd treat him to a pair of shoes. Next thing I know, I've got a bill for two hundred dollars. For *one* pair of sneakers." She waved her hands as if shooing away a fly. "Okay, back to business. Leon Koch is on Facebook. He's not very active, but his posts are all about his family. Here he is with Aubrey on their anniversary."

She turned the screen around, allowing the other three women a view of the happy couple.

"The location of that restaurant is Knoxville, Tennessee." Hester looked at Nora. "Is that where Allie lives?"

"I don't know. She was in Asheville visiting family, which is why she wanted to come to the store for an impromptu signing. The family member wasn't Lara, either. She's from Greensboro."

June continued to peruse Leon's feed. "Here we go. Opa and Oma Koch live in Asheville. Here's a pic of the whole family on a hike. Allie's front and center, sporting a tee shirt that says, FUTURE BESTSELLER. According to the caption, this was taken at the Asheville Botanical Gardens."

Hester leaned closer to the screen. "It's *so* pretty there. Jasper and I went two years ago."

Nora listened for any hints of sadness in her friend's tone but heard none. Hester seemed to be genuinely okay following her breakup with Deputy Jasper Andrews, but her friends were still adjusting to her being single and to Andrews's new relationship with Paula Hollowell.

"I hope he takes Hollowell hiking and she gets bit by a snake," Estella grumbled.

"The snakes are probably scared of her," Nora replied, and everyone laughed.

June kept scrolling Leon's page until the Kochs' two children, Kayla and Kimberly, went from young kids to toddlers to tiny babies.

Glancing up from the screen, June said, "Okay, here's what I've learned from this man's photos. The family lives in Knoxville. They like rescue dogs. Leon is a radiologist who loves golf and cycling. They're real tight with his parents. Aubrey's parents never appear on his feed."

"Can we keep calling her Allie? That's the name I'm used to, and Aubrey isn't sticking," said Hester.

Once they all agreed to revert to Allie, June passed the laptop to Estella and told her to dig around for info on Lara while she topped off her coffee.

Estella explored Lara's website first. "Not much to see here. A summary of her services. Booking times. Testimonials. Purchase links for her memoir. Her bio talks about her childhood in Michigan and how she moved to Greensboro to be with Enzo after meeting him on a singles cruise."

Hester grinned. "That's cute. What about social media?"

Estella's manicured nails tap danced across the keyboard. "She's on Facebook. Her whole page is basically a billboard for her business and her book. There are photos of her in her garden. Some pics of her cats. Not much else. Let's see if she's on any other sites."

Lara also had an Instagram page, but it was basically a mirror of everything she posted on Facebook. Enzo had no social media presence at all that they could find.

Estella closed the laptop and set it aside. "Looks like we've hit a dead end."

"We didn't learn anything that would explain why Allie and Lara acted like strangers, but Allie's expressions during Lara's reading may tell us everything there is to know," said June. "I think they were estranged, just like me and Tyson used to be. Maybe Allie was angry at her mama, like Tyson was before he and I reconciled. Tyson traveled across the country to punish me for ruining his life. And even though his drug addiction played a part in his behavior, it was mostly fueled by anger and hurt. We need to know why Allie suddenly showed up at the bookstore. Was it to confront her mom?"

Or to kill her, Nora thought.

"We still don't know how Lara died, but I'm sure McCabe will talk to Allie. And not just her." Nora's voice sounded a little slurred. The lack of sleep was catching up to her. "He'll talk to all of us."

Hester got to her feet. "I think we should go. You look worn out, and I bet you could use some quiet after the hospital."

"Hester's right." Estella started collecting the coffee cups. "Besides, we all have Lara's memoir. Let's see if it can shed a little light on the mother/daughter relationship."

Without a sound, Higgins appeared from behind the sofa. The cat seemed surprised to find four people in the room but immediately approached June and started sniffing her shoes. A few seconds later, Magnum jumped down from the cat tower where he'd been practically comatose and rubbed his body against June's calf.

"Go away," she scolded. "I don't need the cats around my place to go into possessive kitty mode because they smell you on my shoes. My flower bed stinks of cat spray as it is. You two should focus on Nora—watch over her after we leave."

The cats took June's command seriously. As soon as Nora was alone, they both tried to sit on her lap. Because there wasn't enough room, she stretched out on the sofa with one cat pressed against her belly and another by her feet. Within minutes, she was asleep.

The sound of a cat tussle woke her, and she glanced around the room in confusion. It took her a moment to remember why she was napping in the middle of the day.

Her throbbing head quickly brought everything back to her.

She didn't sit up right away. She felt weighed down by a fatigue that was beyond physical. Her body would heal, but her psyche was a different story. She was still recovering from the trauma of Lucille Wynter's death and the destruction of her tiny house. The idea of being caught up in another murder investigation was too much to accept.

Despite her reluctance, she had to face reality. Lara had died in the middle of the Readers' Circle. Her last words had drifted into the bookstacks to mingle with the scents of coffee and paper. If McCabe launched an investigation, Miracle Books would be at the heart of it.

Stop wallowing. You didn't lose anyone you loved. Think of how Enzo must feel right now.

Though Nora felt sorry for Enzo, a tiny part of her questioned the depth of his devotion. He hadn't tried to help Lara. All he'd done was get in Hollowell's way. Had his obstruction been deliberate?

Allie's reaction had been even worse. While Enzo screamed

in desperation, Allie had stayed with the other customers in the front room while Hollowell tried to resuscitate her mother. By the time she returned to the Readers' Circle, her mother was dead. Allie had just stood there, watching.

Was it apathy? Or had Allie known all along that her mother wouldn't survive the night?

Nora was tempted to conduct a fresh online search on both Allie and Lara but didn't feel up to looking at a computer or phone screen. Instead, she took some Tylenol and fetched Lara's memoir from the nightstand. She made herself a peanut butter and jelly sandwich for lunch and read while she ate.

The introductory chapters focused on Lara's happy childhood and her close relationship with her parents and older sister, Joan. Nora was riveted by the chapter describing the lightning strike, but she had trouble concentrating on the subsequent chapter. Annoyed by this development, she set the book aside and picked up the TV remote.

When McCabe came home at five thirty with bags of comfort food from the Pink Lady Grill, Nora was parked in his recliner, watching *Carrie*.

"The last thing I expected was to find you watching a horror flick."

"I was going to watch *Bridgerton*, but Sissy Spacek sucked me in."

Nora didn't want to admit that she found the mother/daughter relationship combined with Carrie's psychic powers totally compelling. One look at McCabe's face told her that he'd had a rough day, so she wasn't going to mention Lara unless he did.

McCabe deposited the food in the kitchen and returned to the living room. He stood next to Nora's chair, studying her. "How'd it go today? I got worried when you didn't answer my call, but I didn't try again in case you were napping."

"I did nap, and I can't remember the last time I slept in

the middle of the day. The cats loved it, but I woke up feeling a bit confused." She turned off the TV and reached out to hug McCabe. "I'm happy you're home."

While McCabe changed out of his uniform, Nora began plating their dinner of green beans, mac and cheese, and fried chicken. McCabe returned to the kitchen, wearing sweatpants and a Carolina Panthers T-shirt, and grabbed a bottle of beer. He popped off the cap and poured a glass of sparkling water for Nora.

"How was your day?" Nora asked as she carried the plates to the table.

"Longer than I wanted it to be. I kept trying to get out of there—to get home to you—but things kept popping up."

Nora waited until McCabe had the chance to eat a few bites of food before saying, "Were those things connected to Lara Luz?"

"Most of them, yeah." McCabe took a swig of beer and loaded his fork with mac and cheese. "One of the nurses helped us identify the nasal spray. The bottle has a very unique shape, which is probably why its plastic wings were cut off. Someone needed to make it look less like a short sword sticking out of a hilt and more like a decongestant-type nasal spray. Hold on, I'll show you what I mean."

McCabe retrieved his phone from the charger and pulled up an image from his photos app. As she studied the squarish bottle, Nora understood what he meant about the short sword, but she thought it resembled something else.

"Looks like someone flashing their middle finger. What kind of medicine is it?"

"It's called Narcan. It's given to people who've overdosed on opioids," said McCabe. "If someone exhibits signs of an overdose, has taken a large dose of opioids, or combined opioids with alcohol or other drugs, one dose of Narcan can potentially save their life. It's pretty amazing stuff."

"How many doses in a bottle?"

Because he was still chewing, McCabe raised a single finger in reply.

Nora frowned. "Is it harmful? Like, if you use it and you're not using opioids, can it hurt you?"

"It can cause side effects. There's also a list of medications it doesn't interact well with, but the biggest concern involves those with heart or blood vessel disease."

"Like Lara?"

McCabe stabbed his fork into a pile of green beans. "She didn't have a *bad* heart so much as she had a heart that was too big."

"Did it grow? Like the Grinch's?" There was no levity in Nora's tone, so McCabe took the question at face value.

"It did. If she'd been born with an enlarged heart or it had developed when she was a kid, her condition would've been discovered after the incident with the lightning strike. At least, that's what the folks at the hospital told me. The lightning strike happened before records were digitized, so we'll have to call the hospital in Michigan to see if they have paper records. If they do, we'll have to get permission to view them from her next-of-kin or whoever she named as executor of her will. Those details will have to wait until tomorrow."

"Were you able to contact her sister?" When McCabe's brows jerked in surprise, she said, "The gals and I googled Lara. And Allie. And anyone else we could think of."

McCabe flashed her an indulgent grin. "I need to clone you. Then I could have Bookseller Nora and Researcher Nora. Researcher Nora would work for me."

"If I could clone you, I'd have Sheriff Grant and Foot Rubber Grant."

"I can be both of those Grants tonight," McCabe said. "And yes, I talked to Lara's sister. You probably know this already, but her name is Joan Luz Kennedy."

Nora stared at him. "Is that where the Kennedy in Allie Kennedy comes from?"

"I assume so. I had a long talk with Joan, and she told me that Lara and Aubrey—let's just call her Allie for simplicity's sake—have been estranged for most of Allie's life. At age thirteen, Allie boarded a bus in Michigan bound for Roanoke. Joan and her husband raised her from that moment on."

"What happened between Lara and Allie?"

McCabe picked at the label on his beer bottle. "Joan says it's not her story to tell. And before you ask, Allie refused to talk about it. In fact, she didn't have much to say about anything. When I called to officially confirm her mother's death, she thanked me as if I'd been calling to let her know that her dry cleaning was ready. There was absolutely no emotion in her voice."

Nora gazed into the middle distance. McCabe's living room faded away and she was back in the bookstore, standing in front of an audience that included Allie Kennedy. She remembered how Allie had glared at Lara. How she'd kept her face blank during the private readings. She'd done an excellent job of controlling her facial expressions, but her eyes had betrayed her. Nora had seen dislike there. Or had it been a different emotion? Like malice.

"Hey." McCabe touched her arm, bringing her back to the moment.

Nora turned to him. "Was it murder? Did Allie kill her mother in my bookstore?"

"We don't know. It's going to take time to determine if the Narcan was the cause of death. It's a complicated case because there's absolutely no evidence of the medicine in her nasal passages."

"How is that possible?"

McCabe pulled off the rest of the beer label and balled it in his fist. "That's above my pay grade. The medical professionals have more tests to run. More labs to order. It'll take time."

"What about Allie? Is she allowed to go home, as if nothing happened?"

"Until I have evidence proving otherwise, Lara died of heart failure."

Suddenly, Nora needed to move. She pushed her chair back from the table, stood up, and carried their plates to the kitchen. After packing the leftover food into glass storage containers, she started washing up.

McCabe knew she needed space, so he fed the cats and retreated to the living room with another beer.

When the kitchen was spotless, Nora refilled her water glass and joined him.

"Does Narcan require a prescription?"

"Yes. And since I know where you're going with this, I'll tell you that Joan used to work at a drug treatment center as a counselor. She retired last year, but the center keeps plenty of Narcan on hand."

Nora draped a blanket over her lap and sighed. "Our cozy mystery writer is feeling less and less cozy."

McCabe wagged a finger. "There was no trace of Narcan in Lara's nasal passages, remember? We can't jump to any conclusions. Besides, other people at the reading had access to Narcan."

A slideshow of faces moved through Nora's mind. She saw her friends in the Readers' Circle. Her new employee and his mom. Terry Rowe and Deputy Hollowell.

"Grace Kim is a nurse. Terry's a pharmacist."

Magnum jumped up onto the arm of McCabe's chair, nearly knocking the beer bottle right out of his hand. He let out a soft curse and scolded his cat.

"Why would Grace or Terry want to hurt Lara? They didn't even know her," Nora said, mostly to herself.

But McCabe responded as if she'd been speaking to him. "For all we know, they could be former clients. They both lost their spouses, and life hasn't been easy for either of them. Maybe they decided to consult a psychic. Maybe they looked for answers they weren't finding elsewhere."

"Why would they drive to Greensboro? I'm sure we have psychics closer to home."

"I'm just saying that it's possible."

Nora wanted to argue. Not because she believed McCabe was wrong—he wasn't—but because she didn't want anyone from Miracle Springs to be involved in Lara's death.

And what of Hollowell? Just because she wore a badge didn't mean she was incapable of committing a crime. Maybe she and Lara had history. McCabe knew Hollowell as a fellow law enforcement officer, but how much did he know about her personal life? About her past?

We should've googled her too, Nora thought.

"Grant. Did Hollowell tell you why she attended the event? She's never shown any interest in books before."

"I asked and was told that she's into fortune-telling. She has her own tarot cards, checks her horoscope every day, and has had her palm read a dozen times. Apparently, she caught the spiritualism bug from her grandmother. She was excited to get a reading from Lara."

Of course, she had an answer ready for McCabe. I wouldn't expect anything less.

"She asked Grace to buy her ticket—because she had a surprise for me. Did she tell you what it was?"

McCabe pulled a face. "She was going to give you something."

Nora's heart skittered and she sat up straighter in her chair. "Like what?"

"A jumbo-sized bag of Halloween candy for nut lovers."

Nora couldn't help it. She let out a derisive chortle. "She was calling me out for being petty. I guess you told her that I bought all the nut-free candy for the station."

"Only because I was trying to give you the credit," McCabe answered testily. "I had no idea I was adding fuel to a fire that refuses to die."

"But Grace bought the tickets days ago. How did Hollowell know about the candy then?" Nora pressed.

"She saw you at the grocery store. She was in the next checkout lane and heard the cashier ask if you were expecting the whole town to trick-or-treat at your house. You told him you were getting treats for the station. Hollowell's curiosity was piqued, so she looked over to see what you were buying."

"Well, that's one mystery solved," Nora muttered.

Magnum raised his head off McCabe's lap and blinked sleepily at her. Nora wondered if the cat had picked up on her negativity.

Grabbing the TV remote, she said, "Want to watch something?"

"Sure. As long as it's not a horror movie."

"There's a new documentary about the eighties. It looks pretty fun."

McCabe gathered Magnum in his arms, stood up, and placed the disgruntled cat on the sofa. "After today, I think we both deserve some pumpkin ice cream."

Nora wasn't hungry, but McCabe looked so eager that she readily agreed.

"Are you taking tomorrow off?" he asked when he returned with the ice cream.

"Definitely not. The bookstore is my happy place. Even after . . ." An image of Lara's body crept into her head, and she faltered. She blew out a breath and continued. "Even after what happened last night."

McCabe looked skeptical. "See how you feel in the morning before you go in, okay? You really had your bell rung. You might have side effects for days."

Nora turned on the TV, putting an end to the conversation. She made it through half of the documentary before a pulsing headache forced her to retreat to the softer lighting and total quiet of the bedroom.

Propped up in bed, she opened Lara's memoir. After reading the same sentence three times, she laid the book down on her chest and closed her eyes.

She fell asleep cradling the book, as if its familiar size and shape gave her comfort. Later, when McCabe came in to check on her, she stirred when he tried to ease the book out from under her arms. She was dreaming of the birds on the cover. Somehow, she had to keep them from escaping their cage. For their own good, she had to prevent them from flying away.

She mumbled something unintelligible and gripped the book even tighter. The corners dug into her skin, making small, V-shaped indentations—like a child's drawing of birds in flight— between her puckered burn scars.

Chapter 8

I knew beyond all doubt that the dark things crowding in on me either did not exist or were not dangerous to me, and still I was afraid.

—John Steinbeck

When Nora arrived at the bookstore the next morning, Sheldon was already there, even though his shift didn't start until ten.

"How are you, *mi amor*?"

"Still tired, even though I slept for *nine* hours." Nora pointed at the bakery boxes on the counter. "Did Gus bake for us today?"

The Gingerbread House was always closed on Mondays, so Estella's father, a talented bread maker, would often go in just to make muffins for Miracle Books.

"Actually, it was Hester." Sheldon rolled his eyes. "That she-devil called at way-too-early-o'clock to tell me that she couldn't sleep and had gone into work to make some treats called the Monday Blues."

Intrigued, Nora opened the lid of the first box. It was stuffed with turnovers with a pale purple glaze. Hester had written *Blueberry Turnovers* on the inside of the box lid.

Sheldon started scooping coffee grounds into the filter basket. "I'll brew some coffee. We need to sample these ASAP. It's our civic duty to test the quality of our baked goods."

Nora grinned. "Absolutely. I'm sure we need to taste whatever's in the other box too."

The second box contained bright blue muffins dotted with white chocolate chips. Nora found the color a little jarring. "If Cookie Monster was a muffin," she said.

Sheldon peered over her shoulder. "What in the world?"

Nora pointed at the words on the box lid. "Blue Velvet cupcakes? Well, I'm curious enough to try one."

"Let's eat and *then* I'll show you all the goodies I bought yesterday."

Nora washed her hands and cut the breakfast treats in half. The turnover's blueberry filling was still warm and oozed out onto the plate. While she waited for it to cool, she put the remaining pastries in the display case. When the case was full, she made a small sign listing the names and prices of the blue-themed treats.

"The forecast is calling for rain this morning, so that case will be empty by eleven." Sheldon plucked two mugs off the peg board. "Hester's going to swing by later. She wants our after-school crowd to sample some experimental savory items."

Nora carried their plates to the Readers' Circle and sat down. "The high schoolers will love that. They're always hungry."

"I remember when I could eat anything I wanted without paying a price. Now I have a built-in book rest." Sheldon mimed opening a book and propping it on his round belly.

Nora began to snigger and then instantly stopped, as if she suddenly remembered what had happened in the store last night.

Seeing her face fall, Sheldon put a hand on the purple velvet chair. "If Lara's spirit was still here—and I wouldn't blame her for wanting to be a bookstore ghost—she'd tell you to live your life. She tried to help people find closure. So, like my favorite throw pillow says, 'Let that shit go.'"

"It's hard to find closure knowing she might have been murdered in my shop."

"June told me about the Narcan. I'd never heard of it until I became her housemate. One Sunday, I was having a bad flare and was fresh out of Tylenol. June was at church, and I knew she wouldn't mind if I looked for a bottle in her medicine cabinet. When she got back home, I asked her about the funky-looking nasal spray I saw. The red cap made it look dangerous, which is why I wanted to know what it was."

Nora put her uneaten muffin back on her plate. "What did she say?"

"When Tyson finished rehab and moved into the halfway house, he was given a prescription for Narcan. He kept a bottle with him and gave one to June, in case he relapsed and overdosed. He hasn't had a single slip up, but like he told June, he'll be an addict for the rest of his life, which is why he wants her to keep the Narcan."

"Why didn't she tell me?" Nora murmured. "We were talking about which people at the reading had access to Narcan—like Terry and Grace—but June didn't say a word."

"Probably because she left before the reading." Sheldon stared at her over the rim of his coffee cup. "The fact that she has a bottle is coincidence, *mija*, that's all."

Nora passed her hands over her face. "You're right. Of course, you're right."

"You need a distraction," Sheldon said, getting to his feet. "Luckily, I have flea market bounty to show you. Stay where you are—I'm going to wheel it in here and reveal every piece, one at a time. It'll be like an *Antiques Roadshow* show and tell."

While Sheldon was in the stockroom, Nora washed their plates and refilled her mug. Sheldon had given her a mug showing an image of a distraught Cookie Monster staring at a computer monitor. The text bubble over his head read DELETE COOKIES?!

Nora snorted. She'd totally forgotten about the mug, which was no surprise considering the size of their collection. All the pegs on the board were full, and Sheldon had an entire cupboard dedicated to children's mugs. After taking a quick peek in the cupboard, Nora saw that they were running low on rainbow marshmallows and opened her laptop to order more. Cold weather meant coffee for adults and Harry Potter Hot Chocolate for the kids, and if Charlie had his way, they'd soon be adding another drink to the menu—one that would specifically appeal to his peers.

So far, his suggestions had included a Howl's Moving Castle Matcha Latte and a Hunger Games Honey Latte. Nora and Sheldon weren't wowed by either suggestion but told him to keep trying.

Thanks to Charlie's social media posts, Miracle Books had become increasingly popular with teens and new adults, and Nora was eager to make these customers feel welcome in her store.

Having placed an order for marshmallows and striped paper straws, she selected a playlist called Monday Morning Mood and returned to the Readers' Circle just as Sheldon rolled the book cart next to the floral chintz chair.

"First up, we have a beautiful pair of Ming-style vases," he began, sweeping his hand around one of the vases like a *The Price Is Right* model. "Ten bucks says one of the Monday Moms walks out the door with these today."

"Very nice," said Nora.

Next up was a trio of vintage yellowware bowls. The colors—mustard with a brown stripe around the middle—were perfect for Thanksgiving.

"I thought we'd put these in between the cookbooks. And I got *these* for the stoneware crock that hasn't sold yet." Sheldon unwrapped a bundle of old wooden rolling pins.

Nora examined the price tags on each pin and raised her brows. "Is this what you paid?"

Sheldon flicked his wrist in dismissal. "Of course not. I harassed that poor seller until she would've done anything to get rid of me."

"Was she a flea market vendor?"

"Nope. I got the kitchen stuff from an estate sale near Biltmore Village. The sign said the seller would accept all reasonable offers, so I made a pile of the best stuff and convinced her to take my offer." He handed Nora a vintage snow globe. "This was hers too. Everything came from her mountain house, which she's selling because she wants to reno her primary residence in Palm Beach."

Nora gave the snow globe a shake and watched a swirl of white flakes fall on the roof of an alpine cabin. "I've always loved these."

Next, Sheldon placed an assortment of bronze candlesticks on the coffee table. The candlesticks, which varied in size and shape, were in excellent vintage condition.

"I polished them last night because I knew we'd want to put them on the floor right away. What do you think about buying more tapered candles like these?" Sheldon pushed a cranberry-colored candle into one of the bronze candlesticks, but the candle was too skinny to stay in place. It wobbled sideways and then rolled off the table and onto the floor.

"We might have to wedge a little paper under its base," Nora said as she looked for the candle. It was nowhere in sight, so she dropped to her knees and peered under her chair. The candle was resting against the back leg. As she reached for it, she noticed an object under the purple velvet chair.

Nora passed the candle to Sheldon and crawled over to the purple chair. She pulled out the object and held it up to the light.

Sheldon grunted in frustration. "Are people stashing books under the chairs again? Look at that poor thing. I've seen roadkill in better condition."

Nora examined the cover, which was torn in several places.

"I don't think it's one of ours. I've never seen this book before."

She patted the top of her head, hoping her reading glasses were perched there. When her hand met only hair, she wandered into the ticket agent's booth and found her glasses near the coffee maker. She slid them on and took another look at the cover. There was no title—only a strange symbol rising out of the deep purple cloth like a sea creature surfacing from the deep.

"What on earth?" she muttered before opening to a random page.

"Hello? I'm not done out here," Sheldon complained.

Nora didn't reply. She was too interested in the contents of what appeared to be a journal. The pages were filled with names, dates, tiny sketches and doodles. The handwriting was small and dainty, and most of the notes were written in purple ink. As Nora continued flipping through pages, she discovered pressed flowers, sticky notes with a single heart or smiley face, and a slip of paper from a fortune cookie. The message read: YOU HEAR THE VOICES OF THE ANCESTORS.

Sheldon poked his head into the kitchen and glared at Nora. "What is so riveting about that tattered tome?"

Nora handed it to him. "I think it belonged to Lara."

Sheldon flipped through the first few pages. "There's no name. Do you recognize the handwriting?"

"No, but Lara signed her memoirs with a purple pen."

"Hmm. This is like a mashup between a journal and an appointment book." Sheldon showed her a date on the top of one page. "Two dot twenty-three might be February 23. Then we've got the initials *FW* inside a circle. I think these abbreviations stand for 'cheat' and 'divorce.' I think this is some kind of made-up shorthand."

"I don't know how you figured that out. Can you find another appointment?"

Sheldon turned the page, glanced at the drawings of plants and butterflies dancing over the white paper, and located the next date.

"Here we go. March 3. No *FW* this time. We have *EJ* instead. I think the shorthand here translates to 'sister,' and 'car accident.' Oh, and she added 'drunk driver' here, next to this spiral doodle. EJ's initials aren't circled. They're inside a square. Do you think the shapes are a billing code?"

"Maybe. These read like notes taken during a client session." Nora made a gimme gesture, but Sheldon refused to relinquish the book. "Later. Right now, we need to price our new treasures and put them out before we open. Keep your eye on the prize, *chica*."

All Nora wanted to do was look through the purple book, but Sheldon had a point. The Monday Moms would soon be waiting at the front door, eager to come inside, drink coffee, and swap Halloween stories. They'd also trade recipes, discuss school events, and occasionally, talk about books.

"Okay," she told Sheldon. "I'll write the tags."

As Sheldon read off what he'd paid for each item, Nora stared at him in admiration. "I knew you had a good eye, but you did a great job bargaining too."

"I had a ball, but I also know how much you like shopping for shelf enhancers. What are we going to do? We keep selling out before we can restock."

"I'll keep going to the flea market, but if you want to hit the antique malls, estate sales, and local auctions, that's fine by me." Nora held up a warning finger. "But you have to promise to listen to your body. If you overdo it on Sunday, you'll have to call out on Monday. I don't want to start the week without you."

Sheldon beamed at her. "I promise."

They quickly priced the rest of the items. Sheldon was still placing them on shelves when Nora unlocked the front door to welcome the Monday Moms.

Heather, the first woman to enter, gave Nora a weary smile.

"I've been dreaming of your coffee since my daughter woke me up at five. She keeps having nightmares, and neither of us are getting any rest."

"That's terrible—for both of you. Maybe with Halloween in the rearview, she won't see spooky stuff everywhere and will sleep better."

Heather frowned. "This has been going on for months. Do you have any kids' books about not being scared at night? Something I could read to a six-year-old before she goes to bed?"

"I'll take a look. But just so I don't overwhelm you with too many choices, has your daughter talked about what happens in her nightmares?"

"It varies. Sometimes there are monsters in her room. Sometimes she gets chased and falls from a really high place. My therapist said she might be reacting to her dad's new job. He used to be a commercial pilot, but he recently became a cargo pilot because the salary's better. Unfortunately, he's not home every night like he used to be."

Nora could see how the change in routine could cause anxiety for a little kid. After telling Heather that Sheldon would give her a much-needed dose of caffeine, she welcomed the other four moms.

"There'll be six of us today," said a woman named Hannah. "Do you have another chair?"

"I'll grab a folding chair from the back."

After a brief hesitation, Hannah said, "Two other moms have shown interest in joining us, but I'm not sure if we can squeeze anyone else in the circle. I wish we could use your red caboose. We'd have plenty of room, and we could be as loud as we want. But I get that you don't want a bunch of customers in your home."

"Hannah, *she's* not even in her home," chided another mom.

"Oh, my gosh, I totally forgot. I'm so sorry." Hannah looked genuinely mortified. "How are the repairs going?"

Nora thought of the proposal the builder had emailed her. It was great, but she'd yet to approve it. Something was holding her back, but she didn't know what.

"The builder's ready to go, so that's a plus," she said before excusing herself to fetch a chair from the stockroom.

While the moms placed their coffee orders, Nora started gathering picture books for Heather's daughter.

The first book that came to mind featured a little boy who had scary dreams about falling. Nora couldn't remember the specifics, but she believed the child's father was in the military. By the end of the book, the boy faces his fears and learns to fly.

Nora stood in the children's section, waiting for the title to come to her, but it remained elusive.

This was worrisome because Nora had an uncanny memory when it came to books. She rarely forgot titles, authors, or plotlines.

"Must be the concussion," she whispered and continued to scan the shelves.

Then she spotted the book. It was called *Moonpowder* by John Rocco. The cover image was of a little boy in an aviator's cap and goggles who sat on top of a grinning moon.

Luckily, she had no trouble locating the rest of the books. She chose Emma Yarlett's *Orion and the Dark* to help Heather's daughter address her fear of the dark and *The Berenstain Bears and the Bad Dream*, *The Dream Jar*, and *Brave Little Monster* to enable the little girl to render her nightmares powerless.

Nora carried the books to the Readers' Circle and, after catching Heather's eye, signaled that she would leave the pile at the checkout counter until Heather was ready to look at them.

Sheldon had tucked Lara's journal next to the register, and Nora was itching to pick it up and examine every page. She especially wanted to study the most recent entries. Maybe Lara had written about her daughter. Maybe her last entry would reveal the reason behind their estrangement or give some insight as to why they'd acted like strangers at Lara's event.

Instead of opening the book with the tattered purple cover, Nora sent a text to Hester.

Did Lara act like she knew Allie on Saturday? Did she ever stare at her? Allie seemed mad at her mom, but Lara acted like they'd never met before.

She waited for Hester's reply, but when the message remained unread, she put the phone down and hurried out from behind the checkout counter to open the door for an elderly man with a walker.

"Good morning," she said over the jangling of the sleigh bells.

"Sounds like Christmas!" he exclaimed. "My wife is feeling poorly, so she sent me to pick up some books for her. She likes romance novels. The spicier the better. She rates 'em like other folks rate hot wings. Mild, Medium, Hot, Blazing, and Call the Fire Department."

The man cackled, and Nora couldn't help laughing along with him.

"I think we can find her some five-alarm reads," Nora said. "Would you like to take a seat and have a coffee while I pick out books for your wife, or would you rather choose them?"

"Oh, she gave me a list. She'll take any you've got in stock, up to ten paperbacks. I can't fit more than that in my basket and still make it back to my car."

A howl erupted from the back of the store, and the man looked startled. "Somebody yankin' a cat's tail?"

Nora chuckled. "No. It's a group of ladies who get together every week. They tend to laugh a lot."

"That's good. Laughing keeps a person young." He tapped the side of his head. "All the same, I'm gonna turn down my hearing aid and find a little corner to drink my coffee and look at the paper."

"I have the perfect place for you."

Nora settled the old man in the cozy chair in the mystery

section, gave him the local paper, and then headed to the ticket agent's booth to get his complimentary coffee.

Sheldon picked out a mug and handed it to her. "I don't know what Hester put in those muffins, but the Monday Moms are losing it. I can't even look at them because they all have blue tongues. They're not women anymore. They're giggling alien lizard people."

"They know how to kick Monday morning's ass, and I respect that. I also respect a man who comes in with a list of spicy reads for his wife."

"The gentleman with the walker?"

Nora nodded.

"*No!* Gimme that list." Nora handed it over and Sheldon quickly scanned the titles. "Please tell me that we have *Swift and Saddled* in stock. I *need* to see that cover."

"I know we have Kennedy Ryan's *This Could Be Us* and a few others on the list, but I'm not sure about that one." The sleigh bells rang again, signaling the arrival of more moms.

Sheldon darted a nervous glance toward the Readers' Circle. "The alien lizard people's reinforcements have arrived. Save yourself!"

Nora exited the ticket agent's booth just as the Monday Moms broke out in peals of laughter. She had to duck into the romance section to keep from cracking up at the sight of their blue tongues.

The rest of the morning passed in a flurry. Nora moved around the shop, searching for books, recommending books, swiping credit cards, and bagging books.

She was too busy to examine Lara's journal until her lunch break. But the moment she sat down on a stool in the stockroom, she was hit by a headache that felt like a grenade detonating.

You're probably dehydrated, she told herself. *Drink some water.*

After satisfying her thirst, she unwrapped her sandwich and took a bite. Another shock wave of pain hit her, and she squeezed her eyes shut. After swallowing the partially masticated bite of sandwich, she bent over until her chest nearly touched her thighs. She felt nauseous again, and there was a faint ringing in her ears.

Her symptoms had struck without warning. She'd been fine a few minutes ago, and now she couldn't move. She couldn't even open her eyes because the light was too bright.

The store phone, which was on the cardboard box she was using as a table, began to ring.

Nora knew Sheldon couldn't answer it—not with the line of customers she'd passed on her way to the stockroom.

If he got too overwhelmed, he'd interrupt her lunch. But they both endeavored to give the other person a solid thirty minutes of downtime, no matter what was happening in the bookstore. Usually, they explained the situation to their customers and asked for their patience. Most people were happy to oblige.

The phone stopped ringing, and Nora let out a breath. The noise had only added to her discomfort, and when it rang again, she wanted to hurl it across the room.

Hearing the slam of the delivery door, she assumed UPS had dropped off more boxes. She couldn't even call out a greeting to Daniel, their regular driver, because she felt like she had to keep her body folded like a clam.

An eddy of outside air kissed the back of her neck, and she heard someone enter the room. Suddenly, the phone stopped ringing. Someone said, "Hello, this is Miracle Books. How can I help you?"

Hester!

Nora cracked her eyes, but all she saw were strobe lights, so she closed them again.

"Could I take your name and number? We can call you back after we check our inventory. Even better. You can get your cappuccino and browse all the new releases. Thanks so much."

Hester laid a hand on Nora's back. "What's going on? Is it your head?"

"Yes," Nora croaked.

"Should I call an ambulance?"

The thought of paramedics in the store was worse than the stabbing pain inside her skull. "No."

"I'm going to grab a cold cloth from the kitchen. Be right back."

When Hester returned, she draped a towel over Nora's neck and then laid a cold pack over the towel. "Should I call McCabe?"

The cold pack was already helping. "Not yet."

"Let me know when you can sit up enough to swallow some water and Tylenol. I turned off the lights, just in case that would help."

Nora hazarded a peek. This time, there were no strobe lights. She slowly straightened, and to her relief, the wooziness had abated.

After another minute of stillness, she managed to swallow the pills.

Hester said, "Can you sip a little tea? Sheldon has that inflammation-fighting blend in the cupboard next to the fridge."

Nora said she'd try, and Hester bustled off to make her a cup.

When she saw the mug Sheldon had chosen for her, Nora almost smiled. It said, MY FATIGUE IS CHRONIC BUT MY SNARK IS ICONIC.

"Jeez, Sheldon. Read the room," Hester said through a grin.

The tea dispelled the remnants of nausea, and the Tylenol dulled the sharp edges of the headache.

"I don't normally fall apart during my lunch break," Nora murmured apologetically. "It came out of nowhere."

"You should call your doctor."

"I will." Nora ran her fingers over the letters stamped into the mug. "I think I just had my first migraine. I never understood how debilitating they were until just now. I'm really glad you came in when you did."

"I was going to come later this afternoon with those samples, but Estella called to see if I could be here at one. She asked June too."

Lara's journal seemed to thrum from its place in the center of the box. Nora gazed at it for a moment before turning to Hester. "What's going on?"

"No clue. I just do what I'm told." She jerked her thumb toward the door. "I *did* bring some savory treats for you to sample, but I can see that you're not going to want them right now."

"Something must be seriously wrong with me because I *never* lose my appetite," Nora said, trying to sound blasé.

Hester was about to reply when June appeared in the doorway. "Party in the box room!" she boomed, holding her lunch tote in the air. She took two steps forward and halted, her face flooding with worry. "What happened?"

"It's my head," said Nora.

June clucked her tongue. "Did you come back to work too soon?"

"I was fine all morning. Then all of a sudden, I wasn't." Nora waved at Hester. "She showed up just when I needed her, and I feel much better now. Just don't ask me to finish my lunch or do jumping jacks."

"No one's gonna make you do cardio, but you do need to eat. You can't heal without water, nourishment, and sleep."

Nora didn't want to talk about food, so she asked June if she had any idea why Estella wanted to see all of them.

June shrugged. "Maybe it's one of those crazy gender reveals you see on social media. Though that doesn't seem like something Estella would do at one o'clock on a Monday."

As if the mention of her name had summoned her into being, Estella walked in. She wore a green sweater dress, a pair of tobacco-brown boots, and a dazzling smile.

Stretching her arms out wide, she cried, "Guess what? I'm getting married!"

Chapter 9

All my life I thought that the story was over when the hero and heroine were safely engaged... But it's a lie. The story is about to begin, and every day will be a new piece of the plot.

—Mary Ann Shaffer

June let out a whoop. "Oh, my Lord! Married? Tell us everything!"

After receiving hugs from the other women, Estella plopped down on a stool next to Nora.

"For starters, the wedding is happening soon."

"How soon?" asked Hester.

"Not this Friday, but next Friday. We're going to the Justice of the Peace in the afternoon followed by a reception that night. It's perfect because none of you will have to miss work." She looked at Nora. "You might have to close a bit early unless Charlie can handle an hour on his own."

Nora smiled at her friend. "For you? I'd take off the whole day."

"No need for that," Estella said. "It'll just be my dad and Jack's sister at the courthouse—if she can make it. That part will be short and simple. The reception is another matter. I can't celebrate this milestone without my best friends beside me. So what do you say? Can we skip book club just this once?"

"I think we can work something out," Nora said, reaching over to squeeze her friend's hand.

Hester gazed at Estella with a dreamy expression. "I can't believe it. You're a bride-to-be. Tell us the backstory. I want to hear every romantic detail."

Estella laughed. "It wasn't a cinematic moment, but it was so *us*. Me and Jack were painting little yellow stars on the walls of the nursery. We had glasses of mint iced tea and were listening to a playlist of international instrumental music to see if it would be a good choice for when the baby gets fussy. After chatting about this and that, we started sharing names we'd never give our kid."

Nora grinned. "Like Hannibal?"

"Or Brunhilda?" said Hester.

June pretended to mull this over. "You could call her Hildy for short. That's kind of cute."

After agreeing that it was, Estella continued her story. "We were mostly talking about the celebrity baby names we'd never use. Like, we wouldn't name our kid after a food, a cardinal direction, or a math equation."

Hester pointed at Estella's bump. "You mean you don't want your baby's name to be a capital letter? I'm partial to Z."

"There'll only ever be one Z, and that's Zelda Fitzgerald," said Nora.

June gestured for Estella to keep talking. "Okay, so you're painting stars and talking baby names. What happened next?"

"We were totally hamming it up when Jack put his paintbrush down and came over to me. He took the brush I was holding and used it to paint a yellow band on my ring finger. When he was done, he said, 'Let's get married. Tomorrow. Or the day after that. I want our baby to come into the world knowing that her parents were committed to each other in every way—that our lives, hearts, and homes were united.'"

When tears filled Estella's eyes, Nora grabbed the box of tissues from the shipping table and put it within her reach.

"I didn't answer right away," Estella said, pulling a tissue from the box. "Not because I didn't want to, but because I couldn't. The moment felt so *big*. It's the same feeling I get when I read a *really* good book. One of those slow burns that builds to a dramatic, life-changing scene. You know it's coming because you feel the emotion welling up inside. You know it's going to be powerful. It'll probably make you cry. But it's also what you've been waiting for since the first page."

"Go on. Turn the page," whispered June.

Estella dabbed at her eyes. "Jack said, 'Our baby will be with us when we make our promises to each other. We'll be able to tell our kid how they added to our happiness and made us fall even deeper in love. I never knew that was possible, but it's true. I love you more than I did yesterday, and I'll love you even more tomorrow.'"

By this point, there wasn't a dry eye in the room.

"That's way better than a movie!" June exclaimed.

"What is going on back here?" Sheldon demanded from the doorway. "You're all crying and smiling at the same time? Should I be scared?"

Nora waved at Estella, signaling that this was her news to share.

"I'm getting married in two weeks, so polish your dancing shoes because you're invited."

Sheldon released a torrent of jubilant Spanish phrases and rushed into the room. He kissed Estella on both cheeks, gave her one of his famous bear hugs, and offered to be her DJ.

"That's sweet, but I want you to dance and have fun." She gazed around at her friends. "We spend our days serving others, but for one night, we're going to focus on ourselves. I want all of you to eat, drink, and make merry."

Hester held out a warning finger. "I'll gladly party for hours, but I've been thinking about your wedding cake from the moment you and Jack started dating. Just in case it led to this moment. Please tell me I can make it for you."

"Honey, I couldn't get married if you didn't. I'd just tell Jack, sorry, the wedding's off." Estella glanced around the circle. "As a matter of fact, I have requests for each of you. There's no way I can pull this off without your help."

June nodded in encouragement. "Tell us what you need."

"Sheldon, I'm hoping you can find a creative way to do a seating chart. We're capping the guests at fifty, so the reception will be small enough to feel intimate while still big enough to feel like a real party. You're familiar with everyone on the list, which means you know who should sit with who and who should sit at a table for two in the corner."

"Leave the seating chart to me, *mi amor*," said Sheldon.

"June, I'd like you to stand in for Jack's mom for the mother/son dance. I know you're not old enough to be his mom, but Jack adores you."

June put a hand to her heart. "Oh, baby. It would be my honor."

"And Nora, I'd like you to do a literary reading instead of the traditional best man or maid-of-honor toast."

"I'd love to."

Nora felt an immense rush of gratitude for Estella for making her big announcement in the bookstore. She'd swept in like summer sunshine, banishing the shadows and infusing the place with light. Her joy was infectious, and no headache could keep Nora from basking in her friend's glow. Though she still felt a little out-of-sorts, the happiness she felt for Jack and Estella had helped heal her.

"You've given us pretty easy jobs. We can help you with the planning too," she told Estella. "Do you have a venue in mind?"

"I was going to ask June if any of the small ballrooms at the Lodge were available. I love the room that has the fireplace on the back wall and the little white lights hanging from the rafters. It's so cozy."

June was already pulling out her phone. "Give me sixty seconds to text the event coordinator. She owes me a favor, and I'm calling it in right now."

Hester said, "What about food? Is the Pink Lady handling that?"

"We're going to do a buffet. Jack will make the entrees, and his staff will handle small bites and sides. They'll attend the reception as guests, so I need to find a bartender and servers."

June made a check mark in the air. "Done, done, and done. You're booked in the Haven Room with seating for fifty people, a buffet table, cake table, six servers, and a bartender."

Estella jumped up and thrust her arms in the air like a referee signaling a touchdown. "You're better than a fairy godmother!"

"That's for damn sure," June agreed. "When I work *my* magic, it lasts way past midnight."

Sheldon took Estella's hand and slowly spun her around. "You've never been the rags version of Cinderella, but how does a girl get the ballgown and glass slippers in two weeks? Are you worried about finding *the* dress?"

"I am. Especially with this." Estella patted her bump. "I'm forty, pregnant, and getting married in a courthouse. I don't want a traditional dress with the train and veil. I don't want pearl buttons running down my back, an ocean of lace, or loads of beading. I don't even want a white dress, but I *do* want something pretty and ultrafeminine. I also don't want to spend a fortune. I can't imagine how much college tuition will cost in twenty years, but we'll probably have to start saving for it when this kid is still in onesies."

Sheldon cocked his head. "What's a onesie?"

June gave him a playful pinch on the cheek. "You're adorable. And don't you worry, Uncle Sheldon is going to know his way around a onesie very, very soon."

"Why do you make that sound so terrifying?" Sheldon shuddered, which made all the women laugh. Cupping his hand to his ear, he said, "Gotta go. The sleigh bells are playing my song."

Nora's lunch break was almost over. Knowing she had at least five hours of work ahead of her, she thought she'd better get some food in her stomach. While her friends talked about dresses, she took a small bite of her apple and swallowed warily. When her body didn't protest, she ate the rest of the apple and half a sandwich. Between the food, the tea, and the company, she was feeling completely normal by the time she needed to get back out on the floor.

"You can always rent a dress," Hester was saying as the four women headed for the ticket agent's booth.

Estella's face lit up. "Yes, I could! I'll look online tonight and send you gals pics of the top contenders. And if you have any brilliant ideas about flowers for the reception, please share."

"I can ask Val and Kirk," Nora suggested. "I know they mostly deal in plants, but what if they did a wedding version of their blooming baskets? One guest from each table could take the arrangement home, so nothing would go to waste."

"You're a genius." Estella cupped Nora's face in her hands. "Will you call them for me?"

"As soon as I get the chance."

June jerked her head at a man carrying a teal tote bag with a MIRACLE SPRINGS LODGE logo. "Looks like the afternoon trolley is here and you've got a whole mess of tourists with money to burn."

"They can burn all of it right here. Sheldon and I will toast marshmallows." Nora said goodbye to her friends and hurried over to assist a woman who couldn't quite reach a book on the top shelf of the mystery section.

For the rest of the day, Nora concentrated on selling books and connecting with her customers. After Sheldon left at three and the after-school crowd streamed in, there were often lines at both the coffee window and the checkout counter. Nora could ring up books at the ticket agent's booth, but she preferred not to because the counter was usually covered in coffee grounds, milk splatters, and crumbs. This wasn't Sheldon's doing. He never left a mess, but when Nora got busy, the kitchen became untidy.

Her regular customers were used to her flitting between the front and back counters, but several visitors let out impatient sighs or walked away without buying anything.

"If only Charlie could come every day," Nora murmured as she retrieved a fresh carton of milk from the fridge. Thanks to Charlie's social media posts, the store was busier than ever, which was a good thing. But seeing people leave because they had to wait too long to be served wasn't.

By closing time, Nora felt like she'd been hit by a car.

Her head throbbed, and her body ached. She couldn't wait to lie down.

Knowing she had to drive made her feel even more tired. If her house wasn't damaged, she could just walk across the parking lot, unlock the door, and drop onto the sofa. In five minutes, her shoes would be off, her head would be on a pillow, and her eyes would be closed.

But as she turned onto McCabe's street and saw his SUV parked in front of his house, she brightened. All in all, she'd had a great day, and seeing McCabe would make it even better.

When she walked into the kitchen to find him in an apron, stirring something on the stove, her heart swelled.

"You look hot," she said, giving him a saucy smile.

McCabe dabbed his flushed face with a dish towel. "It's pretty toasty in here."

Coming up behind him, Nora slipped her arms around his waist. "I meant the other kind of hot. The you-wear-that-apron-well kind of hot."

"Oh, yeah?" McCabe spun around and kissed her. When he eventually pulled away, he was grinning. "I know what to ask Santa for this Christmas. A big ass box of aprons."

Nora laughed and peered into the pot. "What are we having?"

"Irish stew. There's nothing like red meat and beer to get the week started on the right note." After putting the lid on the stew pot, he studied Nora's face. "How'd it go today?"

"I hit a rough patch around one. Bad headache. Light sensitivity. Upset stomach. Tea and Tylenol helped, but the true healing came from being with my friends. Hester showed up first—she got me the tea and pain meds—then June, then Estella."

McCabe took a Perrier bottle out of the fridge and motioned for Nora to sit in the living room. He soon followed with a glass of sparkling water for her and a Guinness for himself. "Was this an impromptu meeting of the Secret, Book, and Scone Society?"

"I guess you could say that. We were there at Estella's request. She wanted us to be in the same room when she told us her big news."

Leaning forward, McCabe whispered, "Is she pregnant?"

Nora threw a pillow at him. "Smart ass! She and Jack are getting married!"

"Oh, wow! That's wonderful. When?"

"In two weeks. On a Friday night. So, you need to make sure you're off," Nora warned. "No taking anyone's shift."

The corners of McCabe's mouth twitched as he held back a smile. "Are you asking me to be your plus one?"

"You know I am. Who else would eat the inside of the wedding cake and leave all the frosting for me?"

McCabe's laugh startled Higgins, who'd been dozing inside a cardboard box under the coffee table. The cat slunk out from under the table, shot the two humans a dirty look, and padded into the kitchen.

"Sounds like you had a very eventful Monday."

Nora was reluctant to ask McCabe about his day. It had been lovely to forget about Lara for a few hours, and she didn't want the feelings and images from Halloween night to pop the bubble of happiness surrounding her.

McCabe saw the shadow of trepidation in her eyes and nodded in understanding.

"Nothing new to report. It could take weeks for Lara's lab results to come back, which means you should try to put the whole thing out of your mind. I know that's a hard task, but let's look ahead. We've got Estella's wedding. Thanksgiving. The whole holiday season. My sister invited us to visit for Christmas again. I know it's a busy time at the shop, so I'd fly out separately and hopefully, you could join me for a few days."

McCabe had asked her to accompany him to his sister's farm in Texas before, and Nora had gently refused him. The holiday season was the busiest and most lucrative time of the year, but she'd already decided that she'd accompany him this year. She could close the shop for a few days after Christmas, which would give Sheldon a mini vacation too.

"I'd love to come to Texas with you."

McCabe was elated. "Seriously? That's great! Missy will be over the moon. And you can finally visit that bookstore in Houston. The one with the cool name."

"Murder By The Book. I'm hoping the staff can give me some pointers on how to host author events in a small space. They have it all figured out."

As soon as the words left her mouth, Nora wanted to retract them. By mentioning author events, she'd unintentionally brought Lara back into the room. Memories of Saturday night hovered like ghosts.

"The stew should be ready," McCabe said, injecting his voice with forced cheer. He filled two bowls and placed them on the table. On his next trip into the kitchen, he grabbed a basket of Irish Soda Bread, the butter dish, and napkins.

He pulled out Nora's chair and waited until she was seated before realizing he'd forgotten spoons.

"My memory is so bad, I could plan my own surprise party," he joked.

Nora shook her head. "Your memory's better than most. As Bea would say, your brain is fuller than a tick."

"If she printed T-shirts with her expressions, she'd make a killing."

"I told her the same thing. She said she'd add it to her not-to-do list."

McCabe's stew was delicious, but it was almost too hearty for Nora. After half a bowl and a slice of bread, she was full, so she chatted about Estella's wedding while McCabe finished his meal.

"I'll clean up," she said when he was done.

"You're tired, I can tell, but you're also stubborn as a mule." He gave her a tender look. "How about this? I'll do the dishes, and you can pack up the leftovers."

In the kitchen, they moved around each other in a familiar dance of opening cabinets and drawers, loading the dishwasher, and wiping off the counters.

As Nora got ready for bed, she caught sight of the book on her nightstand and her mind instantly flew to the memory of another book—the one in her tote bag.

Lara's book.

Magnum hopped up on the bed and sat on his haunches. Nora stroked his soft fur until he began to purr. He turned in a circle, preparing for a good long nap. But when Nora didn't get under the covers, his purring faltered.

"I'll be right back, baby."

She padded into the living room where McCabe was in his recliner, watching pre-game NFL coverage and working a crossword on his phone. Though Nora hated to disturb him, she had to tell him about the journal. If Lara's death became a murder investigation, the purple journal would be evidence.

"I thought you were turning in," he said, hearing her approach.

"I was, but I found this in the store this morning. I forgot about it until just now, and it can't wait. You need to see it."

He accepted the proffered book and squinted at the faded symbol on the cover. "What is that? An eye?"

"I think so. I've never seen a cover like this before. It's a journal or a diary. Just lined pages and this creepy cover. It was under the chair Lara sat in Saturday night. I'm pretty sure it belonged to her."

McCabe opened to the first page and tried to make sense of Lara's notes. After studying the second page, he began to skim. He paused when he came across an interesting quote or drawing before skipping forward to the final entry.

"I assume the initials represent her clients," he said. "I don't know why some of the initials are circled, some are inside a square, and others are inside a diamond. There's definitely a code of some sort. I can only understand a few words per entry." He glanced at Nora. "Have you looked at this?"

"A bit. Sheldon thought the initials might represent client names too. He thinks Lara created her own kind of shorthand notes for each client session. I didn't have much time to examine it, but I'm curious about the final entries. I thought, I don't know, there might be a clue hidden in one of them."

McCabe took a moment to consider this. "We need to figure out Lara's code. I could ask Enzo, but I'd rather work it out on my own. Could you grab a notebook from my office? I'll play around with this while I'm watching the game."

As a rule, Nora loved word puzzles. Crosswords, cryptograms, riddles—they were her jam. And as much as she wanted to join McCabe in cracking Lara's code, she knew that wasn't in her best interest. She needed rest and she'd never get to sleep if her mind was full of Lara's strange shorthand and miscellaneous doodles.

However, reading was a part of her nighttime ritual, so she picked up Lara's memoir.

She was soon absorbed by the chapter on how Lara's life changed after she'd been struck by lightning. Following the incident at school, where her trancelike state and message from beyond the grave spooked her teacher and her classmates, Lara became a social pariah.

Ostracized or ridiculed by the other children, she sought solace in nature and in books. Nature helped her find peace, and the public library helped her feel less alone.

Surrounded by patrons and kind-hearted librarians, Lara read every book she could find about psychics, spiritualism, magic, those who'd survived near-death experiences or, like her, had been snatched from death's grip and returned to the land of the living.

In high school, she finally made friends with two girls fascinated by Lara's gift. Not only were they impressed by what Lara could do, they encouraged her to monetize her abilities.

"My parents were horrified when they found out I wanted to start a business," Lara wrote. "They thought I'd lose my new friends and spend the next four years of high school being called a psycho. That's when it hit me. My own parents thought I was a freak. They wanted me to be the girl I was before I was struck by lightning. Sometimes, I wondered if my father regretted saving me. I looked like his daughter. I had her eyes and her voice. I had the three moles on my cheek that he said were my tiny version of Orion's Belt. I looked familiar, but I felt like an imposter. I scared my parents, which is why they punished me when I tried to embrace my gift."

Like most teenagers, Lara wanted more independence. Her parents couldn't afford to send her to college, and her greatest fear was living out the rest of her days in her small town, known to all as the local freak.

"When I was a senior, I got a job at the movie theater, working concessions. That's when I met Quincy, the boy who'd change everything," Lara wrote.

Nora heard movement out in the hall. McCabe entered the bedroom carrying Lara's journal.

"Mind if I interrupt?" he asked.

"Not at all." Nora scooched over to make room for him, which earned her a glare from Magnum.

McCabe's expression was grave as he placed the journal on Nora's lap and pointed at an entry with the initials *TR* set inside a circle.

"I think Terry Rowe knew Lara long before she came to Miracle Springs on Saturday. Not only did he know her, but if my hunch is right, he was actually her client."

Chapter 10

Please read my diary. Look through my things and figure me out.

—Kurt Cobain

"How do you know that *TR* stands for Terry Rowe?"

"Because Lara's shorthand is made up of abbreviated words or words without vowels. Let me show you. You read it first, and then I'll tell you what I think it means."

Nora tried to make sense of the entry, which read:

Wf Dnna. Stm. C, 4. Phrm. MS. No kds. Skep. CB/wk. Tur.

Nora glanced at McCabe. "Is she referring to Terry's wife?"

"I believe so. I read this as 'Wife Deanna. Stomach cancer, Stage 4. Pharmacist. Miracle Springs. No kids. Skeptic or Skeptical? Call back in a week.' I'm pretty sure that bit is correct because Terry called a week later."

"What's 'tur'?"

"I haven't figured that one out yet." McCabe flipped a page. "Her writing is so small that she fits a week's worth of session notes on half a page. This journal contains a few years' worth of session notes. This first record of *TR* with a wife with stomach cancer occurred about sixteen months ago. Deanna's diagnosis would've been probably fairly recent then."

Lara's purple scrawl had made the letter C look so insignificant. It was just another letter in the alphabet. A quick swoosh of a pen. A graceful curve like that of a waning moon. But somehow, in the empty space between the instroke where the letter began and the outstroke where it ended, there was a whole universe of fear. Of potential loss.

The next entry showed Terry's initials inside a square instead of a circle. McCabe theorized that new clients were represented by circles while repeating clients were squares. "I'm not sure what gives a client diamond status, but Terry seems to have achieved it during his final session."

Nora didn't respond because she was already reading the next entry. Using McCabe's translation as a guide, she said, "The notes from this session are less detailed. 'Wife declining. Less than two months. Purchased level three tur.' I don't understand that at all."

"Me either. I'm going to visit her website next to look for clues."

"If we're decoding this correctly, then Terry bought something from her," Nora said. "The only things available for purchase on her site are individual readings done over the phone, by video, or in person. Other than that, you can buy a package of readings or a copy of her memoir. Did Terry book more sessions?"

McCabe turned a few pages. "Just one. His initials appear again after Deanna's death. See? He has diamond status now, but this is his final session."

Leaning her head on McCabe's shoulder, Nora tried to puzzle out the meaning of the short line.

Wf d. Rfd rdg. Vy md. E tk ovr.

"Deanna died," she whispered.

"Yes. And not only did Terry refuse a reading, but it sounds like he took his anger out on Lara, so she handed him over to Enzo to deal with."

Nora knew that grief was a powerful force, and anger was often a huge part of it.

Of course, Terry had wanted to rage at the whole world after losing the person he loved most. Nora could see him lashing out at family and friends, Deanna's health-care team, the minister of their church, and anyone else who'd dared to offer him hope.

"If Terry felt like Lara had made empty promises, he probably called to give her a piece of his mind," she said. "Emotional clients were probably a big part of Lara's job, but I bet that side of things could be very draining, especially for an empath."

"Having met Enzo, I'd say he had no problem putting clients in their place. The guy has a presence about him."

Nora nodded. "I think he enjoyed being Lara's protector."

McCabe closed the journal and brushed Nora's cheek with his lips. "I could learn a thing or two from him. Here I am, getting you all wound up when I should be encouraging you to go to sleep."

"If I wasn't so tired, I'd ask you to stay and wind me up a little more." She gave him a crooked smile. "I don't think I'll have any problems nodding off, but if I do, I'll try to think of all the words that contain the letters *t, u,* and *r.*"

"You're going to close your eyes and play a one-person game of Boggle. I guess that's the word lovers' equivalent to counting sheep."

McCabe kissed her, and after giving Magnum a brief scratch behind the ears, left the bedroom with Lara's journal tucked under his arm.

Nora turned off the light and rolled onto her side. She watched the whip-thin branches of the trees outside the window shiver in the wind. There was a sad and lonely quality to the leafless branches. Having lost their foliage, they'd spend the long winter months trembling in the dark.

Winter would be an especially hard time for Enzo. He was about to face the holiday season with its bright lights, merry music, and Hallmark-inspired joviality without the woman he loved.

Though Terry had survived it once, he was clearly still haunted by grief. The holidays wouldn't be easy for him either unless he'd found comfort in the message he'd received from Lara on Saturday night.

Why did he give her another try? Nora wondered. *At the bookstore, he acted like they'd never spoken before. Maybe he was ashamed of his behavior during their last phone session. Maybe he called her a fake or demanded a refund. Did he show up on Saturday to challenge her abilities, only to be convinced by her performance?*

As sleep weighed down on Nora, she tried to think of words starting with *t-u-r*. Her last coherent thought was a word that soon invaded her dreams, filling them with fragmented images of Lara and Enzo. The couple ran a farm stand from which they sold fat purple turnips with lush, leafy stems. Everyone in town lined up to buy them, Nora included. At home, she cut the turnip in half and saw a strange pattern imprinted on its ghost-white flesh. It looked like an eye. And when Nora leaned over for a closer look, the eye opened.

"Hey," McCabe whispered in the dark. "You're okay. It's just a dream."

As if chased off by his voice, the dream fled. Nora snuggled against McCabe's warm chest, waiting for her heart rate to slow. He circled his arms around her and fell asleep almost instantly. She lay awake, thinking about Terry Rowe.

The tap, tap of the branches against the window sounded like a telegraph message. Nora wondered if the universe was trying to tell her something in a language she didn't understand. Finally, sleep returned. And this time, it was dreamless.

The next morning, Nora called Tea Flowers. The shop wouldn't be open for another ninety minutes, but she knew Kirk and Val Walsh would be onsite, preparing for another busy day.

Tea Flowers was one of the newer businesses in town and had been an instant hit with both visitors and locals. Val Walsh was a tea aficionado. On her side of the shop, she sold tea in every variety as well as tea-related gifts. Val's husband, Kirk, was a plant whisperer. His half of the shop focused on gardening and houseplants, but it was his flowering gift baskets that set him apart from other florists or gift shops.

Kirk adopted the Victorian practice of the language of flowers and used it to convey sentiments that could sometimes be difficult to put into words. Nora knew he'd come up with the perfect idea for Estella's centerpieces.

"Val and I are having breakfast at the shop. Please join us," Kirk said after Nora explained the reason for her call.

Twenty minutes later, Nora was sipping a cup of Mozambique Breakfast Blend and trying not to devour Kirk's homemade cinnamon swirl coffee cake too quickly.

"The tea takes the edge off the sweetness," Val said, pouring Kirk another cup.

Nora paused to admire the beauty of the spread. Val had set the table with antique Limoges plates and filled a creamware pitcher with sedum and wild hydrangea. The sun streamed in through the wide front windows, bounced off the water glasses, and scattered rainbows across the tablecloth.

"What a peaceful way to start the day," she said. "I can never let Sheldon know about this or he'll want to do the same thing. And as much as I love my shop, I don't want to spend more time there than I already do."

"This works well for us because we can eat with Tucker before he goes to school," Val said, referring to their young nephew. "When the bus picks him up here, it's only a five-minute ride to school. If he gets on at the stop near our house, it's almost forty-five minutes. That's too long for him. He gets antsy."

"That's a long bus ride for any kid," Nora said.

Kirk nodded. "It's because of the bus driver shortage. They're not getting paid enough. Same goes for teachers, cafeteria workers, and support staff."

"The mayor's almost afraid to shop here." Val gave her husband a playful poke. "Kirk's constantly cornering her to ask what her office is doing to improve the school system."

Kirk aimed an affectionate smile at his wife. "It's true. When it comes to Tucker, I've turned into Papa Grizzly."

They chatted about Tucker's classes, his current LEGO project, and how Derek, his therapist, had given the little boy tools to thrive as a neurodiverse student.

When they'd all finished their food, Kirk said, "Tell us about Estella's wedding. When, where, and how many guests. Does she want flowers for the ceremony and the reception? Are there bridesmaids? Groomsmen? Flowers can play a major role in such a big life event."

"We usually work in tandem with the local florist because we don't deal in cut flowers," Val added.

Nora explained that all Estella needed were centerpieces for the reception. "And the event space at the Lodge has a fireplace. Maybe we could decorate that with candles and greenery."

Kirk paled when Nora told him the date. "I'll have to check with my suppliers right away. I'd like to make centerpieces using one large potted plant and several smaller ones. That way, all the guests have something to take home. We want cost-friendly, low-maintenance plants. By mixing plants with candles and a few lanterns, we can create a magical woodland vibe. It'll be elegant and romantic."

"Without the waste," said Nora. "No throwing away a fortune in cut flowers. I love it, and I know Estella will too. Could you possibly decorate this table as an example and send me a photo?"

Kirk nodded. "I have plenty of philodendron here, which is a great plant for a wedding as it's called the Sweetheart Plant. I could also use a trailing plant called String of Hearts. But the showstopper of each table would be the Fairytale Bride Hydrangea. I have one in stock, but I need to order more pronto if our fairytale bride approves."

"Estella is very decisive. If she likes something, she'll commit on the spot."

"My favorite kind of client." Kirk pushed back his chair. "I'll get started on this right now."

Nora offered to help clean up, and the two women carried their breakfast things to the little kitchen in the back of the shop. They continued talking about Estella's wedding while washing and drying the dishes.

"Before I go, I'd like to buy some tea too. It's for someone who recently lost his partner. It was very unexpected and, as you can imagine, he's having a rough time."

After scanning her shelves of boxed teas, Val selected a blend to aid with sleep and handed it to Nora. "He'll need a mood booster too. I've got a green tea with chamomile, orange peel, elderberries, echinacea, and cinnamon that'll help with depression. It's not a cure. It's just a bright spot—an injection of warmth—to help fight off the worst of the blues."

Nora purchased the tea and thanked Val for starting her day on such a positive note. As she walked to the bookstore, she thought about how much she used to dislike the tea seller.

When Kirk and Val had first moved to Miracle Springs, Nora and Val had gotten off on the wrong foot. Since then, Val had changed. After Tucker's mom lost her battle with cancer and Val became the little boy's primary caregiver, her sharp edges had softened. She'd become more patient and much kinder.

Terry Rowe had also been flattened by grief. Unlike Tucker, who had the unconditional support of his loving aunt and uncle, Terry was alone.

And Enzo? Nora thought. *Does he have anyone?*

At the bookstore, she tucked the tea under the checkout counter and surveyed the display window. It was time to switch out the autumnal theme and install a holiday season display. But Nora didn't want to create one now and one in December. She wanted the next window display to last until January.

When Sheldon arrived, he found Nora transferring the books from the window to a rolling cart. "Good morning, *mija*. I was hoping we'd be working on this today. What are we thinking? Disco reindeer? Pink Christmas trees? Cartwheeling elves? A laser light show?"

"Could we tone it down this year and do something more sedate? I love the idea of incorporating lights, but not so many that we need to post a seizure warning."

Sheldon twirled the tail of his mustache as he gazed into the window. "You know, as much as we like to make fun of Hallmark movies, you can't beat their cozy settings."

Nora arched her brows. "Like a Christmas tree farm or a bakery?"

"Yes, but not those two. It has to be something that allows us to highlight more than one holiday while showing off lots of book genres. A Christmas tree farm is too Christmasy, and we should leave the bakery displays to Hester."

"Okay, let's think. What other elements do these movies have?"

"Hot cocoa. Mittens. Falling snow. Gorgeous gals in hand-knit sweaters. Hunky men in flannel."

Nora shook her head. "Too limited. I'm picturing romance tropes. Keep going."

"Ice skating. Cookies. A farmer's market. Popcorn. Horseback rides. Mistletoe. Dancing. Big family dinners."

"Are you a closet Hallmark Channel fan?"

Sheldon suddenly became very interested in the books on the cart.

"Tell me your deepest, darkest Hallmark secrets," Nora prodded. "Which movie is your favorite?"

"I can't remember the name, but Henry Winkler was in it. You know I love that man. The leading woman was struggling with holiday fatigue, which was super-relatable. All the hustle and bustle was giving her the Grinch syndrome. I think Henry Winkler had a farm. He hired the hot guy, and the hot guy oozed Christmas spirit. The film was especially sweet because it was about a family of two becoming a family of three."

Nora gave Sheldon a light elbow in the gut. "You're such a softie. But I totally get the holiday fatigue feeling. Some people are energized by this time of year. Others want to crawl under a rock and hide until January."

"Your turn. When I say quiet holiday, what comes to mind?"

"Reading in front of the fireplace. Soft music. Hot cider. A scented candle. Fir trees. Something baking in the oven."

Sheldon frowned. "That's a winter window. We need pre-hibernation. We need festive. Lots of color and lights."

"Over the river and through the woods and all that jazz?"

Sheldon grabbed her shoulders. "That's it! To Grandma's house we go! We don't need the sleigh or the snow because it's the *feeling* we want to capture—that anticipation of seeing family. Of eating tons of delicious food and exchanging gifts. *That's* our window."

"How do we convey that scene with books?" Nora began to pace around the front room, her mind leaping from image to image. "Suitcases, boxes tied with bows, a homemade pie, lights shining from a house. Books for travel. Books for entertaining. Books as gifts."

"How about one half of the window shows the journey while the other half shows Grandma's house? The journey side is lit up with stars, and Grandma's house is lit up with lanterns and string lights."

Nora felt a thrill of excitement. "I love that! It would be great if we could find an old suitcase or two for the travel side. We can hang an apron on Grandma's side and surround the apron with cookbooks. Why don't you sketch the background? I'll shelve the stuff on this cart and start pulling road trip books."

She shelved all the books from the previous display and then rolled the cart to the children's section. After grabbing a few car activity books, she pushed the cart into the stacks and began selecting adult books with travel themes. There were lots to choose from, but Nora particularly wanted bright, eye-catching covers or covers featuring maps.

The first book she picked was Sidney Karger's *The Bump*. Next, she grabbed Ben Aaronovitch's *The Rivers of London* and placed it on the cart with Beth O'Leary's *The Road Trip*, Penny Haw's *The Woman at the Wheel*, and Michael Ivanov's *The Cabin at the End of the Train*.

For younger readers, she pulled John Green's *Paper Towns*, Angie Stanton's *Royally Lost*, *The Year the Maps Changed* by Danielle Binks, Morgan Matson's *Amy & Roger's Epic Detour*, and Karina Yan Glaser's *The Vanderbeekers on the Road*.

She made a mental note to hang up a sign encouraging her customers to purchase audiobooks through Libro.fm. Not only were audiobooks perfect for long trips, but a portion of the profits went to Miracle Books.

Tuesday mornings were slower than the other days of the week, and Nora was able to process all the special-order requests before the trolley arrived with a load of guests from the Lodge. When the sleigh bells jangled, a dozen customers streamed into the shop.

"Looks like you were robbed." A cantankerous woman carrying one of the hotel's teal tote bags jerked her thumb at the front window. "That's not exactly welcoming."

Nora pasted on a smile. "We're in the middle of changing it."

The woman smirked. "I suppose you're doing a Christmas display. No one cares about Thanksgiving anymore, but it happens to be my favorite holiday! I don't think any stores should be open on Thanksgiving either. Do we have to shop every day of the year?"

Hoping to find common ground, Nora said, "I definitely feel sorry for people who have to work when they'd rather be celebrating with their loved ones."

The woman nodded emphatically. "Exactly! My Thomas is the assistant manager of a grocery store, and he always works the Thanksgiving shift so that the other employees can visit their families. I wish the damned store would just close. If people run out of milk, it's not the end of the world."

"Come on, Flora," said another woman. "I heard this place has the best coffee in town. I'll treat you to a cup."

The pair headed to the back of the store, leaving Nora to finish clearing out the window.

At lunchtime, she walked to Rowe's Pharmacy and waited in line behind two men in business suits. She didn't catch Terry's exchange with the first man, but she heard him greet the second man with a joke.

"Hey, Gordon. What did the football coach say to the bank employee?"

Gordon shrugged. "What?"

"'I want my quarterback.'"

Gordon's delighted laughter was probably more about Terry making a joke than the joke itself. It was a sign that Terry had finally climbed out from under the cloud of grief, at least for the moment. If he could string more of these moments together, there was a good chance he'd know happiness again.

When Nora reached the front of the line, she gestured at the end of the counter where Terry conducted his consultations. It wasn't completely private, but it was out of earshot of his assistant or any customers who might walk up to the window to collect their prescriptions.

"How are you?" she asked.

"I should be asking you that question." He touched his temple. "How's your head?"

Nora had been so preoccupied with work that she'd forgotten about her injury. "Much better. I brought some tea for Enzo. Val recommended this blend to help with sleeping." She placed the first box on the counter. At Terry's nod, she added the second box. "And this one's a mood booster. I know it's not going to make a huge difference, but maybe it'll provide a little bit of comfort."

"It's worth a try. Thank you."

Fidgeting with the tea boxes, Nora said, "It's incredibly kind of you to invite him into your home. Not many people would do that. Not in today's world."

"That's probably true, but I know exactly what he's going through. And to be honest, it's nice to have someone to take care of. My house has felt so empty. Just hearing water running in the bathroom or the sound of the TV on in the living room— it's been a comfort to me too."

If she hadn't been so focused on the entry in Lara's diary, Nora might have wished Terry a nice day and gone back to the bookstore. Terry was doing better. He'd told one of his famously cheesy jokes. His eyes were bright. He looked better than he'd looked in over a year, all because he wasn't alone in his house. Because someone needed him.

But Nora couldn't forget about the journal. If Terry knew Lara long before she came to Miracle Springs, it stood to reason that he knew Enzo too, especially if Lara had asked Enzo to deal with an angry, dissatisfied Terry.

Terry was keeping secrets, and even though there wasn't an official ruling as to the cause of Lara's death, Nora didn't think her heart had given out on its own. She believed Lara was hastened to the grave, so Terry's pretense made him look suspicious. Nora wanted to confront him before he could fabricate a credible lie.

Moving closer to the counter, she said, "I found Lara's journal under a chair in the bookstore. She kept notes of her client sessions using a unique shorthand. I don't understand her code very well, but she referred to her clients using their initials."

As she spoke, Terry's expression changed. It was like watching a heavy curtain come down over a spotlighted stage. The spark in his eyes went out, and his lips compressed into a tight line.

"Your initials were in that journal, Terry. I wasn't specifically looking for you or anyone else, but I noticed that you contacted Lara when Deanna was first diagnosed. Was she able to help?"

Terry's face darkened. His hands curled so tightly around the tea boxes that they began to cave inward. "Not. One. Bit. I never should've reached out to that charlatan. She was nothing but a swindling witch."

Terry's voice was hoarse with rage. He opened his mouth to continue his tirade when his gaze traveled over Nora's shoulder, and he suddenly paled. Gathering the tea boxes to his chest, he muttered, "I have to get back to work," and disappeared behind a set of tall shelves.

Nora heard a low animal growl and swung around to find Paula Hollowell smiling coldly at her. The low, throaty growl came from her K9 partner.

"Easy, Rambo," Hollowell soothed. "It's just the book lady. She's no threat to us."

There were no other customers in the area, which meant Terry had taken one look at Hollowell and freaked out.

Was he worried about Hollowell overhearing their conversation? Or was it something else?

"Do you bring your partner along on all your errands?" Nora asked Hollowell.

"I do. He's like a security blanket with big, sharp teeth. He's also smarter than half the people in this town. Better-looking too."

Rambo wagged his tail.

"If you hate it here so much, why don't you go somewhere else?" Nora asked. She was in a foul mood now, and it felt good to be snarky. "There must be places in, say, North Dakota where you'd be very happy."

Hollowell's mouth curved into a smug grin. "My *boyfriend* is here, and *he* makes me happy. As long as we're together, I have no reason to leave."

Nora shrugged. "Maybe you'll end up like Estella. She's marrying the love of her life in two weeks. She'll be surrounded by friends, family, and the people in this community who care about her. If you got married, who would you invite? Your coworkers, I'm sure. But what about friends? Or family?"

Hollowell's grin faded, and Nora knew she'd touched a nerve.

She'd seen the same expression cross Hollowell's face the night of Lara's reading. It suddenly dawned on Nora that Hollowell may have lost someone too.

Was she there that night in hopes of reaching a loved one? Or did she have an ulterior motive?

Because Hollowell always had an ulterior motive. She might appear to be the poster child of law and order, but behind the uniform was a woman who thrived on discord and chaos.

A human tornado, Nora thought, recalling the tornado tattoo she'd once seen on Hollowell's flank. The black, spiraling lines on her milky-white skin said it all.

Nora wanted to ask Hollowell her real reason for attending the reading. She wanted to ask why she'd had Grace buy her ticket instead of buying it herself. She wanted to ask if the story about the Halloween candy was a total fabrication, but she hesitated a moment too long. Hollowell stepped up to the counter and began talking to Terry's assistant.

Resolving to search online for information on Hollowell's past, Nora left the pharmacy and headed for the grocery store.

She had just enough time before work to pick up ingredients for one of McCabe's favorite meals, Chicken Piccata. She sent him a text saying that she'd be handling dinner tonight, and he replied with a heart emoji and reminder that he'd be home an hour later than usual because he had several meetings on his afternoon docket.

That was just fine with Nora. She'd be free to read Lara's journal, keeping an eye out for Hollowell's initials. It would never occur to McCabe to search for a *PH*. In his mind, Hollowell was a respected colleague and an upstanding member of the community.

But Nora saw a side of Hollowell McCabe didn't see. A darker, crueler side.

Maybe Lara Luz had seen it too.

Chapter 11

I shut my eyes and all the world drops dead.
— Sylvia Plath

After putting the groceries away as fast as she could, Nora fed the cats and opened a bottle of wine. In the living room, she kicked off her shoes and settled into McCabe's recliner. Lara's journal was right where he'd left it, perched on the side table next to the TV remote and a stack of coasters.

Placing her wineglass on a coaster, Nora studied the cover of the well-used book. She found it endearing that Lara hadn't replaced the ratty journal with a new one, but she also wondered where it had come from. She'd be unable to find a similar journal online, so she searched for the meaning behind the eye symbol instead.

She clicked on articles relating to spiritualism, mysticism, and religion written by college professors, companies selling jewelry, psychics advertising their services, and travel agencies.

All the content generators agreed that the eye was a significant symbol because it was the gateway to the soul. Several academics explained that an eye inside a triangle represented the Eye of God. The triangle was the holy trinity of the Father, Son, and Holy Spirit and was known as the Eye of Providence.

Other experts claimed that the All-Seeing Eye originated in Egypt, and that the trinity referred to Horus, Osiris, and Isis. The more Nora read, the more she understood that the symbol had a presence in many parts of the world and had existed for thousands of years.

Because the lines around the eye on Lara's journal had been partially rubbed off, it was hard to tell if they formed a triangle or another shape. The symbol on the cover could stand for the "third eye," or the center of spiritual insight in a person's brain. Or it could be the "evil eye," or the "eye of protection," which was traditionally worn as an amulet to ward off evil spirits.

Nora clicked on link after link showing an eye in the middle of a hand, the Egyptian Eyes of Horus or Ra, the eye on U.S. currency, Masonic eyes, the eye used by the Illuminati, the blue-and-white evil eye, and many more.

What she gleaned was that the single eye had been used for a very long time to represent divinity, clairvoyance, intuition, protection, and guidance. She couldn't find any negative references to these eye symbols, which is why, when she held Lara's journal in her hands that night, she was no longer creeped out by the dark purple cover and its faded eye. The symbol was a reminder of Lara's desire to help people—to use her gift to bring comfort and closure.

"Let's *see* what secrets are in here," she said to Higgins, who was in his "playing the cello pose" near Nora's feet.

She opened the journal and began turning pages, examining initials as she went. When she saw a *PH* inside a circle, she bolted upright in her chair.

"Well, well," she tittered, sounding like a witch in a fairy tale.

McCabe had made decent headway decoding Lara's shorthand, and by using the list he'd written last night, Nora quickly realized that *PH* wasn't Paula Hollowell. The *PH* in Lara's journal was a military wife with four children. And while Hollowell could've been married and divorced before moving to Miracle Springs, Nora thought it was safe to assume that she didn't have four children.

By the time she went through the whole book without finding any more entries with Hollowell's initials, darkness had fallen, and she needed to get dinner started.

Setting the journal aside, she washed her hands and lined up ingredients on the counter. She melted butter in a sauté pan and lightly floured two chicken breasts. Next, she added olive oil to the same pan, waited for it to reach the right temperature, and then added the chicken. While the meat browned, she dumped a small jar of capers into a colander and gave them a good rinse.

As the liquids in the pan sizzled, Nora cut a lemon into thin slices and chopped a handful of fresh parsley.

She'd made Chicken Piccata so many times that she could think about other things while she cooked, like McCabe's list of decoded words. Unsurprisingly, many of the words described relationships. People reached out to Lara to talk about their loved ones, so there were codes for husband, wife, boyfriend, girlfriend, partner, father, mother, son, daughter, aunt, uncle, cousin, brother, sister, niece, and nephew. Other codes represented illness and disease, accidents, or cause of death.

After seeing all the words written in McCabe's hurried scrawl, Nora thought about the sheer number of sad stories Lara must have heard over the years. In her way, she'd served as a grief counselor.

As the kitchen filled with the scent of hot butter and oil, Nora transferred the chicken breasts to a plate and added minced garlic, bone broth, and lemon slices to the hot pan. She scraped down the sides of the pan and let the liquids simmer until the sauce thickened. Finally, she added lemon juice, capers, and a generous sprinkle of salt and pepper to the sauce.

She was debating whether to return the chicken to the pan

and turn off the heat until McCabe came home when she heard the sound of a car in the driveway.

Seconds later, McCabe called from the hallway, "Something smells good!"

"Your timing is impeccable," Nora called back.

McCabe made a beeline for the bedroom to perform his Mister Rogers ritual. After changing out of his work clothes and slipping on a pair of sweats and a well-worn sweater, he came into the kitchen to kiss Nora hello and wash his hands.

"What can I do?"

"Set the table. I'll just toss the salad, and we're good to go."

A few minutes later, they were seated at the table, eating and talking about their workdays. Nora waited until the meal was almost over before telling McCabe about her visit to the pharmacy.

"Terry was in a good mood when I got there, but I ruined it," she admitted glumly. "I told him that I'd found Lara's journal and that I knew he was one of her clients."

McCabe stared at her. "Why did you do that?"

"Because she died right in front of me, Grant. She was doing one reading after another, and we were hanging on her every word. Yet the only person who acknowledged knowing her was Enzo. Allie is her daughter. Terry is a former client. Maybe everyone in that room knew her. At least two of the people in attendance kept their relationship with her a secret. But Lara is *dead*. That's why I asked."

McCabe jerked his head toward his recliner. "Did you go through her journal in search of Grace's initials? And Paula's?"

"Yes," Nora admitted.

"What did you find?"

"Nothing. I mean, I didn't have time to examine every page, but I read enough to get a sense of just how many people reached out to Lara after losing a loved one."

Magnum meowed and rubbed McCabe's leg. "Sorry, boy. This is Dad's chicken." He gave the cat a quick pat on the head before turning his attention back to Nora. "What I gathered from that journal was that most of her repeat clients were people in the early stages of grief. They either wanted comfort or had questions about money. Wills or real estate. Cash, gold, or jewelry. Questions about where things were hidden or who was supposed to inherit what."

"If all of those people got a personal reading, there must've been a steady stream of clients at her house," Nora said. "Which is in Greensboro. How did Terry, who lives two hours away, hear about her in the first place?"

McCabe looked thoughtful. "That's a good question. An online message board, maybe? Like a Reddit thread?"

"Well, he totally shut down when I mentioned the journal. Either that, or he didn't want to talk because Hollowell showed up with Rambo. He took one look at her and went straight to the back. You should've seen him, Grant. All the color drained from his face. He just stayed in the back, hiding behind the shelves."

"Or he went to fill Hollowell's prescription as a way of ending his conversation with you," McCabe suggested. "You said it yourself. He was in a good mood when you got there. What was his mood like after you told him about the journal?"

Nora's cheeks flamed. "At first, he was angry. Then he became completely closed off, and I couldn't tell what he was feeling."

McCabe splayed his hands as if to say, "There you have it."

"Okay, maybe I didn't handle the situation with delicacy, and maybe there's no hard evidence to prove that Lara didn't die of natural causes, but you've always said that too many coincidences indicate a pattern. And the pattern in this case is that at least two of the people in the Readers' Circle knew Lara but pretended not to."

"Then there's the modified Narcan bottle."

Encouraged by McCabe's comment, Nora said, "Exactly. Terry has access to Narcan. And both Allie and Terry got angry when I mentioned Lara. At least two people had a bone to pick with her, and I want to know what that's about. Don't you?"

"If Terry has a secret, he's unlikely to share it with you. That would be tantamount to sharing it with me. I'm going to swing by his place in the morning to see how Enzo's doing. I spoke with Lara's sister, Joan, before I left the station, too. As the executor of Lara's estate, she wanted to know when she could start planning a funeral."

Nora was surprised that Joan had been chosen over Enzo to handle Lara's affairs. "Does Enzo know that he isn't the executor?"

McCabe shrugged. "I couldn't tell you, but Joan was definitely shocked. Lara never sent a dime to help cover the costs of Allie's care. She sent letters and emails, asking for updates on her daughter, but she never called or visited. Not once. Also, her will was updated early last month."

"This is straight out of a mystery novel," Nora exclaimed. "Whenever someone dies right after changing their will, you *know* they've been murdered."

"I'm going to Terry's tomorrow because I want to see Enzo's face when I tell him about the will. I also want to ask about some of the notes in the journal. There are a few abbreviations I can't figure out. And I still don't know what the circle, square, and diamond mean."

Nora darted a worried glance at the purple book. "What if he wants to keep it?"

"Not gonna happen. That journal could be evidence." McCabe let out a sign of resignation. "I'll also have to tell him that we can't release the body, which won't be an easy conversation. Without a reason to stay, he may decide to go back to Greensboro. Allie certainly didn't hang around. She drove home Sunday evening."

Nora pushed a caper around on her plate. "I just said that this whole thing sounds like the plot of a mystery novel, and now the mystery writer—the estranged daughter of the victim—has run away."

"She wanted to get home in time to finish sewing the costume for her son's school play, which opens tonight. Dress rehearsal was last night," McCabe said.

"What's the name of the play? *My Mom's a Killer?*"

McCabe grunted in amusement. "The kid's a bit young for something that dark. His class is doing *Peter Pan*. He's Captain Hook."

Nora pictured a cute little boy wearing a red pirate's coat and a long, curly black wig. Could Allie sit in the audience while her son stomped around the stage, waving his hook and threatening Peter Pan, and behave as if her mother hadn't just died?

Maybe acting runs in the family.

After dinner and a dessert of apple slices baked with butter, brown sugar, and cinnamon, Nora continued reading Lara's memoir.

Lara and Quinn, the boy she met at the movie theater, fell in love and dated for two years. When Lara found out she was pregnant, she and Quinn got married and moved into a detached garage apartment behind Quinn's parents' house.

Quinn came from a long line of Michigan miners, and for decades, his family profited off their land's iron ore deposits. When those were depleted, Quinn and his father opened one of the first gem mines in the Midwest near a town called Eagle Mills. The gem mine became a popular tourist destination. It was such a success that Quinn and Lara were able to buy a two-bedroom house with an outbuilding. Lara planned to fix up the outbuilding and use it as a place to meet with clients.

At this point in the narrative, Nora expected to read about the birth of Quinn and Lara's daughter, but the next chapter focused on Lara's new business and the trouble it created in her marriage.

"Meeting with clients took most of my energy. Even if I only saw one or two a day. Using my gift as a spirit messenger or channeling my intuition was very draining. Quinn couldn't understand why I was always tired. We were young, and he wanted to go out. I wanted to have fun too, but we had a baby to take care of. Quinn didn't want to stay home, so he went out alone. I saw him less and less, and he started drinking more and more. I started hearing rumors about other women. And drug use. It was a really tough time."

Lara lamented the rapid disintegration of her marriage but saw no way to stop it. After less than two years together, Quinn filed for divorce. Lara got the house, and he moved back to the garage apartment at his parents' house, which was just down the road.

"Are you enjoying her memoir?" McCabe asked when he came in to get ready for bed.

Nora glanced at the clock, surprised to discover how long she'd been reading. A good book could make her lose track of time. It could pull her so deeply into its world that she was barely aware of her own.

"I'm reading about how Lara made ends meet after her divorce. She was quite young and had no support from her parents, who cut off all contact after she married Quinn. Lara and Quinn had shared custody of their daughter, and they remained cordial for her sake. Her name is never mentioned. Not once."

"Maybe Lara was protecting her."

Nora took off her reading glasses and used her pajama shirt to clean the lenses. "Quinn was a high-functioning alcoholic.

Unfortunately, his alcoholism led to diabetes. Fast forward five years. Lara walks down the street to pick up her daughter. She goes into Quinn's apartment to find him unconscious on the floor. He's surrounded by empty liquor bottles, some of which were broken. Lara's first concern is for her daughter's safety, so she takes her home. Assuming Quinn just passed out after a bender, she calls his parents to complain. However, Quinn was unconscious because he'd gone into a diabetic coma. By the time help arrived, he was dead."

"Oh, man."

When Nora closed the book, the pages let out a sigh. The sound was the perfect echo of her feelings. "That's the last time Lara mentions Quinn or their daughter. The rest of the book is about her clients. From this point on, she is completely focused on her work. But where did that leave her daughter?"

Nora put the book on her nightstand and turned off the lamp. The semi-darkness was a relief to her tired eyes, but when she closed them, she could still see the birds on the book cover. If they were meant to be the souls of those who'd died, she wondered if one of them—perhaps one of the black birds—was Quinn.

McCabe was already gone when Nora got up the next morning. She padded into the kitchen and then instantly retreated. The smell of coffee had turned her stomach, and the orb of bright light from the fixture above the sink became an imprint on the inside of her eyelids.

She went back to the bedroom and curled up on the bed until the nausea passed. After a quick shower, she drove straight to the urgent care clinic.

The receptionist gave her a strange look—probably for wearing sunglasses inside—and handed her a clipboard with the usual forms.

However, Nora couldn't fill them out. She got as far as her name, address, and date of birth before she had to put the clipboard aside and shut her eyes.

When she heard the squeak of shoes on tile, she opened her eyes to find Grace Kim gazing down at her.

"Good morning, Nora. Theresa says that your head is hurting and you're experiencing nausea and light sensitivity."

"Yes," Nora said in a near-whisper. "It's like all of my senses are on high alert. Smells are overpowering. Lights are too bright. I can't read or write. Focusing on words makes my headache worse."

Grace picked up the clipboard. "Don't worry about these. Let's get you to an exam room. Are you okay to walk on your own? Any issues with balance?"

"I'm okay."

As if sensing that this was a partial truth, Grace walked very close to Nora. Her presence was a comfort, as was her lack of perfume or scented hair products.

In the exam room, Grace took her vitals and asked for a complete list of symptoms.

"Is this the first time you've felt this way since the initial injury?"

After telling her about Monday's incident, Nora said, "Should I be worried? Am I going to have migraines all the time now?"

"Not necessarily. You're still healing from the concussion. You might have headaches for a few more days or a few more weeks. There's no set recovery time with a head injury."

"Is it safe for me to drive? Did I endanger myself and others by driving here?" Nora's voice was suddenly shrill.

Grace put a hand on Nora's arm. "Doctor Berry will see you as soon as she's done with her current patient. Don't worry, we'll get this sorted out."

While she typed notes into her tablet, Nora rested her aching head against the cushioned back of the exam chair.

"Can I ask you something that has nothing to do with my head?"

Putting the tablet aside, Grace said, "Okay."

"Did you know who Lara Luz was before Saturday's event?"

"Yes. My cousin lives in Greensboro, and Ms. Luz was practically a celebrity there. She had ads all over. Grocery store carts, nail salons, restaurant menus. I knew her slogan just from visiting my cousin. It was 'Providing peace for the present and hope for the future.'"

Nora remembered seeing the same phrase on Lara's website. "It's a good slogan."

Grace stepped into the hallway and flipped the exam room flag from blue to red. Then she closed the door and sat on a stool facing Nora. "After my cousin's best friend was killed in a car accident, she went to see Lara. My cousin never shared details about their session, but Lara really helped her. That's why I called her after losing my husband."

Nora wondered why she hadn't seen Grace's initials in Lara's journal, but what Grace said next explained how she'd missed them.

"I used my Korean name with Lara. It's Hea, which means 'grace.' I called Lara a few months after Ji-hoon died. My parents had gone back to Korea, and I was scared. I didn't know how I'd manage without my husband. I had two children and a mortgage. I was completely overwhelmed. I wanted my husband to continue guiding me, even though he was gone."

"I'm sorry you had to go through that. It must have been so hard."

"It was. It still is," Grace said. "Things are better now, but back then I felt so lost. I drove to Greensboro three times. My cousin watched my kids while I was with Lara. Even though she wasn't able to give me a message from my husband, it helped to have someone to talk to. She made me feel more confident in myself."

Nora thought about the reading in the bookstore. "I wonder why she was able to reach your husband last Saturday when she couldn't reach him before."

"Because I gave her something that was special to Ji-hoon. I didn't want to part with it before—not when he was so recently gone." Grace twisted the band of gold on her ring finger. "I miss him so much. I would've given anything to hear my husband speak to me again."

"Did it sound like him? The message?"

Grace nodded. "Ji-hoon was a kind man. He'd want to assure me that I was doing well by our children because it's what mattered most to both of us. Even if Lara was pretending, I still believe my husband guided her words. I feel like a weight is off my shoulders, and that's good enough for me."

There was a light tap on the door, and Dr. Berry entered the room. Grace summarized Nora's symptoms and explained how she'd been hospitalized Saturday night after being concussed.

Despite looking young enough to sell Girl Scout cookies, Dr. Berry knew her stuff. After asking Nora a series of questions, she said, "Red wine contains a compound called quercetin, which impacts how our bodies metabolize alcohol. The high amounts of quercetin in red wine can trigger headaches. Some patients report that any alcohol can cause a migraine, so try to avoid it for at least two weeks. Other foods you might want to limit or avoid are chocolate and caffeinated drinks. Same goes for artificial sweeteners and foods with MSG. How are you sleeping?"

"I wake up several times a night," Nora admitted. "I don't feel very well rested."

"Try working on your sleep hygiene. No TV, phone, or reading thirty minutes before bed. Turn off the lights and listen to music or an audiobook instead. You want at least seven or eight hours of quality sleep. Sleep is when your brain heals, so make it a priority. That and hydration. We can look into starting medication, but let's see how you do over the next couple of days by being mindful of your diet and sleep routine."

After thanking Dr. Berry, Nora wondered if she could possibly survive without caffeine. This thought was immediately followed by other concerns.

Will the scent of coffee set off a migraine?
What about all the candles in the shop?
What if one of my customers is wearing too much perfume or cologne?

Reading Nora's expression, Grace said, "Stress can be a trigger too. What happened to Lara on Saturday was a very sad thing, but it wasn't your fault. All we can do is hold on to the belief that Lara is at peace now."

She opened the exam room door, and Nora followed her to the reception area. Here Nora hesitated. "I'm sorry if this is overstepping, but you said you gave Lara an item that was special to your husband. Do you mind telling me what it was?"

"A ring made of carved white jade. It's called an archer's ring. It belonged to my husband's great-grandfather." Shame-faced, Grace lowered her gaze. "It was precious to him, and I know he would've wanted Charlie to have it, but . . ."

Nora touched Grace's hand. "Your sessions with Lara gave you comfort when you needed it most. I bet your husband would've traded a thousand jade rings for that."

Tears filled Grace's eyes, and she gave Nora a grateful smile before retreating to a staff room.

By the time Nora left the clinic, she was able to remove her sunglasses and drive to the bookshop without feeling like she might have to pull over to be sick.

Her headache wasn't as intense as it had been an hour ago,

but it was still there. So was the brain fog. Normally, she'd chase that away with a cup of Sheldon's magical Cuban coffee. Instead, she'd have to make do with herbal tea.

As she started her opening tasks, she thought about Grace Kim and the jade ring she'd given to Lara. Nora didn't know much about jewelry, but it sounded like the ring was valuable.

When her tea was ready, she carried it to the checkout counter and powered up her laptop. She then typed "antique jade archer's ring" into Google's search box, and after clicking several links, she called McCabe.

"Grant McCabe speaking," he said in a tone of mild rebuke.

"I know you're with Enzo right now, so I'll be quick. Please ask him if Lara received expensive jewelry from all of her clients, or just Grace Kim. Because Grace gave her a ring worth thousands of dollars to increase the chances of hearing from her dead husband. Terry called Lara a charlatan, which makes me wonder if he gave her something precious. Something that belonged to Deanna. Maybe this made someone really angry. Angry enough to commit murder."

After a brief pause, McCabe replied in his sheriff voice. "Thanks for letting me know. I'll get back to you shortly."

Nora hung up and stared into the middle distance.

The tea was beginning to dispel her brain fog, and her thoughts turned to Lara's journal. Suddenly, the initials inside a diamond made perfect sense. A diamond represented a client's final appointment, and quite possibly, the one in which they handed over a costly piece of jewelry as payment. A literal diamond, perhaps. Or a jade ring. Or another family heirloom. How many people had parted with a valuable item in exchange for a final message from someone they loved and dearly missed?

She walked to the mystery section and stood there in silence, her gaze sweeping over the titles on the book spines.

She believed the clues to Lara's murder were hidden in the purple journal. It was as if the eye on the cover was begging someone to see the truth. Nora believed that someone was her.

Resting a hand on the closest shelf, she whispered, "Once again, the answers are in a book."

Chapter 12

Only fools and charlatans know everything and understand nothing.

—Anton Chekhov

When McCabe dropped by to see if Nora was free for an afternoon coffee, she had to turn him down.

"I have too many customers right now," she said, beckoning him into the ticket agent's booth. "I'm moving slower than usual because I'm running on decaf and herbal tea. Grab a mug and help yourself to the good stuff."

McCabe gave her a puzzled look. "You only drink decaf after four."

"I went to urgent care this morning, and the doctor told me to lay off red wine and caffeine," she said. "Oh, and chocolate. I might as well wear a hair shirt while I'm at it."

McCabe was instantly worried. "If you went to urgent care, you must've felt pretty bad. So why are you here? Shouldn't you be resting?"

"The doctor told me to work on my sleep hygiene. She didn't tell me to stop working. If I feel an episode coming on, I'll go to the stockroom." She wiped drops of milk off the counter and then waved the dishrag. "Let's not waste time talking about my head. Tell me about Enzo."

Plucking a mug off the peg board, McCabe filled it with coffee. "He's going back to Greensboro today. He and Lara have three cats, and their pet sitter isn't available tomorrow."

"What did he say about the journal?"

"He wasn't happy to see it in my hands, that's for sure. He could translate some of Lara's shorthand but not all of it. For example, he didn't know what *t-u-r* was short for. When I asked if he recognized anyone from Saturday's reading by name or face, he got squirmy. The only person he admitted to knowing was Allie Kennedy. He claimed he had very little to do with Lara's business. Turns out, he has his own."

Nora felt a buzz of electricity in her blood. "Does it have something to do with jewelry or antiques?"

McCabe gaped at her. "It's a pawnshop. Did you already know that?"

"Not exactly." Nora repeated her conversation with Grace Kim. "I think the diamonds in the journal mean that Lara asked a client to give her something of value in return for a certain service. If Enzo owns a pawnshop, he could turn those 'gifted' items into cash."

McCabe waved at a teenage girl eyeing the last chocolate-filled book pocket in the pastry case. "Hey, Abigail."

"Hey, Sheriff. Are you guarding that book pocket, or can I have it?"

He smiled at her. "It's yours, and it's on me. Your mom covered for me when I was very, very late for a meeting, so I owe her one. And since she's given up sugar, I'll treat you instead."

"Works for me."

While Nora plated the pastry, McCabe put a twenty in the tip jar. Abigail gave him a thumbs up and pointed at his coffee mug. "Nice choice."

McCabe laughed when he saw that he'd picked a mug that said I HATE PANTS.

Nora waited until Abigail walked away before whispering, "Terry called Lara a swindler. What if he gave Lara something that belonged to Deanna? Something he wanted to get back?"

"He's not going to talk to me while I'm in uniform, so I'll take him out for beer and pizza. Without Enzo around, he's probably feeling low. I sincerely like the guy, and I'm worried about him."

"But you're still going to ask about the jewelry, right?"

McCabe nodded. "I'll be straight with him. I'll tell him his behavior doesn't add up and that he's better off talking to me while we're just two guys sharing a pie and not two guys sitting across from each other in an interview room."

"I hope you learn something. With Allie gone and Enzo leaving town, it feels like the people who knew Lara best are kind of abandoning her." A customer approached the window and asked if she could pre-order the next Jodi Picoult novel. After promising to meet her at the checkout desk, Nora quickly kissed McCabe and said, "I won't see you until later tonight. I'm meeting the girls at the Pink Lady to talk about wedding stuff."

"Have fun. I'm going to duck out the back and do a quick sweep of the parking lot. No one's seen a white van with a Porky Pig sticker, and the mayor isn't happy that the Midnight Dumper is still at large."

Nora wasn't surprised. Miracle Springs depended on tourism, and many visitors chose their bucolic little town for its clean air, hot springs, and pristine forests. They didn't pay top dollar for vacation rentals, hotels, or campsites to stumble on construction debris during a nature hike or plan a fishing excursion to find piles of garbage in the river.

Nora was wondering when she'd be well enough to walk on her favorite trail when the last customer of the day asked for climate fiction with a dystopian slant.

"Everyone always recommends *The Parable of the Sower*," said the young man. "And Octavia Butler is awesome, but I want something new and different. Not *Annihilation*, either. The book was okay, but the movie was a piece of crap."

Nora knew a few titles in this subgenre, but they wouldn't come to her. After running a quick keyword inventory search on her laptop, she led the young man to the fiction shelves.

"I've got three for you. *Pink Slime* is translated fiction featuring a poisonous algae bloom. *The Light Pirate* shows the total destruction of Florida after a series of major hurricanes. And finally, there's *Migrations*. This is a slow burn about a woman following the last Arctic terns migrating from Greenland to Antarctica."

The young man briefly examined the books. "They're all written by women and have a female MC. That's cool. But I'm not into birds, so I'll just get the first two."

Nora rang him up, escorted him to the door, and locked it behind him. After finishing her closing tasks, she drove to the Pink Lady.

Kiesha, the day manager, was just leaving when Nora arrived.

"Your besties are in the back corner booth," she said.

The diner was crowded, and Nora received several dirty looks as she skirted around the line of people waiting for a table. The counter seats were first come, first serve, but every stool was taken by people in navy-blue fire department T-shirts or EMT uniforms.

The bowling rivalry between the Miracle Springs firefighters, EMTs, and sheriff's department was legendary. McCabe didn't bowl, but the absence of other members of his department meant that their team had gone to the alley early to practice.

"Here she is!" cried June as she scooted over to make room

for Nora. "We just ordered drinks. I'm having wine, Hester's having Prosecco, and Estella's having a raspberry milkshake."

When the server arrived, Nora pointed at Estella. "I'll have what she's having, please."

"No wine?" Estella asked.

Nora waited for the server to move away before telling her friends about her visit to urgent care.

"I'm sorry about your symptoms, but it sounds like you were supposed to bump into Grace. Otherwise, she might not have told you about the archer's ring." June frowned. "What is that, by the way?"

Nora stuck out her thumb and tapped the lower part of the pad. "Drawing back a bowstring and releasing it causes friction. Repeating that motion over and over again can be painful. An archer's ring keeps some of that pressure from damaging the thumb."

Estella found several examples on her phone and showed them to Nora. "Looks like there are white and green jade versions. Some are carved. Others are completely smooth."

"And the antique ones are worth thousands of dollars?" asked Hester.

Nora nodded. "And get this. Enzo owns a pawnshop."

June threw up her hands. "There you have it. Lara, may she rest in peace, was a fraud. Why am I not surprised?"

The server returned to take their orders. After deliberating between the herb-crusted salmon and the pot roast, Nora opted for the salmon. As soon as they were alone again, Nora told her friends that Terry had been Lara's client and that he'd called her a charlatan.

"I bet he gave her a piece of Deanna's jewelry," said Estella. "She had a gorgeous pearl necklace that had to be worth a pretty penny. I did her hair for years, and she told me about that necklace. It was made of South Sea pearls from Indonesia and was a wedding gift from her father to her mother. They had a lovely golden color and looked great with Deanna's ash-blond hair."

Hester's hand went to the locket around her neck, which held a photo of her daughter. "What did Enzo say about all this?"

"He told Grant that he wasn't involved with Lara's business."

"Horseshit," said Estella. "The man owns a pawnshop."

Nora made a time-out gesture. "I don't want to hijack our reason for getting together tonight, which is to talk about the wedding. If we have time, we can circle back to Lara and Enzo later. I *do* want to pick your brains about a few things, but Estella comes first."

Estella threw her a grateful look. "Thanks. And thank you for talking to Kirk and Val. I love the plants Kirk picked for the centerpieces. He's going to tape care instructions to the bottom of every pot and will also provide candles and lanterns for the reception. So, I can check decorations off my list."

"And the cake," said Hester.

"And the cake," agreed Estella. "I rented five dresses for a week. They're supposed to come in the mail by Saturday. If none of them work, I'll wear a smock from the salon and Jack can wear a chef's apron."

June grinned. "That's kind of cute."

"But a smock would hide my bump. I don't want our baby to see pics of the wedding and think we were ashamed of them or got married because of them. We want our baby to know that we loved them before they ever set a teeny, tiny toe into this world." Estella gave June a stern look. "Don't get weepy on me. We've got too much to do."

June saluted. "Yes, ma'am. Here's an update on the seating chart. Sheldon is naming every table after a local business. Each business will be represented by a building, and the names of the guests seated at that table will be listed on the building. All the buildings will light up. He's going to surround them with greenery to complement your magic woodland theme."

"I love it," said Estella with a hitch to her voice.

"Don't get weepy on me," June warned, and everyone laughed.

The food arrived, and Nora tucked in with gusto. Her appetite had been off since her injury, but the tender salmon tasted so good that it was almost gone when the server checked in to see how they were enjoying their meals.

"Ten out of ten," Nora said. "This herb crust is delicious."

As soon as the server was out of earshot, Estella put her fork down. Resting her hands on her belly, she gazed at Nora across the table. "We're all set as far as the wedding goes. What can we do to help you?"

"I'd like to know more about Hollowell's background. She told Grant that she went to Lara's reading because her grandmother was into spiritualism. I feel like there's more to it than that."

Hester snorted. "No doubt. That woman has more faces than a roomful of clocks."

"I'll look online while we're talking." Estella reached for her phone. "Do we have any idea where Hollowell lived before moving here?"

"A troll's cave?" suggested Nora.

"One of Dante's lower circles?" said June.

"A viper pit?" said Hester.

Estella's lips twitched with amusement. "I need a place I can find on a map."

Hester jerked a thumb over her shoulder. "I bet the ladies and gents at the counter know. Hollowell's on the bowling team."

"Go talk to that gorgeous EMT who helped me on Saturday," said Nora. "He's obviously into you."

"How would you know? You'd just been whacked in the head."

June made a shooing motion at Hester. "Just go over there and flirt a little. It's for a good cause."

"Okay, but don't watch me," Hester said as she got to her feet. "This is already super-awkward."

June kept her eyes on Nora. "How else can we help?"

"There's an abbreviation in Lara's diary I can't figure out. It's *t-u-r*. I printed out a list of every word starting with these three letters, but none of them seem to fit."

Estella said, "What's the context?"

"Lara used this code during session notes with clients who'd lost a loved one—usually a spouse or a parent—or were in danger of losing one. Like Terry. Deanna had maybe two months left when he first contacted Lara."

After staring at the list for a moment, Estella said, "Maybe it stands for turkey. A turkey is someone who isn't bright or does something foolish. Maybe she thought Terry was desperate enough to do something stupid, like hand over Deanna's pearls. He was a mark. A turkey."

"It's possible," Nora said without conviction.

When it was June's turn to study the page, she placed her finger on a word right away. "What about turquoise? Aren't certain gems supposed to have healing powers?"

Nora mulled this over. "Maybe Lara offered a piece of turquoise in exchange for something that belonged to the client's loved one? Like a jade archer's ring or Deanna's pearls?"

"Does turquoise have mystical significance?" asked Estella.

"No clue. Let's see what the almighty Internet has to say." Nora clicked a few links and shrugged. "Here we go. Turquoise is supposed to have healing properties."

Estella toyed with the straw in her milkshake glass. "Which

might have appealed to Terry, but what about the clients whose loved ones were already gone?"

"Good point," said June. "Does it have other properties?"

Nora kept reading. "It's hard to say. This site says turquoise restores balance and calm. This one says it brings inner peace. Another one says it offers protection, strength, and an increased ability to fight viruses."

Estella perked up. "Now *that's* useful."

At that moment, Hester returned to the booth with pink cheeks and pinpricks of bright light in her eyes.

"Well, well! Methinks there was some flirting at the counter," teased June.

"A little," Hester admitted. "I'm not ready to date anyone, but if Jamie wants to buy me a drink in the future, I wouldn't say no. He might not be a redhead, but he reminds me of the *Outlander* Jamie. He even has a Scottish last name. It's Ballantine."

Nora stole a glance at the sandy-haired man at the counter. "I wonder how he looks in a kilt."

"Let's focus on Hollowell," Hester said. "I learned that she doesn't have any family in the area, she never married, and she worked for the Guilford County Sheriff's Department before moving to Miracle Springs."

"Where's Guilford County?" asked June.

Nora felt a rush of adrenaline. "East of here. It includes the city of Greensboro. Which is where Lara lived."

June let out a soft whistle.

"That's not all." Hester lowered her voice. "We all read Lara's book, so you'll understand why this next tidbit is too juicy to be mere coincidence."

Estella motioned for her to hurry up. "My bladder is too full for theatrical pauses."

Leaning forward, Hester whispered, "Hollowell is from a small town. Near a mine. In Michigan."

June slapped the table. "*Lara* was from a small town. In Michigan. Near a mine. How many of those can there be?"

Nora stared at her. "Hollowell knew Lara. I can feel it in my bones."

"Michigan's a big state. There could be dozens of mines," argued Estella.

Hester rubbed her arms as if she'd caught a chill. "*If* she and Lara were from the same town, the odds of them both ending up in Greensboro, North Carolina, are really slim. It almost sounds like Hollowell was *following* Lara."

The women exchanged stunned glances until Estella broke the spell by hurrying off to use the restroom. Soon after, the friends called it a night.

Back at McCabe's Nora finished reading Lara's memoir. She put the book aside and immediately ran a Google search using the terms "Paula Hollowell" and "Greensboro, North Carolina."

Sure enough, there were several hits from the Guilford County Sheriff's Department. The first announced Hollowell as a new hire. The second was a short article from *The Greensboro News and Record* on the history of the county's K9 officers. This piece included a photo of Hollowell with her partner, a Doberman named Warden.

The Hollowell from four years ago had long black hair pulled back in a bun so tight that the skin on her forehead looked like glass. Her expression was unreadable, and her gaze was guarded.

"Not so crazy about having your picture in the paper, were you?"

Nora kept digging. Because Hollowell didn't use social media, there wasn't much to find other than a White Pages listing of Hollowell's Greensboro address. The listing also included her previous address, which was in Marquette, Michigan.

Plugging Marquette into a map, Nora compared the distance between Marquette and Eagle Mills, the town where Lara had lived. The two towns were less than eight miles apart.

"Whoa," Nora murmured, sinking deeper into the couch cushions.

The White Pages also listed a person's relatives, and there were three people in Hollowell's "related to" field.

Nora decided to look them up. The first two, Donald and Erica Hollowell, age sixty-three, didn't have an address. Neither did Michelle Hollowell, age eighty.

Searching for the names in connection to Marquette, Michigan, led Nora to Michelle's obituary. After reading it, she picked up the phone and called June.

"You caught me dozing off in the middle of *The Bachelor*," said June.

"I'm sorry to call so late, but I had to talk to someone."

She heard a rustling sound, and then June said, "Honey, you know I'm always here for you. What's on your mind?"

"When Hollowell lived in Michigan, she and Lara were only eight miles apart."

"*What?*"

Even though June couldn't see her, Nora nodded. "I know. It's crazy. She lived with her grandmother, who passed away twelve years ago. In the obituary, Hollowell was listed as the only surviving relative. Hollowell's parents died when she was seven."

"Oh, Lord. That's terrible. The woman has her faults, but her behavior makes a little more sense to me now. I think the world broke her heart and it never really got fixed."

"Her situation reminds me of Allie's. As girls, they both lost someone they depended on and were raised by people other than their parents."

June clicked her tongue in sympathy. "Poor babies. At least, they had people to love and care for them. They could've ended up in the foster care system or been taken in by relatives who didn't treat them right. Are you going to tell McCabe about this?"

Nora glanced at his empty recliner. "I have to. There's something here. I don't know what it is, but it's important. It has to be."

"Your voice is dragging, honey. Time to get that sleep you need so badly."

Lara's journal sat on the coffee table. The faded eye on the cover seemed to be looking at Nora, tempting her to stay up a little later. But as much as she wanted to search the pages for a tangible connection between Hollowell and the dead medium, Nora knew June was right. The journal would still be there in the morning, so she wished June a good night and went to bed.

The next morning, the journal was gone.

McCabe had taken it and left a note in its place. All it said was *Call Me.*

Nora complied.

"You left your laptop open last night," McCabe began without preamble. "I saw your search history, and I need you to know that I completed a thorough background check on Deputy Hollowell before hiring her. I spoke to her superiors in Greensboro at length. She is a hard-working, reliable officer of the law. She hasn't received a complaint from a single citizen in this town. The only person who has a problem with her is you. This has to stop, Nora. *Now.*"

"Is that why you brought the journal to work? To keep it away from me?"

"Yes, and this is where it's going to stay," McCabe replied with aggravating calm. "You need to focus on your recovery. Fixating on Lara's death—and on my deputy—is having adverse effects."

Though she was seething inwardly, Nora strived to match McCabe's even tone. "On my health or on our relationship?"

"Both," McCabe said. Softening his tone, he went on. "I'm worried about you. You spent the night in the hospital because of an injury. I should've protected you better by not sharing details of the case with you. That's on me. I love you, Nora. I want you to get better. I want to dance with you at Estella's wedding."

Nora heard a knock followed by low murmuring on the other end of the line. Before McCabe could say he had to go, she said, "I'll talk to you later," and ended the call.

She brewed a cup of herbal tea and sat with her feelings for a moment. She understood McCabe's point, but she hadn't appreciated his delivery. He'd spoken to her like she was a child in need of a firm rebuke.

The cats, sensing her agitation, rubbed her calves and meowed. She gave them a pile of treats and drove to Miracle Books. She lit a caramel apple candle, put on some upbeat music, and shucked off her bad mood as if it were a scratchy sweater she didn't want to wear anymore.

When Sheldon showed up at nine thirty, he presented Nora with one of Hester's homemade pumpkin donuts. Then he told her that Charlie had a teacher workday and would be arriving in twenty or thirty minutes.

"He's going to work a full day. With his help, we can finish the window display and catch up on all our pre-holiday tasks. It'll also give you a chance to pick out a reading for Estella's wedding."

Nora had never been so thankful for Charlie. When Sheldon left at three, the shop was teeming with kids, and they all wanted Harry Potter Hot Chocolates. Charlie cranked out one after another, leaving Nora to focus on selling books.

It had been such a positive and profitable workday that Nora almost forgot about her morning phone call with McCabe. But as she locked the store and crossed the parking lot to where her truck was parked, she caught sight of her tiny home and experienced a lightning-crackle moment of clarity.

She suddenly realized why she hadn't green-lighted any of the builder's renovation proposals. Making a decision about her house meant making a decision about moving in with McCabe. He'd asked her to several times in the past few weeks, and she wasn't certain that she wanted to.

She loved McCabe, but she also cherished her independence. She loved having her own space. She adored every inch of Caboose Cottage and missed moving around her tiny, bright kitchen and reading in her snug living room. She missed the sound of the passing trains and the one-minute walk to work.

You need to decide, scolded her inner voice. *People donated money to restore your house. If you're going to live there, then live there. If not, do something with it to benefit the reading community.*

She was sitting at McCabe's table, working on a list of possible uses for her tiny house, when McCabe came home.

He walked into the living room with his phone pressed to his ear and a troubled expression on his face. "I see. I'll make some calls and get back to you."

He lowered the phone and stared at the keypad, as if unsure which number to dial.

"Everything okay?" Nora asked.

McCabe joined her at the table. "I don't know. That was Lara's pet sitter. Enzo told her to swing by last night so he could pay her, but he didn't answer the doorbell or pick up the phone. She stopped by this morning to check on the cats, and again just now. Still no Enzo. It looks like he never made it home from Miracle Springs."

"And he was definitely headed straight back to Greensboro?"

"That's what he said, which is why I have a bad feeling about this."

Clutching her pinkie, which had begun to throb above the knuckle where the rest of her finger had been amputated, Nora whispered, "So do I."

Chapter 13

To everyone whose favorite color is morally gray.
— Ana Huang

When Enzo failed to return to Greensboro the following day, McCabe initiated a BOLO alert. After sending out a description of Enzo and the make and model of his car, he reached out to the sheriff of Guilford County to update him on the situation. Finally, he asked the pet sitter if she'd continue taking care of the cats until Enzo returned, and the woman kindly agreed.

For the next two days, there was no news of Enzo. Nora was so busy at work that she rarely thought about him. With Thanksgiving around the corner, the town was packed with visitors. They came into Miracle Books searching for hostess gifts, hot drinks, and cookbooks.

Luckily, Nora was prepared for all three. The big display table in the front of the store was loaded with books on cooking and entertaining. A smaller table offered cocktail and mocktail books and a waterfall display near the Readers' Circle featured fiction set on or around Thanksgiving.

Shoppers who came in searching for a pumpkin latte were disappointed to learn that the menu didn't include any espresso drinks requiring bottled syrups.

"I thought *everyone* served pumpkin lattes," a woman whined to Sheldon.

"I have something that tastes much better than those artificial flavors," he told the crestfallen customer. "For one week only, we're offering a brown sugar latte. The syrup is homemade and has notes of caramel and vanilla. Want to give it a go?"

Unable to resist Sheldon's charm, most people ordered the special drink. Later, they'd stop by the pass-through window to tell him how good it was and to add money to the tip jar.

The weather, which had taken a chilly turn, drove everyone indoors. Curls of smoke drifted out of the houses on the hills, and baskets of kindling joined the pumpkins on front porches all over town. The locals dug through their closets, taking stock of their winter clothes and pulling on a favorite sweater for the first time since March.

For some reason, the brisk air was a balm to Nora's head. Her symptoms were decreasing a little every day, but she was at her best in the early morning. She liked to put on a barn coat and carry her coffee out to McCabe's porch. Nestled in one of his wicker rockers, she'd sip her coffee and breathe in the scents of late autumn.

Joggers and dog walkers waved as they passed by, and she'd smile and wave back. She was becoming a fixture in McCabe's house, but she still wasn't sure how she felt about making it her permanent home.

She'd think, *I already have a home.*

Deciding where to live was a complication she didn't want to deal with at present. When she was at work, she put all of her energy into her customers. But during quiet moments like these, her thoughts turned to Lara. This led to a slideshow of faces in her mind. She saw them over and over again. Hollowell, Terry, Grace, Allie, and Enzo.

Sitting outside, where the only noises were the scrabbling of squirrels and the groan of the rocking chair, she felt like she was in the eye of the storm. Lara's death had created a disturbance. This was just a lull—the weightless pause—before the wind howled and the sky blackened again.

The storm returned sooner than Nora expected.

On Friday night, she and McCabe had dinner out and turned in early. After sleeping soundly for eight hours, Nora woke feeling energized and pain-free.

"I'm going on a short hike before work," she told McCabe over coffee. "Wanna come?"

"You sure you're up for that?"

Nora tried not to be irritated by his question. She knew he meant well, but she also knew her own body. "I feel really good. It's such a beautiful morning, and I haven't been on the mountain for ages. Charlie is opening for me today, so I don't need to be at the shop until noon."

"Count me in," he said. "What are you thinking? The path behind your house?"

"How about the Treehouse Trail?" Nora said, referring to the trail that began at a group of hotel rooms built as treehouses and eventually merged into the Appalachian Trail.

McCabe finished his coffee and headed into the kitchen for a refill. "This calls for bacon. We need protein to fuel our exercise."

"I'm having oatmeal with pecans and blueberries." She tapped her temple. "Bacon's not on my concussion diet."

After breakfast, they put on sweaters, sweatpants, and hiking boots and drove to the public parking lot adjacent to the treehouse hotel property. Their boots crunched over the gravel road as they headed for the trailhead, and they passed a family of four returning to their car. Their faces were pink with exertion, and their eyes sparkled as they discussed which pastries to buy from the Gingerbread House on the way home.

"I want an apple cider donut!" the little boy shouted.

McCabe grinned at the boy and turned to Nora. "I had one of those yesterday. Andrews brought in a whole box and left it in the break room. I could smell them from my office, and I practically floated down the hall like a cartoon character following a scent trail."

"I'm glad that he and Hester are friendly. He can still pop into the bakery without any awkwardness."

"Me too. Otherwise, we might have been stuck with grocery store donuts."

Nora was about to ask McCabe to stop so she could retie her boot laces when a woman screamed.

The shrill cry raised the hairs on the back of Nora's neck. McCabe's head jerked to the right, and he scanned the woods like a hound on the hunt. The sound had come from the direction of the trailhead, but farther to the east where a creek cut through a cluster of boulders that looked like a giant's knucklebones.

"HELP!"

The shriek was still echoing in Nora's ears when McCabe broke into a run. She followed behind, but she'd always been a slow runner and it didn't take long for McCabe to leave her in the dust.

By the time she veered off the path and picked her way over the uneven ground to where McCabe stood, trying to calm two very agitated women, she was out of breath.

"I climbed down here to get Waldo's ball! That's when I saw him!" wailed the redhead cradling a Boston Terrier in her arms.

The other woman, a tall brunette with bear-brown eyes, rubbed the redhead's back. "It's okay, babe. This man's the sheriff. He'll take care of this. Just don't look."

The redhead turned away from the creek, which immediately prompted Nora to look in that direction. The rocks blocked her view of the water, but the phantom tingle in her pinkie told her what was down there.

A body.

McCabe confirmed her fears by putting a hand on her arm and whispering, "It's Enzo. I called it in, but it'll take fifteen minutes for the cavalry to come."

"Can we go? *Please?*" the redhead asked in a tremulous voice.

The brunette gave McCabe a plaintive look. "Like I said, we're on our way to see my folks in Winchester. We stopped to stretch our legs, and here we are. But my mom will freak out if we're late, and we really don't have anything else to tell you. If it wasn't for Waldo's ball, we never would've left the trail."

McCabe nodded. "I've got your information, so yes, you can go. You've done this man a service. Because you found him, we can take care of him. Thank you for that."

He tipped his hat in gratitude and stepped back, positioning himself between the two women and the creek.

Nora waited until they were well out of earshot before moving closer to the rocks.

She gazed down at the creek but didn't see a body. As she scanned the opposite bank, she realized that the lumpy, leaf-covered shape was a person.

At first glance, it looked like another rock blanketed by leaves. But the longer she stared at it, the more details she saw. The dark patches under the leaves belonged to a leather jacket. The blur of blue came from mud-stained jeans. Finally, there was the rounded toe of a black boot. What she couldn't see was a face.

"Are you sure it's Enzo?"

McCabe held out his phone. "I zoomed in with my camera. It's him."

Opening the camera app on her phone, she focused on the body and zoomed in.

For a second, the leaves were nothing more than brown fuzz, but then the camera adjusted the focus, and Nora was able to pick out details. She could see the texture of the rocks, a crooked branch, and a hand with thick fingers.

Her gaze moved from the hand to a pale cheek and a jawline covered in dark stubble. She saw a thick, bushy brow resting over a closed eye with a sweep of dark lashes. She lowered her phone and sighed heavily. "How in the world did he end up here?"

"My guess is he was dumped and then covered in leaves." McCabe put his hands on his hips and surveyed the area. "This lot is deserted at night. There are no cameras. The treehouse property has a few, but they're trained on their structures, not the road."

"Whoever did this had to transport him from the lot to the creek. That couldn't have been easy."

McCabe's eyes kept moving. "The strange thing is that the Midnight Dumper dropped a load of garbage very close to where Enzo's body is now. I don't see how the two events could be connected, but it's weird."

Nora stared down at the creek. The current was so sluggish that it looked like the water was frozen. The glassy surface reflected the brilliant blue of the November sky. It was lovely. It seemed like a place where foxes or deer might stop to drink. In the evening, after the humans had gone.

McCabe put an arm around Nora's shoulders. "You okay?"

His touch brought Nora back to the moment. "Yeah. I was just thinking that he's been out here for a few days. And the cats—his and Lara's—have been waiting for their mom and dad to come home. It's stupid, I know. A man was killed, and I'm imagining a bunch of cats looking out the window the way Magnum and Higgins do when they're missing you."

McCabe put a finger under her chin. "Hey. Look at me."

Nora's vision blurred with tears. "Sorry. It's just that . . ."

"It isn't right," whispered McCabe. "The way he was left

here like a bag of trash. It's sad and unfair and wrong. I want to cry every time something like this happens."

"But you never do. You're always so calm. So strong."

"That's because of my training, but I feel things I don't show." McCabe pulled Nora close and pressed his lips to her forehead. "You'll get cold, standing out here."

Nora glanced toward the trail. "I want to stay until your backup comes. It won't be long."

They stood, shoulder to shoulder, watching the path. And even though Nora wanted to know what McCabe was thinking, she didn't ask. For him, this was the beginning of a new investigation. The clock had started the moment he'd heard the woman's scream. For the rest of the day, he'd be collecting evidence, transporting the body, and conferring with colleagues. The least she could do was give him a few minutes of silence before the chaos began.

The first deputy to arrive on the scene was Andrews. He was followed shortly by Fuentes and Hollowell. Hollowell was accompanied by her K9 partner.

Both woman and dog moved briskly over the rough terrain, and Nora stiffened at the sight of them. She heard McCabe's voice in her head, telling her that her enmity with Hollowell must come to an end. She remembered his brisk tone as he reminded her that he'd run a background check, reviewed Hollowell's employment history, read her references, and spoken to the Guilford County Sheriff's Department. But what did he really know about her personal life? About her past?

Like why did she leave a job in a busy city for the quiet and seclusion of a small mountain town?

But if Hollowell needed to relocate in a hurry, she would've been prepared for that question. She would've talked about her love of the outdoors or her desire to have a house with a big yard for her dogs. She may have said that she came from a small town and preferred the slower pace and sense of community found in a place like Miracle Springs.

This story starts in Michigan, Nora thought as she watched a pair of hikers descend from the top of the hill.

Hollowell's grandmother was into spiritualism.

Lara was a medium.

They lived eight miles apart.

Maybe Hollowell's grandmother was a client of Lara's. Maybe Hollowell gave Lara something valuable, but her grandmother died anyway. Would Hollowell chase Lara across the country to retrieve this item?

It was a preposterous theory, and Nora knew it. If there was a connection between Hollowell and Lara, it had to be more significant than a piece of jewelry. If Hollowell wanted revenge, she could have gotten it in Michigan or Greensboro. Why wait until now?

As Hollowell drew closer, Nora saw her own suspicion and dislike mirrored in the other woman's face.

Not mirrored. Amplified.

Hollowell stared at her with unveiled hostility and, not for the first time, Nora wondered why the other woman saw her as a threat. Hollowell had a badge and all the authority that came with it. But for some reason, she'd hated Nora from the moment they'd met.

Nora thought back on her interactions with Hollowell. The woman went out of her way to belittle Nora's business. She scoffed at people who "wasted time" reading books and called bibliotherapy a "total con."

Maybe Hollowell thinks I'm taking advantage of people for my own gain. Maybe she sees me as another Lara. As someone who preys on those in pain. A charlatan.

This felt so right and true that Nora wondered why she hadn't reached this conclusion before.

Hollowell had been raised by her grandmother. After her

death, Hollowell had been left with no family. She'd been completely alone. If she believed that Lara hastened her grandmother to the grave, all the love she'd felt for her sole caregiver could've easily warped into rage.

Hollowell's eyes locked on Nora's face. She looked confused to find a lack of animosity there and immediately shifted her gaze to McCabe.

" 'Morning, Sheriff," she said.

" 'Morning, Hollowell. I'm hoping Rambo can help us find where our perp entered the woods. Fuentes and Andrews can set a perimeter. It's supposed to rain this afternoon, so we need to work fast." McCabe rested his palm on Nora's back. "I'll catch up with you later."

She gave his arm a squeeze. "Good luck. See you at home."

Hollowell glanced down at Rambo, but not before Nora saw the flicker of envy in her eyes.

As she walked away, Nora thought about the contrast between Enzo and Hollowell. Out here, Enzo had unwillingly become a victim to the elements. His body was slowly deteriorating.

But Hollowell was rotting on the inside. The decay might not be obvious to everyone, but Nora and her friends could sense it.

By the time she got back to McCabe's house, Nora was cold and out of sorts. She didn't want to be alone, so she showered and dressed for work. Though she wasn't due in until noon, she showed up at nine thirty.

"What are you doing here, *mija*?" Sheldon asked when he saw her. "You should be snuggled up with your man."

Nora told him what had happened.

"I keep saying that exercise is dangerous, but no one listens." Sheldon shook his head. "Poor Enzo. Is there a chance he just slipped? Strayed off the path and lost his footing? Does it have to be something terrible? Because I don't want that for him."

"He was supposed to be home by now," Nora said. "He and Lara have cats, and he checked in with the pet sitter two days ago to tell her he was on his way home. I can't see him stopping for a hike before leaving town."

Sheldon smirked. "He didn't seem like the hiking type. When I first saw him, I thought he must be a loan shark or a bouncer at a seedy bar. He might've looked like a character from *Goodfellas*, but he was a sweet guy."

"I'm not sure if Lara and Enzo were the selfless, compassionate people I thought they were," Nora said glumly.

"None of us are all good or all bad, which is why the best books have morally ambiguous characters." Sheldon poured her a cup of decaf. "I don't want to diminish what happened to Enzo by moving on with our day, but that's what you need to do for the sake of your mental health. Drink this magical brew and tell us what you think of the display window so far. Charlie's up front, in the thick of it. He's in charge of the glitter."

Nora's eyes narrowed. "I was told there'd be no glitter."

"I'm kidding. We're using sequins instead. Just a few. Less than a thousand. Probably."

"Show me."

Sheldon swept out of the ticket agent's booth and shouted, "Take the sequins and run, Charlie!"

The warning went unheard as Charlie had his earbuds in and was bobbing his head in time to music no one else could hear.

There were sequins, but they were glued to a collection of small stars. Some were in the sky above the car pinned to a snowy backdrop while the others hovered over the roof of the grandmother's house. Charlie was busy hanging a star over Grandma's chimney.

When Sheldon tapped Charlie on the shoulder, the boy gasped and clutched his chest. "You scared me!" Then he frowned at Nora. "Aren't you way early?"

"I was supposed to go hiking, but it didn't work out." She stared at the glittery stars. "I'm loving this window. Who made the apple pie out of felt? And where did we get a fake fireplace?"

Charlie smiled proudly. "Sheldon bought the fireplace. My mom made the pie. She wanted to do something nice for you. She thinks you're awesome for giving me the job."

Nora's heart swelled with gratitude. Not just for Grace Kim and her felt pie but for the gifts she received from friends and strangers alike.

Every day, her work allowed her to interact with so many incredible people. Customers from all over the country sent emails telling her how much they'd enjoyed her book recommendations. Many of these people still shopped for books through the Miracle Books website or followed the store's social media accounts. Nora was connected to a huge network of people whose lives had been changed in some small way because of her store.

Nora had given Miracle Books her all, and in return it had given her a community that reached far beyond the town limits. Before the bookstore, she'd been lost and lonely. She knew how poisonous loneliness could be. How it could diminish hope and make even the most tender heart turn bitter.

She thought about the people at Lara's reading.

Hollowell wasn't alone because she had Andrews. Grace and Allie weren't alone. They both had families. Only Terry was alone.

He took Enzo in after Lara died. Was that an act of kindness? Or part of an elaborate revenge plot?

"They're lining up outside," Charlie said. "Should I keep working on the window or do you want me on the floor?"

Nora glanced at her watch. "Stick with the window. Sheldon and I can handle the initial rush."

The initial rush turned into a morning rush, which continued until two. During a brief lull, Nora grabbed some lunch and tried to pick out an appropriate reading for Estella's wedding.

She sat in the stockroom, eating chicken and wild rice soup and a green salad while searching for literary wedding passages online. She found dozens of swoon-worthy examples, including poetry from Shakespeare, Rumi, and Neruda and lyrical prose from a variety of authors. She read examples from Victor Hugo, Toni Morrison, C. S. Lewis, Charlotte Bronte, and more.

Though the passages were all beautiful, none of them were quite right for Estella and Jack.

Jack had been in love with Estella for years before he finally let his feelings show. Estella, on the other hand, had been with many men. She'd always been attracted to wealthy, worldly types, believing that she could only find happiness if she moved far away from her hometown. But her true love had been in Miracle Springs all along, cooking his heart out at the local diner.

They weren't a young couple in their first bloom of love. At forty and forty-two, they'd been around the block. They were homeowners and business owners. They were about to become parents. Theirs would be a small and intimate wedding. A quiet and tender affair. It would be heartfelt and unforgettable.

Just thinking about it made Nora tear up.

It also made her think about McCabe.

Pushing her salad aside, she sent him a text. She didn't expect him to reply. She just wanted him to know that he was on her mind.

As the text left Nora's phone with a *whoosh*, Sheldon poked his head in the stockroom. "I hope you got enough to eat, because it's starting to rain. You know what that means."

"All the people from the street fair will be looking for shelter."

"And hot drinks. I figure you have five minutes before all hell breaks loose."

Knowing she needed fuel to make it through the rest of the day, Nora finished her soup. While she ate, she came across a website featuring unique wedding blessings. The moment she read the one written in 1947 by a novelist named Elliot Arnold, an idea began to take shape.

She would read a short literary passage meant for Estella and another meant for Jack. Then she would use the blessing written by Arnold to convey her wishes for the couple.

She could hear the rain striking the roof. The tempo was fast and frenzied, and when Sheldon returned a few minutes later, she took one look at his face and got to her feet. "I'm coming! But I want to read you something first. It's for the wedding."

"Read fast."

It wasn't meant to be rushed, so Nora spoke in a soft, measured tone.

> *Now you will feel no rain, for each of you will be the shelter for the other.*
> *Now you will feel no cold, for each of you will be the warmth for the other.*
> *Now you are two persons, but there is only one life before.*
> *Go now to your dwelling place to enter into the days of your life together.*
> *And may your days be good and long upon the earth.*

Sheldon pressed his hand to his heart. "It's perfect. Now get back to work."

Nora hurried over to him and kissed his cheek. "I love you," she whispered.

"*Te amo,*" he whispered back. "Do you need a hug? I should've given you one this morning when you first came in. Instead, I tried to distract you with sequined stars. Do you want one now?"

"Always," Nora said.

As Sheldon's arms curled around her, Nora rested her head against the soft wool of his sweater vest. She could feel his chest expand and deflate as he breathed. He smelled of coffee and peppermint. He was as warm and comforting as a loaf of oven-fresh bread.

"Your man will make it right," he said into her hair. "You'll see. We can't help him today, but we can welcome these people in from the rain. We can give them coffee, books, and comfort."

"What more does anyone need?"

Together, they left the stockroom, ready to greet their newest customers.

Chapter 14

When everything goes to hell, the people who stand by you without flinching—they are your family.

—Jim Butcher

The members of the Secret, Book, and Scone Society exchanged horrified stares as Nora told them about Enzo.

She'd waited until they'd eaten and were preparing to discuss Allie Kennedy's *The Dry Bar Murders* before sharing the grim news.

"*No,*" Hester cried. "What happened?"

"Grant's waiting on the postmortem, but it looks like the poor guy was hit by a car," Nora said gravely. "Whoever killed him must've driven him to the parking lot near the trail and dumped him in the woods."

Estella put a hand over her belly. "First Lara. Now Enzo. Neither one made it out of Miracle Springs alive. Does Grant know why?"

"Not yet."

June held up Allie Kennedy's book. "She's one of three people with a reason to kill Lara. Terry and Grace are the other two."

"Don't forget Hollowell," added Hester.

Nora gestured at her copy of *The Dry Bar Murders*. "There

are no clues in this story. Allie's killer uses poison. Her sleuth has a network of supportive friends and family members. The sleuth's mother is mentioned exactly once, and she died of cancer when the main character was a baby. Nothing in this plot hints at Allie's feelings toward Lara."

"I wish we could read her work in progress," said Estella.

Hester pointed at an image on her phone screen. "Look at this. Here's proof that Allie couldn't have killed Enzo." She put the phone on the center of the coffee table. "Allie's running the Scholastic Book Fair at her son's school. Her Facebook feed for the last four days is full of pics of her working with other parents. Here she is setting up, selling books, and posing with teachers."

The other women leaned over as Hester scrolled through the photos.

June fanned her face with her hand. "Whew! I didn't want to find out that she was a murderer. I like her, and I like her book. I love how the community she created comes together to seek justice for a veteran, especially after he was wrongfully accused of stealing from a homeless shelter."

Nora gazed at the author photo on the back cover of Allie's cozy mystery. "I hope she's innocent of Lara's murder too. I don't want to believe that someone who loves words and volunteers to run a book fair is capable of matricide."

"What does Grant think?" asked Estella.

"We talked a few minutes before you guys got here, so I know that Terry was brought in for questioning. Grace wasn't, which makes me think she's in the clear. I didn't dare mention Hollowell."

Nora told her friends how McCabe had basically ordered her to stop finding fault with his deputy.

"But what about the Michigan connection?" spluttered Hester. "Does he know where Hollowell's from or that she moved from Michigan to Greensboro?"

"I was going to drop the subject for the sake of our relationship, but I can't do that now. I have to force the scales from his eyes. I don't know how Hollowell does it, but the men at the station see her in a completely different light than we do."

Hester drained the rest of her wine and said, "I've given this lots of thought, and I think the dogs make her more likeable. Animals are supposed to be good judges of character. And maybe she *is* different with dogs. She can trust them. They won't leave her. As long as she has a dog, she'll never be alone. They're probably the truest partners she's ever had."

June sighed. "I hate the idea of a two-faced animal lover. And yes, Paula Hollowell's tough, but could she move Enzo's body by herself? Maybe the killer had an accomplice."

"Maybe," said Nora. "It would have been doable for Terry. As a matter of fact, he has a hand truck in the pharmacy. I noticed it the last time I was there."

Silence descended as the women conjured images of a shadowy form loading Enzo's limp, heavy body onto a moving dolly.

"Can we talk about something positive?" Hester pleaded, reaching for Estella's hand. "Like a wedding? Or a baby?"

Estella nodded. "We can. I can tell you that my dresses came today."

"And?"

"One of them is absolutely perfect. It makes me feel, well, bridal."

Hester clapped. "I can't wait to celebrate you and Jack. And, if it doesn't totally mess up the seating chart, I'd like to bring a date."

"Oh, we can make room!" Estella exclaimed. "Who is it? Jamie?"

Hester's cheeks turned Barbie-pink. "He came into the bakery to buy bread. He's never been in before, and I was pretty sure he was there to see me. I mean, Gus's bread is amazing, but

Jamie spent a long time chatting with me after he paid. So, I just came right out and asked him to be my plus one."

June's eyes flashed with mischief. "Is he going to wear a kilt?"

"Forget about *him*. What am *I* going to wear? I don't have time to order something, and I have a ton of baking to do to get ready for the parade."

"Can my dad help?" asked Estella.

Hester shook her head. "Not any more than he already is. Your dad is the best thing that ever happened to me."

Estella smiled tenderly. "He loves you too. You're like a second daughter to him."

June snapped her fingers. "Hester, you haven't treated yourself to new clothes in ages, so we're going shopping in Asheville tomorrow. I'll take you after church. Once you've found something to wear, we can tackle your Gingerbread House list."

The two of them ironed out the details of their shopping excursion while Estella recommended specific shops and looked up business hours on her phone. Nora sat back and let their chatter flow over her. She wanted to store the sound of her friends' voices and laughter in her heart. She wanted to use it to light her from the inside like a torch. That way, when McCabe came home later tonight carrying the weight of a man's murder, she could lend him strength. She could comfort him as he spoke about medical reports and motive.

By the time he climbed into bed, Nora was on the brink of sleep. But she was awake enough to listen when he told her that Lara's lab tests had come back and Narcan had been found in her bloodstream.

"Someone injected her," he whispered. "The needle was probably very thin. She would've felt a little pinch, that's all. It could've happened when the lights went out, or when she went to the restroom. Did she make a noise of surprise or discomfort? Did she rub her arm, or neck, or leg at any point?"

"I heard a woman cry out, but I don't know if it was Lara. Terry sat next to her. Do you think he did it?"

McCabe went quiet for so long that Nora wondered if he'd fallen asleep. Finally, he murmured, "He has access to Narcan, and he was furious with Lara for swindling him out of his wife's pearls in exchange for a lump of tourmaline."

A minute ago, Nora had been struggling to stay awake. Now she was completely alert. "Is that what *t-u-r* stood for?"

"Yes. Lara brought a bag of gems with her from Michigan. Her ex-husband's family gave them to her back when they were still married. They came from the family's mine, and Lara had so many that she started giving tourmaline necklaces to her clients in exchange for pieces of their jewelry."

"I assume she sold their jewelry."

"I can't prove that until I gain access to Enzo's business records. God knows how long that'll take." He breathed a weary sigh into his pillow. "Is Terry guilty? I don't know. He told me that he felt Deanna's presence during Lara's reading. He said he felt at peace for the first time since her death. That he feels a glimmer of hope. He's going to get a dog. He wants to help coach the Little League team."

"That doesn't sound like a murderer talking, but he could be lying."

McCabe slipped his arm around Nora's waist. "We questioned him over and over. His story never changed. He said that he loved taking care of Enzo and would never hurt him. He saw him as a brother—as another man who'd lost the love of his life. He gave me the keys to the pharmacy and the passwords to his computer system. He told me to check his Narcan inventory."

"Did you?"

"Fuentes did. It was all accounted for, but that doesn't mean he didn't have some stashed away. He knew exactly when Enzo left town and could've easily followed him. However, Terry's truck shows no signs of damage. No traces of blood. Enzo's DNA is all over the front seat, but that's because Terry drove him home from the hospital after Lara died."

Nora didn't see how Enzo could've been hit by a car unless someone convinced him to pull over and exit his own vehicle. She was barely conscious as she conveyed this thought to McCabe. He said something in reply, but Nora didn't hear it. Her brain was too tired to listen. Her body went limp and she dropped off to sleep.

On Sunday, Nora and Sheldon shopped the flea market together. After loading up on vintage holiday items, they went to the Pink Lady and treated themselves to a short stack of blueberry pancakes.

"We did good work this morning." Sheldon saluted Nora with his coffee cup. "What's next? Antique malls? Estate sales? I didn't see anything exciting in the paper this morning."

"No more shopping for me. I've got an advanced copy of Michael Connelly's new book and it's just going to be me, Michael, and the cats chilling out on the sofa."

Sheldon took a sip of coffee, grimaced, and signaled for the waitress. "Can I trouble you for a cider?" Flashing an angelic smile, he pointed at his mug. "This isn't doing it for me today."

"We can't hold a candle to your bookstore blend," she said, glancing at the nearly full mug. "I wish you could talk Jack into offering it here. Our customers would be thrilled. Where on earth do you buy it?"

"I'll never tell," Sheldon said, pretending to zipper his lips.

The waitress winked at him. "And I'll never stop trying to get it out of you."

After she walked away, Nora quirked her brows. "I think she likes you."

"Naturally. I'm adorable. I'm also a mystery folks want to solve. Especially the ladies. I mean, how can a devilishly handsome silver fox such as myself be happy on his own? What they don't realize is that I'm not on my own. At work, I have you, Charlie, and my book club buddies. At home, I have June. My life is full." He studied Nora for a moment. "Speaking of houses, have you decided what to do with yours?"

Nora said, "I have an idea to run by you, but it's a little out there."

Sheldon's eyes sparkled. He sat up taller and twirled the tails of his mustache. "I love out there. Let's hear it."

An hour later, Nora headed back to McCabe's with a page of notes in her purse. With Sheldon's help, her seed of an idea had quickly grown into something that felt both right and necessary.

Sitting at McCabe's dining room table, she took out her laptop and composed an email to her builder. After outlining her plan, she attached a dozen images and Pinterest links. Then, she sent a group text to Hester and June, suggesting they throw an intimate bridal shower dinner in Estella's honor.

I can host, June wrote. **How about Wednesday? I don't have knitting club this week.**

When Nora and Hester both replied with thumbs-up emojis, June said that she'd call Estella to be sure she was free that night.

A few seconds later, she wrote, **It's a date! She's craving spicy, starchy comfort food, so I'll make my zesty Tex-Mex chicken casserole.**

Hester volunteered to whip up virgin margaritas and Nora offered to handle the group gift. The three friends had been batting around gift ideas since Estella had told them about the wedding, and while they all wanted to treat the newlyweds to a weekend getaway, they couldn't seem to find the perfect place.

"Estella's too high maintenance for glamping," June had said when Hester had proposed they rent a custom Airstream.

Nora had shot down the luxury cabin June had found just outside of Asheville, even though it had all the amenities, including a chef's kitchen, an outdoor fire pit, and a hot tub.

"They shouldn't have to cook or clean on their honeymoon," she'd argued.

After researching several high-end resorts and hotels, the friends decided on the Grove Park Inn. The historic hotel boasted stunning mountain views, a golf course, a spa, and fine dining. Nora purchased a weekend package that included a room in the adults-only area of the resort, a couples massage, and a champagne dinner at the Sunset Terrace. Split three ways, the total cost was still on the steep side.

"If you're going to splurge, do it without regret," said June.

"Exactly," agreed Hester. "We all work hard, so why not use our hard-earned money to spread a little joy?"

Not for the first time, Nora was moved by her friends' generosity. Every conversation they had reminded her of exciting things to come. A wedding. A baby. Holiday celebrations. A trip to Texas with her man.

And finally, a decision about where she was going to live.

Nora was going to accept McCabe's invitation to make his house her own. Now that she knew exactly what to do with Caboose Cottage, she was ready to move forward. She would tell McCabe once the murder investigations were behind them, but come Monday, she would start making plans for the future.

The week began with McCabe working a twelve-hour shift. He and his team found no useful evidence at the scene of Enzo's death. It had rained twice since Enzo had driven away from Terry's house, and their only hope of discovering clues was the postmortem. McCabe was anxiously awaiting the results of the trace evidence and fiber analysis tests but knew he could be waiting for some time.

As for Terry, he'd been released on Sunday after lengthy questioning. He was still a person of interest, but there wasn't enough evidence to charge him with a crime.

McCabe came home Monday night looking completely defeated.

"I interviewed Grace today. Her story is very much like Terry's. She gave Lara a valuable piece of jewelry in exchange for a tourmaline necklace worth around fifty bucks. Grace regrets giving a family heirloom away but bears no grudge against Lara."

Nora thought about her conversation with Grace the day she went to urgent care. "She believes Lara's help was worth the cost."

"Terry, on the other hand, was furious with Lara. However, he claims that he had a change of heart after her reading at Miracle Books. He felt Deanna's presence that night and feels more hopeful about his future. Enzo was staying with Terry. He could have killed him and dragged his body into the woods, but there's no evidence to back that up."

Nora didn't think Grace could carry a bag of mulch into the woods, let alone a man's body. She shared this thought with McCabe.

"No," he agreed. "She'd need an accomplice."

This was the moment to mention Hollowell's hometown, and Nora did so as calmly and respectfully as possible.

"I know where she's from," McCabe responded wearily. "She was a kid when she lived there and had never heard of Lara. She had no idea if her grandmother was a client or not. Hollowell moved to Greensboro because she was tired of the Michigan winters, not because she was following Lara. She applied for jobs in North Carolina, Virginia, and Tennessee. When Guilford County offered her a position before the other departments did, she took it."

Hollowell had a logical explanation for everything, but Nora didn't share McCabe's faith in her. However, she didn't argue the point. She had no desire to drive a wedge between them.

On Tuesday, Allie Kennedy returned to Miracle Springs.

This time, she hadn't come to promote her cozy mystery or attend her mother's reading. She'd been ordered to appear at the station for questioning. According to the text McCabe sent, Allie had lawyered up.

Though Nora was curious about the interview, she preferred to focus on work. With Thanksgiving over a week away, there was a festive vibe in the bookstore. The window display was a huge hit, influencing customers to buy road trip or entertainment-themed books by the handful.

As closing time approached, Nora let her remaining customers wander the store or linger over the books they were sampling while she ordered more copies of the most popular titles from the window display.

The travel bingo cards that had been around since Nora was a kid were still in high demand. She'd sold a dozen that day and knew her current supply wouldn't last until Thanksgiving, let alone Christmas. She was trying to decide how many to order when the sleigh bells rang, and Allie Kennedy entered the store.

Unlike the bubbly, upbeat Allie Kennedy who'd stood in front of an audience to talk about *The Dry Bar Murders*, this Allie was fraying at the edges. Wisps of blonde hair floated around her face, her cardigan was misbuttoned, and her rosy-brown nail polish was chipped.

"Hi," she said.

"Hello."

Allie's gaze fell on the travel bingo cards. "I remember these. My aunt and I used these on road trips. My uncle did all the driving. My aunt was in charge of the map, the music, and keeping me entertained."

Nora waited for her to continue, but Allie just opened and closed the little windows on the bingo card until the man who'd been reading in the sci-fi nook appeared at the checkout counter to buy two books and a Friendsgiving candle.

Allie feigned interest in the spinner rack of bookmarks until he finished paying for his purchases and left the store.

"I'm sure you know why I'm in town," she said. "And even though it's been one of the longest days of my life, and all I want to do is collapse on my hotel bed, I had to come here." She gestured at the front door. "I know I only have a few minutes, but could we talk?"

"Sure. Would you mind coming to the back? I need to see if anyone needs help before I close."

Allie followed Nora to the Readers' Circle. At six o'clock on the dot, Nora turned off the music. The remaining customers took the hint and exited the store.

Nora locked the front door and returned to the Readers' Circle to find Allie staring at the purple velvet chair. It was the chair Lara had been sitting in the night she died.

Allie said, "I want to apologize for my behavior. You hosted a wonderful event for me, and I repaid your kindness by being weird and deceitful. I didn't kill my mother, but I *was* going to kill her in print. My plan was to create a character who had her looks and mannerisms and then bump her off."

"Using what murder weapon?"

Allie touched the shade of the reading lamp. "I was going to use electricity. It would represent the lightning strike that resulted in her *gift*. I gave the sheriff a copy of my current manuscript, as well as a copy of the proposal I sent to my editor six months ago. It outlines the whole book. I'd already written the murder scene, but I needed to see Lara in action because I'd never witnessed one of her readings."

"One sec." Nora stood up and fetched a bottle of wine and two coffee cups from the ticket agent's booth. She placed the mugs on the table and said, "Would you like a glass of extremely mediocre chardonnay?"

"I'd love one."

After filling their cups, Nora raised hers in the air. "To the quiet comfort of being surrounded by books."

Allie smiled. "I'll drink to that."

Hoping the wine wouldn't bring on a headache, Nora took a tentative sip.

As if guessing her thoughts, Allie tapped her temple. "Whoever stitched you up did a great job. How are you feeling?"

"Much better than last week."

"I'm glad. That whole night—it was so awful. I feel like it was all my fault too. Like, if I had never come, she might still be alive. Like my hatred caused her death."

Nora shook her head. "It happened because someone came to that reading with murder in their heart."

"I obviously wasn't the only one who wanted to punish her, but I also fantasized that I wouldn't need to. A part of me was hoping she'd say that she was sorry for letting me go—for letting someone else raise me. I wanted her to tell me that she thought about me every day." Allie dabbed at the corners of her eyes and gave a hollow laugh. "I didn't think I had any tears left."

Gently, Nora said, "Was Halloween the first time you'd seen her since you left Michigan?"

Allie shook her head. "She came to my event. She wore a wig, but I recognized her. She looks just like my aunt. She came in late, during the Q & A session, and it was so hard to act normal after I saw her."

"I bet. Did you two talk?"

"Yes. I thought she was there to give me what I'd been waiting for my whole life. A grand gesture. I thought she was going to beg my forgiveness. But no. She wanted to see me. She wanted to reconnect. But she was not there to apologize."

Allie's voice was raw with pain. Nora could see her as a scared but determined teenager boarding a bus with a backpack and a broken heart.

Nora wasn't a mother, but she couldn't imagine how anyone could let their child leave like that.

"Did you ever find out why Lara let you go?"

Allie grunted. "It was her *gift. Everything* was about her gift.

She told my aunt that she couldn't think clearly after client sessions. She had to rest and recharge after each one. In the meantime, she neglected me. She didn't make regular trips to the grocery store. She didn't do laundry. I was always hungry. I was always asking other kids for the leftover food on their lunch trays."

"Were you close with your dad's folks?"

"I was until he died. After he was gone, they didn't want to see me. They told my aunt that I reminded them of the worst day of their lives." Allie sagged deeper into the chair. "But what no one knows is that Lara sensed my dad was in real trouble and left him there—on the floor, anyway. She'd had a *feeling* that he couldn't be saved, so she didn't even try."

Nora absorbed this news in silence. She ached for the child who'd lost both parents to addiction. Her father had been an alcoholic, but Lara's addiction was more difficult to define. All of her energy had gone into curating her reputation as a psychic medium. Everything else in her life had taken a back seat to this goal, including the well-being of her only child.

"The hurts piled on hurts," Allie continued softly. "Lara never came to my aunt's house to check on me. Her letters sounded so fake and flaky that I stopped reading them. Then her memoir came out, and it was clear that I was just an insignificant blip in her life. She didn't even mention my name."

"Why did she come to your event?"

Allie tilted her face toward the ceiling. "She was curious about me. That's what she told me in the parking lot after it was over. She said she was doing an event at the store in a few weeks and asked if I would come. I said I would, but if she let on that she knew me, I'd cut ties with her forever. By this point, I no longer hoped for a reconciliation. I only wanted to punish her, and to do that, I needed to study her in action."

Suddenly, Nora understood what Allie had intended. "You were going to expose her."

"Yes."

"How?"

"She started doing that tourmaline swindle back in Michigan. When I googled Enzo's name and saw that he ran an online pawnshop, I knew exactly what was going on. In Michigan, Lara used to sell the precious things she got from clients on eBay, but in North Carolina, she had someone to do that for her. Enzo."

Allie rummaged around in her purse and pulled out a plastic baggie, which she handed to Nora. Inside was a simple pendant with a black gemstone.

"I was going to tell everyone at the reading about her scam. I was going to write about it in my next book. Word would get out, and she'd be ruined." Allie pointed at the pendant. "That's the only weapon I needed. I didn't want to kill her. I wanted to destroy her career—the thing she'd chosen over me. I'm actually furious at the asshole who took her life because now, I can't make her feel the pain I felt."

Nora believed every word. Allie had been deeply wounded. She was angry, bitter, and bereft, but she was no murderer.

"Did you tell all of this to the sheriff?"

Allie nodded.

"No wonder you're exhausted." Nora held out the baggie, and when Allie moved to take it, Nora captured her hands and held them tightly. "Do you have someone to talk to?"

"For years, I had the most amazing therapist. She recently moved away, and I haven't looked for a replacement. I thought I'd be okay . . ." She smirked. "Obviously, I'm not okay. For the sake of my family, I'll find a new therapist."

Allie shoved the necklace into her bag and got to her feet. After saying that she'd meet her up front in a minute, Nora hurried to the children's section to grab a picture book. The one she had in mind was Bob Raczka's *You Are a Story*.

"This is for the girl who boarded that bus in Michigan and

the woman you are now," Nora said, tucking the book into Allie's bag. She hoped Allie would go back to her hotel, flop on the bed, and start reading. Nora wanted her to read one line in particular. The one that said, "No matter who your family is, you deserve all the love you get."

Nora hoped the book would serve as a comfort and a companion until Allie could return to all the people who loved her.

Chapter 15

Suspicion often creates what it suspects.

—C. S. Lewis

Thursday's storytime was just wrapping up when McCabe walked into the bookstore.

Nora didn't notice him right away because she was busy ringing up picture books about turkeys, families, food, and manners.

Sheldon's storytime had been a huge hit, and the shop was still buzzing with excitement. He'd started off by reading Zanna Davidson's *Table Manners for Tigers*. Then he had the children make a paper-bag tiger puppet. Finally, he'd placed a pretend bowl of cotton-ball mashed potatoes on the ground in front of the kids.

"How does your tiger ask for this bowl of mashed potatoes?" he'd asked.

"ROAR!" shouted a little girl. "Gimme the potatoes!"

Sheldon had cowered in fear. "*Wow.* I really believed you were a tiger for a second there. Who else?"

The children had taken turns bellowing for the potatoes. After that, the puppets pretended to stand on their chairs, throw food, eat with their mouths open, and be generally loud and rude.

"You've done it, tigers," Sheldon had declared when the noise rose to rock-concert levels. "You've ruined Katie Crocodile's party. After this, the tigers won't be invited to any more parties. No one wants to have them over because they have *no* manners. They're going to miss all the fun. Unless..." He'd pretended to think. "Unless we tigers can prove that we have good manners. Let's start this party over."

After laying out photos of common Thanksgiving dishes on the alphabet rug, he'd said, "Okay, tigers. It's Thanksgiving, and we're super-excited. All of our friends are coming to our house for dinner. I'm going to pretend to be a tiger who *didn't* go to Miss Molly's School of Manners, and *you* need to tell *me* when I'm doing something wrong. Ready?"

Sheldon had delighted the children by producing a white napkin and depositing it on the top of his head.

"It goes in your lap, not on your head!" cried a boy.

After the children had corrected a number of dinner table infractions, Sheldon gave them each a tiger treat. The kids accepted their tiny bags of animal fruit snacks with exuberant thank yous.

"Sheldon's the best," a woman told Nora as she fished in her bag for her wallet. "I look forward to Thursdays as much as my son does. When I think of the things I'm grateful for this Thanksgiving, this store and that wonderful man are pretty high on my list."

Nora heard similar sentiments from other parents. By eleven, her face hurt from smiling so widely.

"Can I buy you a cup of coffee, pretty lady?"

Nora slotted Cynthia Rylant's *In November* into its appropriate place on the picture book shelf and turned to McCabe. "Well, hello. This is a surprise."

"A good one, I hope. I have interesting news."

"Hold that thought," Nora said, ducking into the ticket agent's booth to tell Sheldon to take a break. He happily acquiesced, untied his apron, and poured McCabe a coffee before heading to the stockroom.

McCabe examined his mug and snorted with mirth. It showed Jesus peeking out from around a corner and the text, I SAW THAT!

"Is Sheldon trying to tell me something?"

"The storytime parents might think he's the second coming, but his powers have their limits. The Children's Corner is a mess."

Taking a sip of coffee, McCabe let out a sigh of pleasure. "Nothing short of miraculous."

Nora made a hurry-up gesture. "I have about ten minutes until the start of the lunch rush, so what's your news?"

"We caught the Midnight Dumper."

McCabe looked pleased as punch, but Nora was a trifle disappointed. She was glad the litterer had been apprehended. Of course, she was. But she'd been hoping for a positive update on Lara and Enzo's cases.

"That's great," she said.

McCabe failed to notice her lack of enthusiasm. "It is. Not only because no one has to stumble on construction waste in our woods anymore, but also because the suspect had a curious possession in his van."

This got Nora's attention. "Which was?"

"Enzo's watch. It's a Patek Philippe, which is on par with if not more expensive than a Rolex. His was a few years old, but it's still worth around twenty-four grand."

Nora was baffled. Why would the Midnight Dumper have Enzo's watch?

"We're still processing the van, which was recently cleaned, but we have reason to believe this was the vehicle responsible for Enzo's death."

Nora imagined a cargo van possessed by an evil entity. Like the car in Stephen King's *Christine*, the sentient van was destined to kill—to mow people down without discretion.

The van hadn't killed anyone, though. Its driver had. And for some reason, McCabe wasn't naming the driver.

"How did you find the van? From the stickers?"

McCabe shook his head. "They were gone. The guy probably took them off during its recent cleaning. He hasn't said a word in English—only a few in Spanish—so Fuentes is taking the lead on this one. But the guy doesn't want to talk, no matter what language we're using."

Nora wanted to know everything there was to know about this man. Most of all, she wanted to know how this Spanish-speaking litterer was connected to Lara and Enzo.

"Where was the van found?"

McCabe brushed some sugar granules off the ledge of the pass-through window. "It was Hollowell's discovery. She was on patrol and saw it turn off on the road leading to the river ridge trails. It was getting dark, and there are no houses on that road, so she figured he was up to no good. She was right."

"She caught him dumping trash?"

"Yep." McCabe didn't smile, but a satisfied gleam appeared in his eyes. "Luckily, Rambo was with her. The guy took one look at the dog and practically jumped into the back of her patrol car."

Is it over? Nora wondered as she wiped off the counter. *Is the litterer also a murderer? Was he another victim of Lara's tourmaline scam?*

The sleigh bells banged against the back of the door, and an elderly man carrying a teal tote bag approached the ticket agent's booth. "Howdy! I sat in the front of the bus so I could be the first in line. These old bones could use a hot coffee. I didn't sleep very well last night, and I'm plum tuckered out."

"We'll put the wind back in your sails," promised Nora. "Have a seat in one of those comfy chairs, and I'll bring you a cup."

The man glanced at McCabe, dipped his chin in greeting, and placed a twenty on the window ledge. "I'd sure appreciate a sweet treat to go with that coffee. Anything you've got is fine. I'm not picky."

Nora warmed a chocolate book pocket, which was basically a book-shaped chocolate croissant, and carried the pastry and coffee over to the Readers' Circle. She warned the man to wait a moment before sampling either or he might burn his tongue.

"Thank you, darling." He immediately slurped his coffee, and his lined face crinkled in delight. "That's the stuff. Life is all about little moments of joy. Like this one."

Nora smiled at him before returning to her station behind the espresso machine. Other hotel guests were heading her way, which meant she'd have to curtail her conversation with McCabe until later. But there was something she wanted to know first.

"Is there a chance the van driver was in the audience the night Lara died? Do you think he killed her?"

"At the moment, there's no evidence linking this man to her. We'll see what Fuentes can get out of him, but I can tell he's going to be a tough nut to crack. I wanted to give you an update because I know it's been weighing on you—what happened to Lara and Enzo. Hopefully, when I see you tonight, we'll have a clearer picture."

He gave her a quick kiss and slipped out of the ticket agent's booth. After tipping his hat at a group of elderly ladies lining up to order coffee, he disappeared around the corner of the fiction shelves.

The woman in the front of the line watched him walk away. Then she turned to Nora and said, "If I steal a book real fast, will he arrest me? Because I wouldn't mind one bit."

The women behind her cackled.

At that moment, Sheldon returned from his break. McCabe was instantly forgotten as they took in Sheldon's waves of silver hair, debonair mustache, and big brown eyes.

One of the women fanned her face and murmured, "Oh, my."

"He looks like a mustachioed Don Johnson," her friend whispered. "I think I'm in love."

Sheldon gave Nora a wink. "Don't worry. I've got this."

Nora smiled distractedly at the women.

She was feeling conflicted.

On one hand, she was grateful to McCabe for telling her about the break in the case. On the other hand, she was mildly irritated because she wasn't focused on selling books. She was thinking about the van driver.

Had the Midnight Dumper hit Enzo by accident and then left his body in the woods to avoid being caught? If that was the case, why had Enzo gotten out of his car to begin with? Did he have a flat tire? Where was his car now?

Questions fluttered like winged insects in Nora's brain until a customer approached the checkout desk with a stack of books in his hands. He placed them on the counter and asked if Nora would hold them while he grabbed more items. A few minutes later, he reappeared with an armload of shelf enhancers and a huge grin on his face.

"I'm doing my Christmas shopping early. My girlfriend says I leave everything to the last minute, and she's right. I want to be a better man for her, so here I am, being better."

"Are these gifts for her?" Nora asked.

He pointed at a Limoges picture frame painted with delicate pink, blue, and yellow flowers. "I'm going to put a photo of us inside from the night we met. It was at a wedding. We were seated at the same table with a family who was arguing very passionately in Polish. We didn't know where to look or what to do, so we started talking. The rest is history."

As Nora wrapped the frame, she told the young man that he had great taste. "One of my best friends is getting married tomorrow," she added. "I wonder if anyone will fall in love at her wedding."

The interaction had successfully refocused Nora's attention, and she spent the rest of the workday helping customers and humming along to music as she tidied the store.

When everything was shipshape, she drove to June's house for Estella's impromptu bridal shower dinner.

Unsurprisingly, June had everything under control. The casserole was in the oven, the table was set, and Benny Goodman was on the record player.

While Nora washed her hands, Hester placed a tossed salad in the middle of the table, and Sheldon filled flute glasses with sparkling grape juice.

"How was work without me?" asked Sheldon.

"I barely made it through," she teased. "It was a busy day, but a good day."

The doorbell rang, and Hester shouted, "I got it!"

She returned to the dining room with her arm hooked through Estella's. "Here's our beautiful bride."

Estella glanced around and mimed wiping her brow. "Thank God. There isn't a Bride-to-Be sash or baseball cap in sight."

"No kitschy apparel. No party games. No strippers," said June.

"Damn," muttered Sheldon.

Estella arched a brow at him. "No sex toys either?"

Sheldon's shoulder moved in a hapless shrug. "I *almost* ordered you a bag of gummy penises, but they wouldn't get here in time, so you'll have to settle for a list of the best marriage advice ever."

The women groaned in unison.

Pulling out Estella's chair, Sheldon said, "They'd be funnier if we were all drunk, but it's all I've got."

June put steaming squares of casserole on plates in the kitchen, and Nora delivered the plates to the table. After everyone had been served, June signaled for her guests to raise their glasses.

"To the bride!" she shouted.

"To the bride!" echoed her friends.

The casserole was hot, spicy, and delicious. Strings of melted cheese clung to every forkful, and June told her guests that this was a meal best served among friends.

"Good thing we've seen each other at our worst because we're all gonna have cheese hanging from our mouths. There's no way around it."

To Nora, the taste was well worth the mess. The food warmed her body just as sitting at this table surrounded by her friends warmed her soul.

"Feeling any pre-wedding jitters?" Hester asked Estella.

Estella pursed her lips. "Not really. I guess the only thing I'm anxious about is our honeymoon weekend. Jack won't tell me where we're going, so I don't know what to pack. I am *not* the type of woman who can throw a few things in a duffle bag and be ready to go in ten minutes. I need a suitcase the size of a telephone booth and an hour to pick out my clothes."

June, Hester, and Nora exchanged conspiratorial glances. Hester grinned at Estella and said, "Jack doesn't know where you're going either. Tell her, Nora."

"The four of us organized your romantic weekend. You don't have to drive far, and once you reach your destination, you won't have to lift a finger."

Nora placed an envelope on the table and slid it over to Estella. "This is your wedding gift. We love you and Jack and couldn't be happier for you both."

Estella's eyes were glistening with tears before she even picked up the envelope.

"Go on," prompted Sheldon. "Don't keep yourself in suspense."

"I already know this is going to be amazing because it's from all of you," she said. But when she looked at the sheet containing photos of the resort and the weekend's itinerary, she let out a gasp of surprise. "A suite at Grove Park Inn! A sunset dinner! And a couples massage! This is way too much!"

"In the immortal words of Goldilocks, this is just right. You deserve it, babe." June blew Estella a kiss. "Now, who wants dessert?"

When she received no takers, June opened another bottle of sparkling grape juice instead.

"Okay, Sheldon, let's hear your marital advice," she said while refilling his glass.

Affronted, Sheldon put a hand to his chest. "It isn't coming from *me*. This is the list of the *worst* wedding advice ever given. It's totally snarky, which is why it's perfect for us."

Estella laughed. "That's totally on point."

Sheldon produced a small notebook, put on his reading glasses, and cleared his throat. "Topping the list of the worst marital advice is this gem: 'If you're having problems, just have a kid. That'll fix everything.'"

Pointing at her baby bump, Estella said, "Check!"

"'It's important to win arguments. Keep a tally and see who wins the most each month. The loser has to clean the toilets. We've been married for three months, and I haven't cleaned a single toilet. Guess I married a loser.'"

June's mouth fell open. "Is this for real?"

Sheldon squinted at the tiny font. "Yes. This person also admitted that they're in the middle of divorce proceedings."

"Shocker," said Nora.

Sheldon adjusted his glasses and moved on to the next one on the list. "'You need to be honest with your wife. If she asks if she looks fat in those jeans and she does, tell her it's time to hit the gym.'"

Hester nearly choked on her drink. "Holy shit. I'd kill that man."

"Here's one for you, Mama Bear," continued Sheldon. "'If he can push a mower, he can push a stroller.'"

The women chortled and gestured for Sheldon to keep going.

"'If you don't like what your partner is saying, just pretend you can't hear them.'"

The more he read, the louder the women's reactions were.

Sheldon loved being the center of attention. He used different voices and accents with every piece of bad advice for optimum effect.

For the next entry, he adopted a deep Southern drawl. "'If she yells at you, tell her to calm down over and over again until she leaves the room. Boom. You win. Now you can get back to the game.'"

Estella covered her face with her napkin.

Sheldon delivered the last piece of advice in a high, whiny voice. "'Spend your man's money on whatever you want. That's why you married him in the first place.'"

June waved a hand in front of her face. "Good Lord. These people!"

"That list read more like motives for murder than marital advice," said Nora.

All four women praised Sheldon for the entertaining list.

He did his best to bow from a seated position and then gestured at Nora. "Today was so crazy that I didn't get the chance to ask you about McCabe's visit. He seemed like he was bursting to tell you something. Care to share?"

Nora hesitated. She didn't want to dampen the mood by mentioning the Midnight Dumper. She could tell her friends that he'd been apprehended, but she knew they'd ask follow-up questions. And then they'd be talking about Lara and Enzo again.

Hester raised a warning finger. "Hold up. Was it good news or bad news?"

"They caught the guy who's been dumping construction waste all over the county."

June pumped a fist. "Yes!"

Estella eyed Nora thoughtfully. "There's more to the story,

I can tell. Don't worry, you're not going to ruin the party by telling us what's going on. This is who we are. It's what we do. We tell each other everything."

Giving in, Nora briefly explained how the van driver was caught, and that Enzo's watch was discovered among his possessions.

June's face creased in puzzlement. "Do you think this man hit Enzo on purpose or by accident?"

All Nora could say was that she didn't know.

Hester rolled her eyes. "Now that Hollowell's the hero of the hour, she'll be absolutely unbearable. I can already picture that smug look she gets. Every time I see her, I want to push her face into a coconut cream pie."

Suddenly, Estella winced and pressed a hand to her belly. "Oof. Easy there, baby black belt." She rubbed circles on the side of her bump. "Guess my Karate Kid doesn't like Hollowell either."

"What if Deputy Dour isn't the hero?" challenged Sheldon. "She has more connections to the victims than anyone else at the reading. Including Allie." He began ticking them off with his fingers. "She lived near Lara in Michigan. She lived near Lara in Greensboro. She attended Lara's reading but made Grace buy her ticket, which is weird, no matter what ridiculous reason she made up for that. She tried to resuscitate Lara and failed. She tracked the litterer, who just happened to have Enzo's watch in his van. I'm sorry, Nora, but why isn't your man seeing what I'm seeing?"

Heat rushed to Nora's cheeks. "I'm sure he is. He's just not talking to me about it."

"If Hollowell hands him the solution to two murders and illegal dumping on a silver platter, he might not look at her too closely," June said.

Nora immediately leapt to McCabe's defense. "That's not how he operates. He won't close the case because it's convenient. I've never met someone with more integrity than Grant. I trust him to do the right thing."

"I do too," said Estella.

"But you've also told us that he has a blind spot when it comes to Hollowell," June gently pointed out.

Unable to deny this, Nora said, "I saw McCabe this morning. All kinds of developments may have happened since then. Let's table all talk of murder until after the wedding, okay? Tomorrow is all about Jack and Estella."

Her friends agreed, and the conversation shifted to matrimonial topics.

Despite what she said at dinner, Nora hoped McCabe would give her an update as soon as he got home, but he walked through the door in a very different mood from the one he'd been in that morning.

Shucking off his jacket, he dropped into his recliner and murmured, "What a day."

Knowing he needed to gather his thoughts before sharing them with her, Nora kept quiet. Higgins vaulted onto McCabe's lap and settled down for a petting session. As McCabe stroked his cat's fur, some of the tension drained from his face and shoulders.

Eventually, he looked at Nora and said, "The guy won't talk. Fuentes tried everything but got nowhere. We didn't even know his name until we called his employers. He works for a place called Gonzalez Painting and Carpentry, a business owned by two brothers, Emilio and Javier Gonzalez. The van is registered to their company, and our suspect has been working for them for a few months. He's applied for a green card, and the Gonzalez brothers are trying to help him get his citizenship. His wife is also a Gonzalez. She and the brothers are cousins."

"Do you think he's refusing to talk because he's afraid to go to jail or because he's afraid of being deported?"

McCabe turned to her in surprise. "Funny you should ask.

He didn't react when Fuentes warned him of the legal ramifications for obstructing justice. Not a single twitch. But when Fuentes asked why he and his family left Mexico, he got scared. I could see it in his eyes. Zamora, the city where he's from, has become extremely violent due to cartel activity."

Nora put a hand on McCabe's arm. "What's your gut telling you?"

"That this man would do anything to avoid going back to Zamora, even if that means serving time."

"Is that what'll happen to him if Enzo's DNA is found inside the van?"

McCabe rubbed his eyes. "It won't look good, that's for sure."

"What about his wife? Did you talk to her?"

"Yes." Frown lines sprouted across McCabe's forehead. "She says he's a good man. Works hard, goes to church, hardly ever drinks, and saves every penny so their three kids can have a better life. She got so overwrought that her cousins had to physically support her when she left the station."

When Higgins jumped off McCabe's lap, Nora took his place.

The day's events had worn on her man. He wasn't relieved by the turn the case had taken. He was saddened by it. Tonight his sleep would be fitful. It would be haunted by the faces of both the dead and the living.

Nora put her arms around McCabe and rested her head on his shoulder. "You once told me that some investigations feel like swimming in murky water, and that it's hard to tell what you're looking at until the rain comes along and makes things clear again. You're in the murky part now, but the rain will come."

McCabe raised her chin and kissed her. Then he pulled her closer and held her for a long time.

The cats were ready to call it a night. They trotted into the bedroom and summoned the humans with their cries. Nora sent McCabe to bed while she turned off lights, tidied the kitchen, and started the dishwasher. By the time she slipped under the covers, he was already asleep.

Nora gazed out the window, probing the night for stars, but the sky was a smudge of clouds. She'd seen hundreds of stars the night before, glimmering between the tree branches, and if she concentrated hard enough, she felt like she could see them still.

The steadfast line of Orion's belt. The brilliance of Betelgeuse. And Sirius, bright as a beacon in a storm.

She wished on the memory of these stars, believing in the unwavering power of a light that had traveled through a million miles of space to reach someone like her—an ordinary human looking for a little hope.

Chapter 16

Any day spent with you is my favorite day.
—A. A. Milne

Nora started her workday by hanging a sign in the front window announcing their early closure.

"Big plans?" asked a man who came in every Friday for a cappuccino and a mystery novel.

"One of my best friends is getting married."

A wistful look came over the man's face. "My wedding was a bit of a blur. There was the church, then a buffet, then a lot of drinking and dancing. I remember catching sight of myself in a mirror at one point and being shocked by the thought that I was now someone's husband. That's the moment I remember most because I felt like such a grown-up." He glanced down at his ring finger and smiled. "Anyway, I hope your friend enjoys every second of it."

"Thank you. I'm sure she will."

Other regular customers who were also Estella's clients peppered Nora with questions. They wanted to know about the wedding dress, the cake, and the length and location of the honeymoon.

When Nora replied that the honeymoon would be a weekend at the Grove Park Inn, the women sighed in collective relief.

"We can't live without her during the holidays," one woman explained. "She makes us look and feel like we can conquer the world. I know that sounds silly. I mean, we're cooking Thanksgiving dinner, not brokering a peace treaty in the Middle East, but she gives us the confidence and energy to juggle all the stuff we need to juggle between now and January."

Another woman said, "Without Estella, we'd survive. *With* her, we thrive. It's as simple as that."

The first woman nodded enthusiastically. "Exactly! I don't know what we'll do after the baby comes."

"Tell her we'll take turns watching the baby at the salon. Really, I would gladly come in early for my appointment to feed or change the little darling while Estella cuts and styles someone else's hair."

"That's genius," said the first woman. "I'd be willing to do that too. Estella could put a crib and a changing table in the smaller treatment room. I bet the spa music would send the baby right off to sleep. We should talk to her other clients—see who else would help out."

Nora doubted Estella would be interested in her clients overseeing her childcare, but then again, she had no idea what Estella's plans were for after the baby was born. She'd mentioned coming up with a schedule where either she, Jack, or Gus would be home with the baby, but Nora hadn't been listening too closely.

"A wedding and a baby—all before New Year's. Can you imagine?" one woman said to the other as they headed out of the shop.

Nora wanted to recognize Estella's new identities one at a time. Tonight, her friend would become a wife. In December, she'd be a mother. And while Nora was excited to celebrate these milestones, she wondered if these life changes meant that Estella would be less available. Would she stop coming to book club, for example? Would she be too busy to meet for dinner or pop by the bookshop?

Am I going to lose the Estella I know?

During her break, Nora walked across the parking lot to her tiny house. She stood outside, drinking in its boxy shape and cheerful Christmas-red paint. Last night hadn't been the right time to tell McCabe she'd decided to move in with him. Maybe tonight, during a slow dance, the moment would feel right. And if she could embrace this change, she could welcome others, especially a positive change like Estella's wedding.

"What are you so chipper about?" Sheldon asked when she reentered the store.

"The future," she said.

The sleigh bells jingled, and a large group of tourists streamed into the shop. When Charlie showed up at two, looking frazzled from his calculus exam, Nora told him to step into the stockroom whenever he needed to decompress.

"I don't think I can," he said. "Tons of high schoolers are heading our way. They want to chill out after a day of exams. I told them we were closing early, but they don't care." He inhaled deeply and glanced around. "They just want to hang out and feel that weekend vibe, you know?"

Nora did know. As Friday afternoon waned and twilight hovered, she gently reminded her customers that the shop was closing early.

"Don't make us go!" protested one of the teenagers. "It's a mean, cynical, judgmental world out there."

A friend of Charlie's grunted in agreement. "She's right. We're safe in here."

Thanks to the young man's remark, Nora's workday ended on a high note.

At McCabe's, she fed the cats and then took her time showering, doing her makeup, and styling her hair. She was still in her robe when McCabe rushed into the house.

"Sorry!" he called, turning on the shower. "I'll be quick. We won't be late."

He kicked off his shoes, unbuttoned his shirt, and gave Nora a kiss. "You look beautiful."

"I'm not even dressed!"

"You could wear that robe to the reception, and you'd still be the prettiest woman in the room."

Nora traded the robe for a dark green midi dress with a round neck and a cinched waist. The green complemented her whiskey-brown hair, which fell in soft waves to her shoulders.

"Wow," McCabe whispered when he saw the final look. "Just wow."

Admiring the dashing figure he cut in his new mulberry twill suit, Nora said, "Same goes for you. You could be a duke or an earl on the next season of *Bridgerton*."

"Now *that's* high praise." He held out his arm. "Ms. Pennington, might I have the pleasure of escorting you to the wedding of the season?"

"I would be honored, kind sir."

As they drove to the hotel, Nora was tempted to ask McCabe about the case. She'd thought about the Midnight Dumper and his wife several times during the day. She couldn't shake the image of the man's wife being half-dragged, half-carried out of the station by her cousins. She wanted to know if McCabe's team had found Enzo's DNA in or on the van. She wanted to know if the man had talked or asked for a lawyer. She wanted to know everything, but not now. Not tonight. Tonight, she wanted to focus on new beginnings, champagne toasts, and tearful speeches.

Jack and Estella stood outside the Haven Room, waiting to greet their guests.

Jack looked debonair in a black tux and Estella was resplendent in a ballet-slipper pink gown with an off-the-shoulder neckline, Empire waist, and voluminous skirt. Her red hair was combed back into a low bun with face-framing tendrils. Her makeup was natural, with just a hint of shimmer.

"You're beautiful!" Nora cried, kissing Estella's cheek.

Estella hugged Nora and showed her the gold wedding band on her ring finger. "It's official. Jack is stuck with me for the rest of his life."

Jack beamed at his bride. "Which makes me the luckiest man in the world."

After McCabe congratulated the newlyweds, Estella waved at the room behind her. "June and Sheldon are already here. June wanted to make sure everything was perfect, which it is, and Sheldon had to set up his seating chart. Wait until you see what he made."

"Where's Hester? In the kitchen with the cake?"

Estella laughed. "You guessed it. She wanted to add the decorations on-site and is stressed because she wants the cake to be on display before the guests arrive. Will you go to the kitchen and make sure she's not freaking out?"

"Straight away."

A stylist from Estella's salon squealed and rushed toward the newlyweds with her arms outstretched, so McCabe took Nora's elbow and led her into the reception room.

Sheldon stood just inside the double doors next to the three-dimensional seating chart he'd created. He'd painted a landscape of green trees, blue mountains, and a starry sky on a large sheet of plywood. Next, he'd affixed narrow shelves to the board and added colorful little wooden buildings to each shelf. Each building had been hollowed out and fitted with a tea light.

"Look at this!" exclaimed McCabe. "They're named after local businesses. See? Here's Miracle Books."

Nora moved closer to the tiny yellow building and saw the number four and a list of names written above the doorway in neat block letters. She and McCabe were at a table with Hester, Jamie, June, and Sheldon.

"Best table ever," Nora said. "Sheldon, this is absolutely darling. And very clever."

He grinned. "Just like me, right? And you, *mija*! You're dazzling. Give me a squeeze before the D.J. turns the music up and I transform into a half-Cuban Kevin Bacon."

When Sheldon finished hugging Nora, he reached for McCabe next. "You clean up real nice, Sheriff. Forgive me for not including your place of work in my little seating chart town. I didn't want folks thinking of subpoenas or speeding tickets tonight."

"Fair enough," McCabe said without rancor.

As they wandered through the room in search of their table, Nora took in the décor. Kirk and Val Walsh had done a phenomenal job with the centerpieces. Not only did the arrangements of plants, candles, and lanterns create the enchanted woodland vibe Estella had wanted, but the space smelled clean and crisp, like a sunlit forest.

McCabe pointed to the opposite end of the room. "How cool is that mantel?"

Nora followed his gaze to where a dozen lanterns of all different sizes and shapes jutted out of a garland made of tree fern, magnolia leaves, and baby's breath. The hearth was filled with a cluster of white pillar candles. They cast a warm, soft glow from the middle of the room, like a beating heart made of candle flame.

When Nora looked up, she saw a netting made of hundreds of tiny lights stretching from the corners of the room to the central chandelier. It was like walking under a galaxy of stars.

Someone called McCabe's name. He waved at Andrews who stood at the bar.

Nora said, "Why don't you grab a beer? I'll meet you at the table after I find Hester."

A waiter stepped through a door on the rear wall carrying a platter of chicken and waffles. He was closely followed by another waiter holding a pitcher of syrup and a bowl of butter balls.

Nora waited for them to pass before entering the hallway that led from the kitchen to the conference rooms. She headed toward the noise and delicious aromas coming from her right and entered a kitchen that was bigger than her entire bookstore.

"You're here!" June shouted cheerfully. "Damn, girl. You look like a forest goddess. A gorgeous Celt like Guinevere or Morgan Le Fay. I love the dress."

"And I love yours. That purple is stunning. It reminds me of Scottish heather."

June clapped in delight. "That's the name of the shade! And listen to this craziness. The color of Hester's dress is Scottish Lake blue, and her date looks like an extra from *Braveheart*. She's around the corner, washing her hands, but her masterpiece is ready."

Nora turned to where the wedding cake sat on a stainless-steel counter and gasped.

A cascade of delicate flowers wound around the outside of the three-tiered confection. Pale pink cherry blossoms mingled with creamy white dogwood flowers. The petals had been so meticulously crafted that Nora thought they were real.

"How did she do this?"

Hester appeared from behind a set of shelves. "They're sugar flowers. Handmade. The dogwood represents Estella and the Sakura—the cherry blossom—represents Jack. Each cake tier is a different flavor. The bottom is Hazelnut Praline. The middle is Coffee Cream. And the top is White Chocolate Raspberry, Estella's favorite."

Nora couldn't stop staring at the cake. "It's a marvel. You should be really proud of yourself."

"I've made so many wedding cakes, but I didn't love any of those brides like a sister." Hester's eyes moved over the cake. "I conjured so many memories of Estella while I was making this—I just hope those memories enhance the taste."

Nora seized her friend's hand. "You're worried that this cake might turn out like one of your comfort scones. When you bake someone a custom scone, you know it'll evoke a powerful memory, but you can't guarantee that it'll be a happy one. But Hester, this is different. Your cake will taste like love. I can't wait to try it."

Hester smoothed the front of her blue maxi dress and nodded. "Okay, I'm ready. Let's bring this thing in so I can spend the rest of the night flirting with Jamie."

Together, Hester, June, and Nora slid the cake onto a wheeled cart and slowly pushed it down the hallway to the reception area. A pair of servers transferred it to the cake table with practiced ease and then departed with the cart.

The D.J., who was tucked in the opposite corner, started playing, "Cake by the Ocean," and several guests let out a cheer.

When the song was over, he asked the guests to make their way to their tables. Then he announced the bride and groom.

Jack and Estella entered to whistles and applause. They walked to their table next to the fireplace and signaled for the guests to be seated. Servers moved around, filling champagne glasses, while the D.J. handed Estella a microphone.

"Thank you for coming tonight," Estella said. "Our happiness wouldn't be complete without having our friends and family here for our first meal as husband and wife."

"She's glowing," McCabe whispered to Nora.

He was right. With her blush-colored dress and red hair, Estella looked like a sunrise. Jack couldn't take his eyes off her, and when she passed him the mic, the first thing he said was, "Can someone pinch me? Because I must be dreaming. If you'd told me five years ago that I would marry this amazing woman, I'd have thought you'd downed too many glasses of the diner's house wine."

Several guests laughed. Others smiled at the couple, honored to be sharing in their tender moment.

"As everyone here knows, I really loved my mom," continued Jack. "Mama grew up in Alabama, and she believed in God, good food, and family. When she married my dad, a shy, Japanese math nerd, it caused a bit of a scandal. They were ostracized by many, and they struggled financially for years. Even though they ended up going their separate ways, Mama never stopped believing in love. Seven days a week, she fed people heaping platters of love. She gave love and she received love."

When Jack paused to compose himself, Estella reached for his hand. He clasped hers to his chest and said, "I know Mama's with us tonight. She's sitting on a cloud that looks like a mashed potato, smiling from ear-to-ear. If she was here, she'd say, 'You found a real peach, Jack. Don't ever let her go.'" He raised his glass toward the ceiling. "I won't, Mama. Not ever."

He kissed Estella, which elicited a fresh round of applause.

Together, the newlyweds shouted, "Let's eat!"

The buffet was a feast of Southern comfort foods. In addition to the chicken and waffles, there was hanger steak with blistered tomatoes, pimento mac and cheese, bacon-wrapped asparagus, shrimp and grits, and green beans.

Jack and his team had prepared the entire spread, and every bite was delicious.

Sheldon admired the mac and cheese on his plate. "We're going to pop some buttons tonight!"

"You know it," agreed June. "If my shapewear gets any tighter, I might turn blue. Good thing we have a trained medical professional at our table."

Jamie made a show of inflating his chest. "In my professional opinion, you should eat what you want, then hit the dance floor. None of this stuff will stick as long as you move and shake."

"From your lips to God's ear," said June.

After dinner, Estella and her father took the floor for the first dance. After several turns around the floor, Jack and June joined them. When the song ended, Jack led June to her seat and asked his sister, Reika, to dance. Jack's sister moved stiffly and wore a serious expression. She and Jack weren't close, but Jack was clearly pleased that Reika had flown across the country to be a part of his big day. Sheldon had seated Reika at the table with the bride and groom, Gus, Deputy Andrews, and the mayor.

Nudging Sheldon in the side, Nora whispered, "Andrews looks miserable. Why did you put him at that table?"

Sheldon shrugged. "I figured he has a thing for ice queens."

"At least the mayor's happy. We all know she has a thing for Gus. Maybe this will be the night he makes his move."

"He'd be a fool not to. There's magic in the air."

The first few notes of "It's a Wonderful World" tripped through the speakers, and McCabe asked Nora to dance.

When she was in his arms, she told him that she'd finally decided where she wanted to live.

"It's okay if you don't want to move in with me," he said. "I just like coming home to you, and it doesn't matter to me where that is."

"I want to make your house our house, but I have two conditions."

McCabe's eyes crinkled in amusement. "Name them."

"My name needs to be added to all the bills. Otherwise, I'll feel like a roommate. I'm your partner, and once I move in, you're stuck with me."

"That's an easy request to fulfill. Also, the guest room is yours. Turn it into a second office. A home library. I don't care. I'd put everything I own out at the curb if it meant being under the same roof as you."

"Even your recliner?" Nora teased.

McCabe looked aghast. "No way! Deal's off." After spinning her around, he immediately pulled her back into his chest. "What's the second condition?"

"I'm not going to sell Caboose Cottage because I want to turn it into a community meeting space. The town raised the money for the renovations, and their generosity meant so much to me. And since I have a place to live, I want those donations to serve the community. Caboose Cottage can be a cozy place for book club meetings. AA meetings. Teacher planning sessions—you name it."

McCabe tucked a strand of hair behind Nora's ear. "I love the idea, and I love you."

The song ended, and the D.J. announced that it was time to cut the cake. Nora and McCabe returned to their table.

"Why do some couples shove the cake in each other's faces?" asked June. "I just don't get it."

Hester grimaced. "I am *not* a fan of that tradition."

"Jack wouldn't dare mess up Estella's makeup," said Sheldon. "The woman is holding a carving knife."

After the couple cut the cake, Estella picked up the mic and praised Hester's creation. She told the guests that they'd be sampling all three flavors and then explained the significance of the flowers winding around the outside of the cake.

"Even though they look real, they're edible. Hester is *that* talented."

Jamie squeezed Hester's hand, and she blushed furiously. Across the room, Andrews stared at his ex and her date. He looked wretched.

While the cake was being served, Gus moved to the center of the dance floor and gave a short, sweet speech. He made it all the way to the end before his voice became thick with emotion and his eyes grew wet. Too overcome to speak, he simply kissed his daughter and new son-in-law and waved at Nora to come forward and accept the mic.

After dabbing her eyes with a napkin, she accepted a hug from Gus and faced the audience. "Seriously, Gus. How am I supposed to follow that?"

The guests laughed in understanding, which helped Nora relax.

"When Estella asked me to do a reading, I thought it would be easy to find the perfect passage. After all, every book is essentially about love. But none of the famous literary quotes about romance or marriage were quite right for Jack and Estella. Their story is so unique. So beautiful. No writer could do it justice."

Some of the guests looked confused. They didn't know if they were going to hear a reading or if Nora had something else in mind.

"A marriage is a joining of two individuals, so I'm going to read a passage for the groom and another for the bride. Don't worry, I won't keep you from that amazing cake for long." Turning to Jack, she said, "Your reading is from *Love in the Time of Cholera* by Gabriel Garcia Marquez and tells the story of how you loved Estella from afar for a long time before telling her how you felt."

Jack shot a quick glance at Estella before focusing on Nora again.

> To him she seemed so beautiful, so seductive, so different from ordinary people... He had not missed a single one of her gestures, not one of the indications of her character, but he did not dare approach her for fear of destroying the spell.

Nora shifted her gaze to Estella. "Your reading is from Chimamanda Ngozi Adichie's *Americanah*. These words tell the story of how you learned to love and trust Jack. They speak of how you came to realize that he was your person."

She waited until one of the guests finished talking before reciting Adichie's quote.

> *He made her like herself. With him, she was at ease; her skin felt as though it was her right size. It seemed so natural, to talk to him about odd things. She had never done that before.*

Estella nodded and pressed her napkin to her face.

"Finally, I want to read a blessing from a book published in 1947. These words celebrate your story as husband and wife."

Nora had to blink away tears to see the words she'd written on the paper, but she drew in a deep breath and began to speak. Her voice became a benediction, a song of joy echoing through the room.

> *Now you will feel no rain, for each of you will be the shelter for the other.*
> *Now you will feel no cold, for each of you will be the warmth for the other.*
> *Now you are two persons, but there is only one life before.*
> *Go now to your dwelling place to enter into the days of your life together.*
> *And may your days be good and long upon the earth.*

She switched off the microphone and hurried over to embrace Jack and Estella.

"Thank you," Estella whispered into her ear. "Thank you for being my friend."

The D.J. waited until the guests had the chance to eat their cake before playing "Dancing Queen." For the next hour, Nora and the people she loved best danced, laughed, and drank champagne.

When the evening waned, and Nora knew it was almost time to go, she sat down next to Andrews and asked how he was doing.

"Not gonna lie, this has been hard. I keep thinking about how Hester and I used to talk about getting married. I miss what we had."

Andrews looked so young and vulnerable that Nora couldn't stop herself from putting an arm around his shoulders. "I'm sorry."

"Estella and Jack have always been so nice to me, which is why I came tonight, but it's tough to see Hester on a date. It's even tougher to know that half the people in this room don't like the person I'm dating."

"The only one who needs to like her is you."

Andrews stared at his empty beer bottle. "It doesn't really matter because she's not into me anymore. She's been acting weird lately. Not returning my calls. Cancelling plans at the last minute. Like tomorrow. We're supposed to go camping, but she sent a text saying that something came up and she can't go now."

Nora felt a ripple of unease, which only intensified after Andrews said his goodbyes and left.

She's been acting weird lately, he'd said.

Hollowell was pushing Andrews away. Not because she'd grown tired of him, but because the secrets she'd been hiding for so long were bubbling to the surface. Even if no one in the sheriff's department thought she had anything to hide, Nora and her friends believed otherwise.

She wasn't going to spoil this magical night by asking McCabe about the case, but in the morning, when the light streamed through the kitchen windows and the scent of coffee hung in the air, she would listen to what he had to say. She fervently hoped that he was looking at all the key players without bias, but if he refused to see Hollowell as a suspect, he'd have a fight on his hands. Someone had to speak on behalf of the two victims, and Nora wasn't afraid to raise her voice.

But there was no need to think of such things until tomorrow. Tonight, there was time for one last dance.

There was time for one more kiss under a net of stars.

Chapter 17

Time always sounds like a parade ... as though with enough time and all that fearful energy and virtue you people have, everything will be settled, solved, put in its place.

—James Baldwin

The next morning, Nora woke to a silent house.

McCabe's side of the bed was partially occupied by two sleeping tabby cats, neither of whom stirred when Nora sat up. This meant they'd already been fed.

Nora listened for sounds from the kitchen. The clink of a spoon against the side of a coffee cup. The splash of water in the sink. McCabe tried to be as quiet as possible when he got up before her, but she couldn't hear a single noise.

Bleary-eyed, she shuffled into the kitchen to find that McCabe's car keys, phone, and wallet were not in their usual place in the blue pottery bowl. A yellow sticky note sat next to the coffeepot, which was tragically empty.

She carried the note over to the window. She squinted, trying to decipher McCabe's hasty scrawl without the aid of her reading glasses.

> *Grace Kim called the station and asked for me. She said it couldn't wait. Sorry I didn't have time to make the coffee.*
>
> ♥G

Nora's brain was too sluggish to puzzle out why Grace would call McCabe early on a Saturday morning to request a meeting. As she scooped coffee grounds into the paper filter, eager to resume her relationship with caffeine, she replayed everything Grace had told her the day Nora's headache had driven her to the urgent care office.

Grace had talked about the archer's ring, how Lara had been a source of comfort after her husband died, and that she'd learned about Lara from her husband's cousin.

A cousin who lived in Greensboro.

As the coffeemaker gurgled and hissed, Nora wished she'd asked Grace more questions about this cousin. Had her husband's relative been scammed by Lara? Had she also traded a valuable piece of jewelry for a cheap tourmaline necklace? That seemed unlikely, considering the cousin had recommended Lara.

Maybe this has nothing to do with the cousin. Maybe Grace called McCabe because she had a confession to make.

After pouring herself a cup of coffee, Nora wandered into McCabe's office. She wished he owned a big bulletin board like the investigators on TV crime shows so she could create a timeline and cover the board with photos of the key players and index cards full of important facts. Using a piece of red yarn, she could connect the objects and stare at the board until she had an epiphany.

Unfortunately, this was real life, and she wasn't privy to all the details and facts. She'd been certain that Hollowell had orchestrated the murders, but after reading McCabe's note, she was no longer sure.

Nora sat down at McCabe's desk and gazed out the window. As she watched brown, brittle leaves cartwheel across the lawn, she wondered if Grace had been keeping secrets to protect her husband's relative.

"Another person from Greensboro," she mused aloud. "Lara and Enzo. Hollowell. And now, this cousin. Is there a connection between this person and Hollowell?"

She couldn't come up with a reasonable theory and knew that she'd simply have to wait for McCabe to call when he was finished talking to Grace. She hoped it wouldn't be long. She didn't want to spend the rest of the day speculating.

An hour later, Sheldon stormed into the ticket agent's booth and grumbled, "I hate parades. It doesn't start for another ninety minutes, and the parking lot is already full. Good thing we're not getting any deliveries today because I'm in the loading zone."

"Technically, you had bakery boxes to unload. Twice as many as usual too. I don't know how Hester found the time to make so many parade treats for us."

"You should see her kitchen. Every surface is covered with cupcakes and cookies. Chocolate turkey cupcakes, pumpkin pilgrim hat cupcakes, pecan pie cupcakes, and vanilla cupcakes with cranberry filling. And the cookies? They're shaped like wedges of pie. She's packaging eight wedges together to make them look just like a real pie. The woman is a culinary genius."

Nora pried open the lid of the closest box. The scents of pumpkin and cinnamon wafted out from inside.

"These muffins will sell in two seconds," she said.

Sheldon popped open another box. "So will these maple chocolate chip beauties. Wanna split one of each?"

"Does a one-legged duck swim in a circle?"

In between bites, Nora told Sheldon about McCabe's note.

"We could ask Charlie about it when he comes in," Sheldon suggested.

Nora shook her head. "He's just a kid. We shouldn't drag him into this."

"Fair enough." Sheldon glanced at his watch. "¡Dios mío! We open in five minutes, and the coffee isn't ready. You need to go up front and hold back the stampede."

"Yee-haw!" Nora said as she mimed twirling a lasso.

The shelving cart was loaded with the same books found in the display window. Nora pushed it behind the checkout counter before taking a quick peek outside.

Seeing the crowds gathering on the sidewalk, she knew Sheldon had every reason to panic. The moment she unlocked the door, a line would form at the ticket agent's booth. People wouldn't even look at books until they got their hands on something hot to drink and something sweet to eat.

Nora wasn't worried about lines of customers. She was worried about Sheldon's joints. Even though the new JAK inhibitor he'd started taking in September was working miracles on his inflammation, he still had bad days. Today, the air was chilly and damp. It was the kind of weather that could cause a flare, especially in his knuckles and wrists.

Keep an eye on his hands today, she told herself.

Luckily, Charlie was scheduled to work from ten until closing, and Nora was counting on his youthful energy.

However, ten o'clock came and went with no sign of Charlie. By ten thirty Nora was concerned. She quickly checked her phone to see if he'd sent her a text, but he hadn't.

She didn't have time to call him because too many customers needed her attention. Customers wanted to check out. They wanted book recs. They wanted directions to the restroom. They wanted a comfy place to sit. They wanted to stay inside the warm, cozy bookstore until the marching band at the front of the parade was a block away.

It was almost eleven when Sheldon slipped behind the checkout counter. He reached for a customer's candles and began to wrap them in tissue paper.

"Charlie's here," he whispered to Nora. "His sister isn't feeling well, and he didn't want to leave her until his mom got home. She was stuck in traffic on the way back from the station. He texted me an hour ago, but I didn't see it. It's been hella crazy back there."

"Does he seem okay?"

Sheldon passed the bag of candles to the customer and wished her a lovely day. "He feels really bad about being late. I told him that if this is the worst thing he's done this month, he's not trying hard enough."

When the customer with the candles opened the door to leave, the rumble of drums and the peal of trumpets swept inside.

Nora let out a sigh. "The parade's underway, which means we have about an hour of relative calm until mayhem resumes."

Hearing the music, most of their customers rushed out of the bookstore. Nora took advantage of the momentary lull to pick up strays, empty the trash, and refill the paper towel dispenser in the restroom.

After finishing these tasks, she sent Sheldon to the front to sit down for a few minutes while she and Charlie tidied the ticket agent's booth.

"Can you wipe off the counter?" she asked Charlie. "I'll reload the pastry case."

"Yeah, sure." Charlie grabbed the rag and cleaning spray. "Sorry I was late this morning. Sheldon said you were really slammed."

Nora washed her hands and opened a bakery box. "You made the right call. You couldn't leave your sister."

"I think it's just a cold, but she sounds terrible. My mom will know how to make her feel better."

Nora offered Charlie the last maple chocolate chip muffin, which he happily accepted. Reaching for the other bakery box, she said, "Grant told me that he had an early meeting with your mom this morning. Is she okay?"

Charlie peeled off the muffin wrapper and squeezed it into a tight ball. "I don't know what's going on. She was on the phone with Auntie Mae—my dad's cousin—when she started freaking out. I was still in bed, so I didn't hear the details, but I could tell she was upset. I guess she thought the sheriff needed to hear what Auntie Mae said because she got dressed really fast and left." He tossed the muffin wrapper in the trash. "We didn't talk about it when she got home because I was already late."

Nora couldn't resist the urge to check her phone for a message or missed call from McCabe, but he hadn't reached out to her. She was about to tell Charlie to brew more coffee after he finished his muffin when she realized that he'd already devoured it.

She laughed. "Do you even chew?"

"You should see me eat a donut. Two bites. That's all I need."

"You'd better have a pumpkin muffin before they're gone. It's going to be a long day." She held out the box so he could select the muffin of his choice, watched him gobble it down within seconds, and then turned her attention to the dirty mugs in the sink.

She'd managed to wash a dozen mugs when her phone rang. She expected McCabe's name to pop up on her screen, but the call was from the Pink Lady.

"Nora? It's Jack. Have you seen Estella?"

Jack's voice was taut as a bowstring. He'd barely said anything, but Nora was on high alert. "I haven't. What's going on, Jack? Aren't you two supposed to be on your way to Asheville by now?"

"That's just it—she was supposed to meet me at her place two hours ago. I figured she got caught in parade traffic, but she's not answering her phone."

She's eight months pregnant, and he doesn't know where she is. No wonder he's scared.

"We'll figure this out," Nora said matter-of-factly. "What did she need to do before you guys headed out of town?"

"Two things. First, there was something with the computer system at the salon. She had to reset it so the other stylist could use it this afternoon. After that, she was going to swing by and see you. She wanted to get a book for this weekend and a latte for the road."

Estella knew what town was like on a festival or parade day. She wouldn't have dropped by Miracle Books after ten. She would've come before business hours.

Nora scrolled through her missed calls. "She didn't call me this morning. Can you track her phone?"

"I usually can, but her phone isn't visible anymore." After a pause, Jack blurted, "I don't know what to do. She's two hours late for our *honeymoon*. This isn't like her at all. What if she's hurt? Or the baby—"

"We'll find her," Nora interrupted. She was worried now too, but she wasn't going to let it show. "Have you asked Gus?"

"Yes. He hasn't heard from her, and neither has Hester. I came to the diner thinking she might've parked here. None of the staff or customers have seen her. Can you ask June? I'm heading to the salon to check there."

Nora promised to make the call right away and was relieved when June picked up after the first ring. Skipping the pleasantries, Nora told her that Estella was missing.

"We haven't spoken since last night," said June. "But I don't like the sound of this. You'd better ask for McCabe's help. I'm going to walk into town and look for Estella's clients along the parade route. Maybe one of them has seen her."

"Great idea. Text me with any news, and I'll do the same. I'm going to loop Hester in too. She can ask the locals who come into the bakery, and I'll talk to those who come in the bookshop."

Nora's next call was to McCabe. The phone rang and rang,

and she was just about to give up when he shouted, "Hang on! I need to get to a place where I can hear you."

The din of crowd noise filled her ear followed by sudden, blissful quiet.

"Sorry about that," McCabe said. "I'm a few blocks away, maintaining order by smiling at babies and picking up trash. This is a very well-behaved crowd. They're definitely feeling the holiday spirit. I just ducked into the post office lobby to talk to you."

"Grant, I think something happened to Estella."

Nora's words tripped over themselves in her rush to repeat everything Jack had said.

"We'll find her," McCabe said, his calm and measured tone a balm to Nora's anxiety. "I'll alert the deputies on patrol to be on the lookout for her. Let me go, so I can call Jack. I'll be down your way soon. Hang tight."

Despite McCabe's reassurances, Nora wanted to take action. She wanted to rush out of the shop and comb the crowd for a flash of red hair. She wanted to stop people on the street and ask if they'd seen Estella.

She drove from her house to her salon. Next, she planned on coming to Miracle Books. What kept her from reaching me? Unless she never left the salon. Will Jack find her inside? Is she okay?

To stop herself from catastrophizing, Nora walked to the front of the store and told Sheldon about Estella.

"Maybe she spent too long messing with the computer—you know how they can be—and her phone died," he said without conviction.

"There's a phone at the salon. If she was running behind because of the computer, she would've let Jack know." Nora passed her hands over her face. "They were supposed to leave two hours ago. It's their honeymoon weekend. She wouldn't be late for that. She just wouldn't."

Sheldon glanced out the window at the parade crowd. "What can we do?"

Nora was tempted to hang the CLOSED sign, lock the door, and rush outside, but it made more sense to learn what Jack found at the salon first. When she shared this thought with Sheldon, he closed his eyes and began to pray in Spanish.

It was impossible to focus on anything while they waited. Though Nora managed to reshelve a few strays and push the manual floor sweeper over the rugs, she kept pausing to look at her phone.

Finally, a text from Jack appeared on her screen.

Estella's car is at the salon. Everything looks fine inside, but she's not here. Calling the sheriff now.

She heard from McCabe next.

"Her purse is in her car," he said. "But no phone. I've asked every officer on duty to search their immediate areas and report back to me."

"Including Hollowell?"

After a slight pause, McCabe said, "She's off today."

In the hallway outside the stockroom, Nora leaned on the handle of the floor sweeper. "Something's wrong, Grant. I can feel it. Why did Grace come to see you this morning?"

This time, he didn't hesitate. "Her husband's cousin, Mae, the one who lives in Greensboro, was talking to Lara about her biggest fears during one of their sessions. Lara admitted to being scared of dogs. Especially Dobermans. She said she'd had a bad experience with a police dog. When Mae asked if she filed a complaint against the dog's handler, Lara responded by saying that it was safer to avoid them both."

Safer, thought Nora. *Safer to avoid the police dog* and *its handler.*

She felt her mind sharpening like a stick. She wanted to use it like a weapon. To scratch away the extraneous details until the truth was revealed.

"Why did she feel compelled to tell you this first thing this morning?"

"Grace forgot about this conversation until a few days ago when she saw Hollowell on patrol with Rambo. That brought it all back. On a whim, she took a photo of them and sent it to Mae. Mae didn't recognize Hollowell or her partner."

Another dead end, Nora thought.

But she was wrong.

"Last night," McCabe continued slowly, as if it took a superhuman effort to push the words out, "she attended a community function with a retired officer from the Guilford Sheriff's Department. Mae showed him Hollowell's photo, and this man remembered her. When she worked for Guilford, her partner was a Doberman named Warden. Lara's neighborhood was on her routine patrol route."

Lara knew Hollowell! She knew her and was afraid of her.

Nora returned to the Readers' Circle and dropped into a chair. "Where is Hollowell right now?"

"We're looking for her."

They're looking for Hollowell.

Estella is missing.

"Oh, God," she whispered.

Seeing the anguish on her face, Charlie came out from the ticket agent's booth and sat across from her.

Up front, the sleigh bells banged as customers entered the shop. A little girl ran past Nora's chair, making a beeline for the Children's Corner. She pulled a book off the shelf and plunked down on the alphabet rug.

"This one!" she cried as her parents joined her on the rug. She climbed into her father's lap, and he opened the book and began to read while the mom snapped photos with her phone. Dressed in their fall sweaters and warm jackets, with their apple-red cheeks and sparkling eyes, the little family was everything that was good and right in the world. Watching them, Nora's heart constricted.

"It was Hollowell, wasn't it?" she croaked. Her voice was hollowed out by fear. "Lara. Enzo. And now—what about Estella? Does she have Estella, Grant? *Does she?*"

"There's no reason to assume she's done anything to Estella, but I'm going to find them both. Listen to me, Nora. Are you listening?"

Her reply was a feeble, "Yes."

"The parade just ended. When the crowd clears, my team will do a thorough search of the area. Fuentes and I are five minutes away from Hollowell's house. Just sit tight."

Sheldon stepped into Nora's line of sight and pointed at his phone. "I called the hospital and our local urgent care. They haven't treated anyone with Estella's name or description."

Nora just stared at Sheldon. She didn't hear the sleigh bells or the laughter of the little girl in the children's area. Her body buzzed with anger. She was furious with Hollowell, with McCabe, and with herself. But she couldn't hold on to the fiery heat of her anger. Not when her heart was icy with terror.

"What's going on?" asked Charlie.

Nora couldn't look away from Sheldon. She fixed her gaze on the familiar lines of his face and the cheerful curve of his mustache. Searching his warm brown eyes, she found exactly what she needed. His wonderful mix of softness and steel. He didn't blink as he knelt beside her and took her hands in his.

"I think Hollowell took Estella," she cried. "She's a killer. And she has our friend."

Chapter 18

I've learned that waiting is the most difficult bit.
— Paulo Coelho

Nora paced behind the front windows, her gaze darting from her phone to the street and back to her phone again.

Two deputies had begun removing the barricades at the end of the block. It wouldn't be long before traffic was allowed to flow freely, and the post-parade crowds clogged the roadways.

Those watching and participating in the parade had gotten lucky. The morning had been weighed down by cold, damp air, but there'd been no rain.

Now clouds threatened. They swam low in the sky like a shiver of gray sharks in an angry sea.

"Andrews is out there," Nora told Sheldon when he joined her at the window.

She didn't notice that he was holding her jacket and purse until he pushed them into her hands. "Go."

Outside, she jogged straight for Andrews. He finished loading the last barricade onto a county truck and gave his partner a thumbs-up. The partner held up his palm, signaling that he'd hold the traffic until Andrews had the chance to drive away.

Nora couldn't let him leave without her.

She ran to the cruiser and banged on the passenger window. When Andrews lowered it, she said, "Let me in. Please."

Andrews darted a glance at the line of cars waiting for the other deputy to let them pass and unlocked the door.

"Where's Hollowell?" Nora demanded as she slid into the seat.

"Put your seat belt on," Andrews replied, turning right onto Main Street.

Nora did as he asked and then repeated her question.

"Not at her house," he said as the first raindrop struck the windshield.

"Then where?"

Andrews stopped at a red light and turned to Nora. "She must've taken the SIM card out of her phone. We can't track it. Same goes for Estella."

Seeing self-recrimination in Andrews's eyes, Nora said, "Right now, you might feel like you didn't know Hollowell at all, but you were the only one who truly got close to her. There has to be a place she'd escape to. A place with lots of privacy? Or one that was particularly peaceful?"

The light turned green. Andrews accelerated, but his mind was traveling much faster than the car. "She felt the net closing, you know. That's why she's been acting so weird. She told me so many lies. I got the feeling she was playing me, but I was too much of a jackass to call her on it. I didn't want to face the fact that another woman was about to dump me. I didn't want to be a two-time loser."

"You can feel sorry for yourself after we've found Estella," Nora's voice was dagger-sharp. "She's eight months pregnant, and she needs your help. Please, Andrews. *Think*. Did Hollowell ever talk about a place around here that was special to her?"

Suddenly, Andrews made such an abrupt left turn that Nora was thrown sideways in her seat. Over the screech of tires, he shouted, "There's a cabin! A small rental cabin just north of Paint Rock. It's a stone's throw from the Tennessee border and looks over the French Broad. Paula stayed there when she was living in Greensboro. She could see the river from the back deck, and the owner let her use his boat. She said the key to the front door is in a turtle statue right on the porch."

Nora whipped out her phone and started searching for rental properties on the French Broad. She zoomed in on a map of the area, trying not to get carsick as Andrews merged onto the highway. He sped west, deeper into the mountains.

"I found two rentals overlooking the river. One's a tiny house. Pretty new. It has a front porch and a back deck. The other's a log cabin. They're both on wooded lots at the end of gravel roads. Tons of privacy. Did she mention any other details?"

"I don't remember. Can you read the descriptions? Maybe something will ring a bell."

Clicking on the tiny house rental, Nora read the listing out loud. "'Secluded tiny house with tons of charm. One bedroom, one bath. Kitchen has all the amenities. Back deck looks out on the French Broad River. Easy access for canoeing or trout fishing. Wi-Fi. TV with standard cable.'"

Andrews shook his head. "That's not it. Her place was off the grid. No Wi-Fi."

Nora moved to the second listing. "Quaint log cabin. Riverfront. Perfect place to unwind, barbecue, or fish. Stone fireplace. One bedroom. One bath. Antique furnishings. Back deck has gas grill and hot tub."

"That's it," Andrews said, his tone leaving no room for doubt. "I'm calling the sheriff."

"Don't tell him I'm with you," Nora pleaded. "It might distract him, and the only thing that matters is getting to Estella."

Andrews asked the dispatch officer to patch him through to McCabe. When McCabe's voice crackled through the speaker, Andrews said, "I think I know where Hollowell went."

After listening to Andrews, McCabe told him not to approach the cabin.

"We're ten minutes behind you, so park and wait for backup. We have no idea what we're walking into, and we don't want anyone to get hurt. We need to proceed with caution. Do you hear me, Deputy?"

"Yes, sir."

Andrews drove in silence for several minutes before casting a warning look in Nora's direction. "Once we get there, you need to follow my orders. I can't have you running off half-cocked. You heard what the sheriff said. We need to be careful."

Nora raised her hands in surrender. "I wouldn't do a thing to put my friend's life in jeopardy. I promise to do whatever you say."

"We're all assuming Estella's with Hollowell, but no one knows that for sure. We don't know if Paula's at this cabin or if she's out on a hike. The reality is, we don't know shit."

Nora didn't respond. She watched the windshield wipers crush the raindrops for a while. Then she raised her gaze to the mountains. She'd felt protected by them ever since she'd moved to Miracle Springs. Not a day passed when she didn't revel in their majesty or take comfort in their permanence. But now, shrouded in mist and storm clouds, they looked cold and unknowable.

Somewhere, at the foot of one of these blue hills, was a small, brown cabin hidden by a palisade of trees.

Somewhere, her friend was waiting to be rescued.

Nora knew the women were together. They'd both vanished without an explanation. Their phones were suddenly untraceable. Andrews had said that the net was closing for Hollowell, which meant she was guilty of a crime. Or several crimes.

A trapped animal lashed out. Panic made it unpredictable. This was what scared Nora the most. What would Hollowell do when she realized there was nowhere left to run?

As the car flew over the rain-slick asphalt, Nora prayed that Estella was okay and that McCabe knew how to handle the situation. She prayed that everyone would walk away from whatever confrontation lay ahead.

She didn't understand why Hollowell had taken Estella in

the first place. The two women had only interacted when Hollowell had been Estella's client, which hadn't lasted long. Hollowell had soon moved to another salon, and Estella had been more than happy to see her go.

Why didn't you come for me? I'm the one you hate.

Glancing over at Andrews, she saw the set of his jaw and his tight grip on the steering wheel and could only imagine how many questions were stampeding through his mind.

Quietly, she asked, "Did Hollowell ever talk about growing up in Michigan?"

He pulled a face. "I never knew she was from Michigan, or that she'd been raised by her grandma. She didn't talk about her past. I didn't do much asking, either."

Nora thought about Andrews and Hester. They'd spent years swapping stories. They'd spoken of their childhoods. Their fears and dreams. They'd planned a future together. They'd talked of houses and holidays, family and finances.

They hadn't been able to make things work. And not long after the breakup, Andrews had started seeing Hollowell.

"We didn't care about each other's histories," continued Andrews. "We were a temporary thing. We both knew it. We were both okay with it being super-casual."

"I get that."

"Everything I know about her past I learned in the last twenty-four hours. Her parents died when she was a little kid. Her grandma raised her. I knew that she worked for Guilford County before she came here, but I didn't know that she used to have long, dark brown hair."

Nora remembered Hollowell's photo in the paper. The hair pulled back into a fist of a bun. The thin, unsmiling mouth. Those dark, guarded eyes.

"Last week, after the sheriff asked her some basic questions about her past, she started avoiding me. Not at work. She was normal there. But she didn't want to hang out after work." He grunted. "I didn't really care. But if I *had* cared just a little more, I might've asked her what was going on—why she was acting so cagey."

"But you didn't have that kind of relationship," Nora reminded him. "Whatever she's done—none of that is on you."

She could tell that Andrews didn't believe this, so she let it drop. He didn't speak again until they exited the highway and drove on roads that grew narrower and curvier as they headed northwest toward the French Broad.

Nora watched their progress on the dashboard map. One more turn and they'd reach the gravel lane leading to the cabin.

The lane was marked by a metal mailbox affixed to a crooked pole. Andrews parked right next to it and cut the engine.

Nora stared down the lane. She couldn't see the cabin, only a cluster of pine trees arrowing into the shale-gray sky.

She sent a thought down the lane and into that gray sky. She thought it over and over, like a silent line of Morse code. *Please be okay. Please be okay. Please be okay.*

The wait for backup seemed interminable. Finally, after what felt like an hour but was more like eleven minutes, McCabe's SUV and another cruiser pulled in behind Andrews.

"You have to stay here," he said sternly. "No matter what, you have to stay here."

"I will."

Andrews got out of the car and slammed the door, hard, as if to emphasize the directive. Twisting in her seat, Nora watched him walk toward McCabe's SUV. She saw McCabe exit his car and grab a spare rain jacket from his back seat. He passed it to Andrews, who slipped it on and then pointed at his car.

McCabe frowned and said something to his team. A moment later, he slid into Andrews's seat and grabbed Nora's hand.

"We don't have time to chat, but I can't do my job if I'm worrying about your safety. I need to know that you'll be right here, in this car, at all times. I need you to give me your word that you won't move."

"I promise." She squeezed his hand. "Please, Grant. Go get Estella."

He nodded and turned away, but not before she saw the fear in his eyes. She knew he wasn't scared for himself. His fear was for Estella and his colleagues. Including Hollowell.

Nora watched him jog down the lane toward a cabin she couldn't see and an outcome she couldn't predict. How she wished she believed in psychic powers and that someone with a gift for fortune-telling could assure her that everything would be okay.

She was tempted to call June. Or Hester. She wanted to hear a familiar voice—to have someone to wait with her—to offer her distractions and hope.

But Hester would be far too busy at the bakery to field such a call, and June was probably on her way to Estella's place to sit with Jack. She would make him coffee and tidy the kitchen. She would pray over him and hold his hands when they started shaking.

Nora couldn't reach out to Sheldon either. He and Charlie had too many customers to handle. Not only did they have the post-parade crowd to deal with, but they now had rainy Saturday shoppers too. Miracle Books would be thrumming with people, and the two men holding down the fort would be running themselves ragged trying to serve them.

You have to wait this out on your own.

Even though there was nothing to see, Nora stared out her window. The trees flanking the lane began to blur as the rain fell faster and harder. It hammered the roof of the car, but Nora thought she heard another noise behind the rain. It sounded like the whine of a small engine.

Suddenly, a black four-wheeled vehicle appeared on the gravel lane. It scuttled over the ground like a cockroach, heading straight for Andrews's car.

It carried two people, and as it drew near, Nora saw a spark of red hair.

"Estella!" she cried.

The ATV hurtled past.

Estella sat in front of Hollowell, pinned between Hollowell's body and the handlebar. Nora caught a fleeting glimpse of her friend's pale face. Estella's features were slack with shock.

Nora burst out of the car, but the ATV vanished behind a copse of trees before she could take any action. She chased after the two women, her fingers fumbling with her phone.

"They just passed me on an ATV!" she shouted at McCabe. "There's a trail up here!"

"Don't—"

Nora hung up before he could tell her not to follow Hollowell. She knew she could never keep pace with the ATV, but the only way she could help Estella now was to see where Hollowell was taking her.

She broke into a run, her every movement fueled by that glimpse of Estella's waxen face.

She's alive.

Alive and seemingly unharmed. Nora had to ensure that she stayed that way.

The trail snaked through the trees, and while Nora couldn't see the ATV, she could hear its engine. It climbed higher and higher, leaving Nora behind.

Her legs and lungs burned, and she felt the hopelessness of her efforts.

Don't stop, she told herself. *Don't you dare stop!*

But she couldn't run uphill indefinitely. She didn't have the strength or the stamina.

As she slowed to a walk, her face crumpled in despair. What hope did she have of helping Estella now?

Don't stop.

Picking up her pace, she shoved aside a pine branch blocking the trail, which released a shower of water from the higher branches. It rolled off the needles and dripped down her face and back. She swiped at her eyes, nearly colliding with another tree.

Only it wasn't a tree. It was a woman in a green dress.

Estella cradled her belly with one arm and reached out for Nora with the other.

"Oh, my God!" Nora cried, rushing forward to support Estella before she collapsed. She put her arm around Estella's back and murmured, "I've got you. I've got you."

"She let me go. I was sure she was going to . . ." She didn't complete the thought. Instead, she staggered.

Nora tightened her hold.

"You're safe," she said. "McCabe is here. So are Andrews and Fuentes. Can you make it to the car?"

"I feel sick. And it hurts. Here." She pressed a hand to her belly and wailed, "*My baby!*"

Nora couldn't show any fear. She had to be brave for Estella's sake. "We're going to get off this trail and get out of this rain. You can do this, okay? I know you can."

She took as much of Estella's weight as she could while simultaneously holding her phone to her ear. The connection was bad. McCabe's voice was little more than a series of staccato bursts. Still, Nora shouted, "Call an ambulance! I have Estella! We're on the trail."

She dialed 911 next, but the call failed.

"You're doing great," she told Estella. "You're so strong. So brave. We're going to make it to that car and then to a hospital. It's just a little bit farther, love, just a little bit farther."

Estella let out a sob. "I can't lose my baby! Please, God, I can't!"

"Your baby is strong. *You* are strong." Nora coaxed Estella into putting one foot in front of the other. She kept saying that the car was just around the next bend. Through the next gap in the trees. Downhill a little more. Not much longer now. Almost there.

Then, suddenly, Andrews appeared on the trail ahead.

"Man, am I glad to see you," he told Estella as he strode toward her. "Put your arms around my neck. I'll carry you the rest of the way. And don't worry, an ambulance is coming."

Nora couldn't believe the pace Andrews was able to maintain as he scrambled down the trail.

"Where's McCabe?" she asked, unable to keep her voice from trembling.

"Pursuing Deputy Hollowell."

His tone was as cold and unrelenting as the air. His face was as hard as mountain stone. His expression only softened when Estella rested her head against his chest. He whispered something to her as the rain dripped off his chin, and she managed a tiny smile.

In that moment, Nora loved Deputy Jasper Andrews with her whole heart.

This is what a hero looks like, she thought. Rain-drenched. Neck muscles taut with strain. Eyes filled with equal measures of anguish and determination.

If Hester saw him now, she'd fall in love with him again.

When they reached the cars, Andrews eased Estella into the back seat of his sedan. He gave Nora a bottle of water and told her to get Estella to take tiny sips. Then he grabbed an emergency blanket from his trunk and two more from McCabe's SUV.

He jumped into the driver's seat, turned on the engine, and cranked up the heat.

"If you can, help her out of her clothes," he told Nora. "If nothing else, unzip the top of her dress and cover her with the blanket. Put another one over her head. I'm going to sit in McCabe's car to give you some privacy and check on the ETA of the ambulance."

As soon as he was gone, Nora unzipped the back of Estella's sodden dress and peeled it off her shoulders. She pushed it down, but it got stuck around the widest part of her belly. Not wanting to cause her friend any discomfort, Nora wrapped her in the blanket and briskly rubbed her arms and back. Then she toweled her hair as best she could with the second blanket. It wasn't until Nora had removed Estella's shoes and socks that her friend stopped shivering.

It was a small victory, and Nora tried not to focus on Estella's pallor or the low moan she released as she bent over in her seat.

Wiping off her wet phone, Nora called Andrews. "I think she's going into labor!"

"EMTs are four minutes out. Try to get her to relax. Tell her help is coming." Andrews sounded so calm that Nora felt her panic subside a fraction. Infusing her voice with the same calm, she repeated what he'd said to Estella.

"You're safe. Your baby's safe. Help is coming."

Exactly four minutes later, the ambulance arrived in a whirl of sound and flashing lights. While a female EMT held an umbrella over Estella, Andrews gently picked her up and carried her to the ambulance.

Nora waited outside its open doors while Estella was secured in a stretcher and the EMTs checked her vitals.

"Can I ride with her?" she asked through chattering teeth.

"There's no room," said Andrews. "Get in my car. We're going to escort them to the hospital."

Another blanket was conjured up for Nora, and she pulled it around her chest before buckling her seat belt.

Only then did her thoughts turn to McCabe.

"Where are McCabe and Fuentes?" she asked as Andrews pulled onto the road and hit the siren. "Where's Hollowell going?"

"We think she's crossing the river into Tennessee. There's a park not too far from the opposite bank. If she left a car and a go bag there, she could make a run for it."

"What happened in the cabin?"

Andrews merged onto the highway. The ambulance was

right behind them. Its red lights glowed on the wet highway. Its siren spilled into the sky, amplifying Andrews's siren. It was too much noise. Too many bright lights. Nora wanted to close her eyes until it was all over.

Let her baby be okay. Let her baby be okay.

"Hollowell must've seen us coming because she called the sheriff on the phone and told him we all had to stay on the front porch. If we moved, she'd hurt Estella. She said she was leaving and would let Estella go, unharmed, if we didn't pursue her. If we gave chase or raised our weapons, it would be our fault if Estella died."

Nora covered her mouth with her hand.

"The sheriff tried to convince Hollowell to give herself up. He talked to her like she was still one of us. Like she hadn't crossed every line. He asked her to put justice and duty before her own needs. He reminded her that Estella was a citizen of their community. A person they'd sworn to protect."

Nora looked for the ambulance in her side mirror. "Why Estella? Of all the people to take hostage, why her?"

"I don't know. But when the sheriff said that bit about protecting citizens, Hollowell got really pissed. She yelled something about how no one had ever protected her. Except the dogs she trained."

"Protected her from what?"

Again, Andrews said that he didn't know. "The sheriff told her that he wanted to hear her story. He said they could talk, just the two of them, about what happened with Lara and Enzo. He offered to lay down his weapons and phone and go inside the cabin with his hands up. She laughed and said that she wasn't going to have a nice, cozy fireside chat while Fuentes and I called in the staties."

"And then?"

"She stopped answering his questions—probably because she was pushing Estella out the back door and onto the ATV."

Nora could easily picture Hollowell grabbing Estella's arm

and shoving her out into the rain. "I hope she breaks her neck on that thing."

"She didn't," Andrews said. "I talked to Fuentes when I was sitting in McCabe's car. Hollowell left the ATV on this side of the river and crossed by boat. I don't know where she got the ATV or the Jon boat, but she obviously had an escape plan in place. I don't think Estella was originally part of it, either. I think she took her at the last minute, but I don't know why."

"Has someone called Jack?"

"Yes. He's meeting us at the hospital."

One of the few things Nora disliked about Miracle Springs was its distance to the nearest hospital. Even with a law enforcement escort, the drive took over thirty minutes. If it felt long to Nora, she couldn't begin to imagine how it felt to Estella or to Jack.

When they finally pulled in front of the Emergency Room entrance, Nora jumped out of the car and watched the EMTs unload Estella's stretcher. Between the EMTs and the hospital staff, Nora couldn't get close enough to see Estella's face, let alone hold her hand.

Words and phrases were carried to her by the rain-lashed wind. She heard "approximately thirty-four weeks" and "labor pains" and "unconscious."

Nora dug her fingers into Andrews's arm. "She's unconscious?"

Andrews steered Nora toward the entrance doors.

"She's in good hands," he said. "The best hands. Come on, you need to get out of the rain."

Nora didn't realize she was crying until she tasted salt. "I can't leave her!"

Andrews put his arm around her and led her inside. In the waiting room, he sweet-talked a nurse into loaning Nora a pair of scrubs. She changed into them mechanically, shivering the whole time. She kept shivering even after she was in dry clothes with a blanket draped around her shoulders. She shivered as she paced outside the doors dividing the waiting area from the emergency room. She didn't stop until McCabe showed up and enfolded her in his arms.

"Estella," she whispered into his chest. "She has to be okay, Grant. She has to be okay."

He didn't say anything. He just stood, solid as a tree, and held her until the doors to the inner sanctum opened and a man in scrubs called out, "Family of Estella Sadler?"

Nora raised her head and looked around for Jack. Seeing that he hadn't arrived yet, she rushed over to the health-care worker and said, "That's me. Estella is my sister."

Chapter 19

When you begin a journey of revenge, start digging two graves: one for your enemy, and one for yourself.

—Jodi Picoult

The man in scrubs was a nurse. As he led Nora through the automatic doors, he told Nora that Estella was one centimeter dilated and that the baby's heart rate was strong.

"So she *is* in labor?"

"She was probably experiencing Braxton-Hicks contractions." Seeing the blank look on Nora's face, the nurse said, "They're practice contractions, but they can feel like the real thing. Estella might deliver tomorrow. Or in a few days. Or weeks. As soon as a room in the labor and delivery ward becomes available, we'll move her up there. In the meantime, we're making her comfortable and giving her fluids."

Unsure of what all of this meant, Nora sought clarification. "But she's okay? And the baby? They're both okay?"

The nurse pushed a button on the wall, and a pair of doors opened to reveal another corridor. "We're not seeing anything to cause us alarm at this point, but the doctor wants to run more tests. Mom is clearly upset, and we're hoping a familiar face will help calm her down. We'd rather not administer a sedative if we don't have to."

Nora said, "Estella's husband will be here any minute. The two of us will do everything we can to make her feel safe. She's been through a terrible ordeal, and she thought she might lose her baby. If you can show her there's no danger of that happening, she can relax a little."

"We'll work together as a team to do that."

The nurse paused in front of a curtained cubicle and drew back the curtain. "Estella, your family is here."

Another nurse had a hand on Estella's belly. She didn't turn when Nora entered the cubicle as she was completely focused on Estella.

"We'll do an ultrasound next," the female nurse told Estella. "For now, I want you to focus on the number on the screen. A normal fetal heart rate is between 120 and 160. Your baby's heart rate is exactly where it should be. Keep watching that number, and I'll be back with the ultrasound machine."

After the woman stepped out, Nora took her place by Estella's side. She cupped her friend's hand in hers and whispered, "Listen to that heartbeat. Strong and steady, just like yours."

Tears sprang to Estella's eyes. She couldn't look away from the fetal heart rate monitor.

"You're safe now," Nora soothed. "You're safe."

When the tears cascaded down Estella's cheeks, Nora searched for tissues. The ones she found weren't very soft, but she folded them into a square and tenderly wiped Estella's tears away.

"Jack will be here any minute, and McCabe and Andrews are already here. No one's getting within a mile of this bed unless they're wearing a hospital badge. You're safe."

Nora smoothed Estella's hair and tried to distract her by talking about how her child would brag about this one day.

"This'll be the story your son or daughter tells on the school bus or at the playground to prove what a badass you are."

Estella was about to reply when the curtain parted and Jack launched himself into the small space. His face crumpled as he leaned over to kiss his wife. They clung to each other for a long moment. Suddenly, it was Estella comforting Jack, and not the other way around.

"We're okay," she murmured to him. "They're going to do an ultrasound. In just a few minutes, we'll be able to see our baby."

To give them a little privacy, Nora offered to locate the nurse. She knew Estella's fears wouldn't be extinguished until she saw an image of her baby on a monitor. Words weren't enough at this moment. She needed the unwavering evidence provided by a machine. By the unshakeable honesty of science.

Fortunately, Nora didn't have to go far before she saw a middle-aged woman with a butterfly print scrub top approaching. She pushed a cart with a laptop and an attachment resembling an electric shaver to the cubicle next to Estella's and poked her head in.

"Doctor Kessler? I'm ready when you are."

Seconds later, the two health-care workers entered Estella's cubicle.

Nora waited in the hall until the doctor emerged. He grinned at Nora and told her exactly what she wanted to hear. "Baby looks great. We're going to move Mom upstairs, where she'll be more comfortable. It'll probably take thirty minutes because patient transport is running behind this afternoon."

"Thank you."

She wanted to say more, to convey her gratitude to everyone in the ER, but the doctor ducked into another cubicle before she could come up with anything profound. She returned to the waiting area to share the good news with McCabe.

McCabe stood in a far corner, speaking quietly but urgently into his phone. Catching sight of Nora, he lowered the phone and closed the distance between them.

"They're okay," Nora cried as she crashed against his chest. Holding her tight, he whispered, "Thank God."

When they broke apart, McCabe said that he needed to finish his call. "Then we can go to the cafeteria and talk."

Nora sat down and watched McCabe as he spoke into the phone. At one point, he passed his hand over his face and looked utterly dejected.

Did Hollowell get away?

The thought sparked Nora's anger. She fanned the spark, allowing the emotion to create a fire inside her chest. Her heart felt like a volcano, pumping lava into her veins.

She couldn't stand the thought of her nemesis escaping. She wanted her to be hunted down and caught. She wanted her punished.

"Where's Hollowell?" she asked as she and McCabe headed for the cafeteria.

"In custody. In Tennessee. I was just talking to the sheriff of Greene County. The Forest Service helped apprehend her. Paint Creek is part of Cherokee National Forest, and she might've slipped away if they hadn't acted so quickly."

The heat in Nora's body abated. Hollowell had been captured. Justice would be served.

McCabe bought two cups of coffee and joined Nora at a table overlooking the courtyard garden. He opened his lid, allowing the steam to escape, and put a hand on Nora's knee.

"You look adorable in scrubs, but are you warm enough?"

"I'm getting there." Nora gestured at his uniform shirt. "Is that your spare?"

He nodded. "They tease me about it at the station, but I can't tell you how many times I've used the extra uniform I keep in the car. I need to add socks to that kit. Mine were soaked, so Andrews asked a nurse for a pair of those nonslip hospital socks."

"He got the scrubs for me too. He was incredible today, Grant. The way he carried Estella down that trail to the car and took charge—you would've been so proud."

McCabe took a sip of coffee. "I *am* proud of him. I'm proud of everyone who wears this uniform, which is why it hurts so much to have someone I trusted betray it. You tried to tell me about Hollowell, but I never saw that side of her. I saw a dedicated professional. I saw a young deputy who tried to get along with her colleagues and had a genuine bond with her K9 partner."

"There's nothing wrong with seeing the best in people."

"There is when it's your job to see the truth," McCabe answered sharply. Nora knew his anger wasn't directed at her. He was mad at Hollowell. And himself. "We were short-staffed when I interviewed her, and she seemed like a great fit. Hiring her meant that it was no longer DEFCON 1 every time someone called out sick. I was grateful she came aboard."

Nora knew how many extra hours McCabe had worked over the past year to make up for the staff shortage. He hadn't been the only one, either. It had been hard on the whole department.

"I didn't ask many questions about her personal life," McCabe went on. "I remember one thing, though. She said that she liked to live near train tracks. Her parents were killed in a train crash, and the grandmother who raised her used to say that whenever a whistle blew, the sound was her mom and dad, saying hi to her. Saying that they loved her."

Though Nora loathed the woman Hollowell had become, she pitied the little girl she'd once been. "It's a lonely sound."

"She was a lonely kid, I think." McCabe drank more coffee and stared at the rain. "I made a bunch of calls, trying to find folks from her hometown who remembered her. Teachers and neighbors and such. They painted a sad picture."

"It was just her and her grandmother? There wasn't anyone else? No other family?"

McCabe shook his head. "Just the two of them. Hollowell's mother was an only child, and after the train crash, the grandmother spent most of her time and money trying to contact her. It sounds like the grandmother had some mental health issues."

"How did she try to contact her daughter? Through Lara?"

"Lara was one of several mediums. Remember the Psychic Hotline?"

Nora recalled the late-night commercial with its 1-900 number and catchy name. "The Psychic Friends Network? Wasn't Dionne Warwick in the commercials?"

"That's the one. They got all of the grandmother's money. When that ran out, she used the monthly payments from Mr. and Mrs. Hollowell's estate earmarked for Hollowell's clothes, education, food, and so on. One of Hollowell's teachers said that she often came to school with dirty clothes, no lunch, and once, in the middle of a snowstorm, without a coat."

"Did social services get involved?"

McCabe grimaced. "They did. Hollowell became a ward of the state. Less than two months after this happened, her grandmother died."

Nora listened to the rain for a moment. "What a sad history."

"She's had more than her fair share of loss, that's for sure. And I see why she demonized psychics. Because of her grandmother's obsession with them, Hollowell looked like a Dickens character for most of her childhood."

Nora shook her head. "She *was* a Dickens character. A poor, undernourished orphan. A girl living in Michigan with no winter coat. Her grandmother was her only connection. Her only family. Unless she found a foster family?"

"No. She stayed in a group home until she was eighteen."

"And then?"

"She went to junior college, majored in criminal justice, and got a job with a police department in Michigan. Not in her hometown, but not far from it."

Nora imagined Hollowell receiving her first uniform. How proud she must have been. She'd never have to wear dirty or tattered clothes again. She'd have warm coats and heavy boots. She'd have a family of men and women in blue.

"She left the police department to become a deputy in Guilford County, North Carolina. When I asked why she'd made such a major move, she said that it was because of the dogs. She'd always loved them, and it was her dream to be a K9 officer and to live in a place where she could spend more time outside and less time freezing her ass off. There was nothing to tie her to Michigan, so when she saw the Guilford posting, she jumped at the chance."

Nora took McCabe's hand. "I would've believed her story too. Did she tell you she wanted a dog when she was a kid?"

McCabe nodded.

"After talking to these people from her hometown, did you begin to doubt her reasons for moving to Greensboro?"

"I began to doubt lots of things, but the job was one of them. After listening to the Midnight Dumper's confession, I knew that he, Zeke, had been coached. Not by his construction company bosses, either. He was terrified of messing up, but his story about accidentally hitting Enzo with his van didn't ring true. It was too rehearsed, and he didn't know certain key details."

Nora noticed June making her way over to their table. Her face was lit by such a jubilant smile that Nora automatically smiled back.

"I've been looking all over for you two! I have *amazing* news!"

McCabe pulled out a chair in invitation. "We sure could use some."

Ignoring the chair, June bent over and gave Nora a hug. After releasing her, she immediately hugged her again. "I had to hug you twice because I couldn't do this to Estella. I am overflowing with gratitude and relief, and I need to share it."

"You can squeeze me if it helps," McCabe offered.

June was happy to oblige. When she finally sat down, Nora said, "What's the amazing news?"

"Estella hasn't gone into labor. Not yet anyway. They're going to keep her overnight, make sure she's hydrated, and monitor her and the baby. If she feels better tomorrow, she can go home. She'll have to take it easy, but that sweet cinnamon roll in her oven can go on cooking."

"The ultrasound was good?"

"Right as rain. I already called the hotel and got their honeymoon weekend postponed until February. I figured they'd have their hands full until then, but if we all help out with the baby, they can have a romantic Valentine's getaway."

It seemed like a lifetime ago that Jack had called Nora, looking for Estella, but it had only been a handful of hours. The newlyweds were supposed to be enjoying a couples massage or having afternoon tea at this moment. Instead, they were in a hospital.

June waved a finger back and forth between McCabe and Nora. "I interrupted a serious conversation, didn't I? Was it about Hollowell?" She pinned McCabe with her gaze. "Please tell me that woman is behind bars."

"She is."

"Why on God's green earth did she take Estella?"

McCabe shook his head. "I don't know. Until she's interviewed, that question will remain unanswered. Among many others."

June scowled. "Including the burning question, Did she kill Lara and Enzo?"

"I believe she killed Lara. We had Narcan in the evidence room. It came from Clem Wynter's apartment and was taken into evidence as part of the investigation into his death. Hollowell was one of the deputies who processed the scene, so she knew about the Narcan." McCabe returned June's frank stare. "Even though it's missing, I can't prove that she took it. I also think she knew about Lara's heart condition, but I can't prove that either."

Nora got a sick feeling in her stomach. "Is she going to get away with murder?"

"What about Enzo?" June asked, her words tripping over Nora's.

McCabe made a time-out gesture. "Here's what I know. It's going to be Hollowell's word against a man apprehended for illegal dumping. Zeke isn't a U.S. citizen. His work permit is about to expire, and his story sounds like a tall tale."

June said, "What *is* his story?"

"That Hollowell promised to turn a blind eye to his illegal dumping in exchange for a favor. All he had to do was come to her house, load an item into his van, and dispose of said item in a remote place far from Miracle Springs."

"And that item was Enzo?" asked Nora.

McCabe dipped his chin. "Zeke made a terrible mistake by agreeing to Hollowell's demands. His English is limited, so he didn't understand that she wanted Enzo's body left miles from town. Zeke's plan was to dump the remains in the woods, return the van, and go into hiding."

"Which he couldn't do because Hollowell arrested him."

June folded her arms across her chest and frowned. "I bet she scared the bejesus out of him on the ride to the station."

"According to Zeke, she threatened his family. If he told

anyone what she'd made him do, she'd kill his wife and children. He believed her, which is why he refused to talk, despite hours of questioning. If Deputy Fuentes hadn't finally earned his trust, he never would've opened up."

"What will happen to him now?" asked Nora.

McCabe glanced out the rain-spotted window. "Hollowell's an officer of the law with an impeccable record. Enzo's DNA was found in Zeke's van. He's under arrest for illegal dumping. Things don't look good for him."

Nora was suddenly electrified by rage. "But she *will* go to prison for what she did to Estella, right? She kidnapped a pregnant woman. She held a gun to her head. She's obviously capable of extreme violence."

"We recovered her firearm, which was left in the cabin." Reluctantly, McCabe added, "It was unloaded."

June narrowed her eyes. "Are you telling me that she's going to walk because her gun wasn't loaded?"

McCabe's reply was swift and sure. "No. I'm saying that we have our work cut out for us. And by us, I mean my department and the outside agency I've called in to assist us. We need an impartial party to take charge of this case. My department can't interview Hollowell. She would only try to manipulate us."

A voice came over the speaker system, calling for a hospital employee to report to a room on another floor. When the announcement was over, low conversations from other tables resumed, but McCabe, Nora, and June stayed silent, each lost in their own thoughts.

Finally, June said, "What did Lara and Enzo do to her?"

"Lots of people contributed to Hollowell's desire for vengeance," Nora said. "Many of them were strangers. They were voices on the other end of a phone line. But Lara represented all that Hollowell lost due to her grandmother's obsession with spiritualism. Hollowell was still a kid when she lost her ability to trust. Her willingness to love. All that pain and loneliness twisted her."

June gave her a pointed look. "You sound like you feel sorry for her."

"I feel sorry for the child she once was." Nora's voice hardened. "I do *not* feel sorry for the adult she became. She could've made different choices. She could've found a home in the sheriff's department. In our town. She could've become a part of a family."

McCabe's phone buzzed. A text message floated on the surface of his screen. He read it and pushed back his chair. "Estella's ready to talk."

"We're coming too," said June. "She might need moral support."

They took the elevator up to the L&D ward and were buzzed in by a nurse. After escorting the trio to Estella's room, she told them she'd be back in fifteen minutes to check on her patient.

They entered to find Andrews inside, standing near the window. His body language signaled that he felt more than a little awkward.

"Do you want us here, or is it too crowded?" Nora asked Estella.

When Estella said, "please stay," June sat down in the recliner in the corner of the room. Nora perched on the arm of the chair.

McCabe asked Estella to begin by telling him about the salon.

"Our software has been buggy all week, which happens whenever there's a major update. This morning, it was so bad that I had to call tech support. The call took longer than I thought. It was a little after nine by the time I finished. I knew I needed to get out of town before the parade started, so I hurried to my car. I'd just opened my door and tossed my purse inside when a car squealed to a stop next to me. I saw the sheriff's department seal and got this sick feeling."

Estella's lip began to tremble.

"Take your time," McCabe said gently.

Jack offered Estella a cup of water, but she waved it away. "Hollowell put the window down and shouted my name. She said, 'There's been an accident at the bakery. You need to come with me.'"

June let out a cry of horror.

Estella nodded at her. "That's the noise I made. A thousand things were going through my head at once, so when Hollowell opened the back door for me, I got in. When I asked her what happened, she told me that my father needed me. She looked upset and scared, which made *me* upset and scared. As soon as she shut the door, I was trapped."

She was in a cruiser, Nora thought. *A wire mesh partition. No door handles. It was a mobile cage.*

This time, Estella accepted the water cup from Jack and took a drink. When she was done, she put a hand on his arm and went on with her story. "I thought there'd been a fire or something equally terrible. I thought my dad was seriously injured. Or worse. I begged Hollowell for information, but she said I'd find out soon enough."

"Did she drive straight out of town?" asked McCabe.

"Yes. And when she didn't drive past the bakery, I lost it. I started yelling and kicking the back of her seat. Told her I wouldn't stop until she answered me." Estella let out a puff of air. "She told me that my ex-con, bread-baking daddy was fine and to calm down or I might hurt my baby. When she looked at me in the rearview mirror, I knew I was in trouble. Her eyes were wild. And she was sweating. When we got on the highway, I asked her why she'd picked me up."

McCabe held very still. "What did she say?"

"That she'd waited too long to leave. That I could buy her some time. She said that all I had to do was listen to her and I wouldn't get hurt. She made me remove my SIM card and throw my phone and card out the window."

"But why you?" blurted Nora.

Estella let out a humorless laugh. "I wasn't her first choice. You were. But she didn't think she you'd fall for it, even if she faked a story about Hester being hurt. When I drove past her on my way to the salon, she decided I'd make a great hostage. A pregnant woman is the ideal human shield."

McCabe shot Nora a warning look before turning back to Estella. "Did Deputy Hollowell say anything else on the drive to the cabin?"

Estella stared into the middle distance. "She was muttering to herself, but I couldn't understand a word. At the cabin, she pulled her gun and pushed me inside. She let me use the bathroom while she watched and then handcuffed me to a chair in the kitchen. She left me there and did something in the bedroom. I couldn't see anything. I just heard her moving around. I tried talking to her, but she never responded."

Watching Estella, Nora knew that her friend was back in that kitchen, feeling the cold metal of the handcuffs biting into her wrists and her baby shifting in her belly.

Andrews spoke next. "Did she interact with you again before you got on the ATV?"

"She came to the kitchen and looked out the window. Then she *totally* freaked out. She started crying. One second she sounded heartbroken, and the next second she was furious. She yelled stuff like effing Fuentes and effing Andrews. Then she cried harder and said she was sorry over and over." She looked at McCabe. "I think she was talking to you."

"What makes you say that?"

"She was staring out the window when she said, 'you believed in me.' She also said, 'if not for *her*, you might have picked *me*.' I think the *her* was Nora."

It was difficult for Nora to picture Hollowell in tears—to imagine such a cold and hostile person breaking down.

She saw her colleagues and knew that the price she'd paid to have her revenge was too high.

Nora almost shared Hollowell's fate. The night she'd guzzled a bottle of booze before getting behind the wheel, determined to confront her cheating husband, had almost ended in the deaths of two innocent people.

It was why Nora understood the all-consuming power of rage. She'd almost sacrificed her future on its altar but had been luckier than Hollowell. Fire had burned away all thoughts of vengeance. It had left her yearning for a new life. A better life.

When Hollowell's rage was spent, she'd gained nothing. All she had was regret.

But it was too late.

She'd gone too far.

Estella walked McCabe through the end of the ordeal, starting from the moment Hollowell forced her to straddle the ATV until the moment she stopped on the trail and told her to get off.

"The last thing she said was 'tell them I'm sorry.'"

McCabe closed his notepad and thanked Estella. "You were very brave today. I am deeply sorry that you were put in a dangerous position and incredibly relieved that you and your baby are safe and well. Is there anything I can do for you other than let you rest?"

Estella pointed at Andrews. "Give that man a promotion."

McCabe glanced at Andrews, his eyes shining with affection. "I'll see what I can do."

No one knew that Andrews was about to receive a different kind of reward. As soon as he exited the L&D ward, Hester threw herself into his arms.

"I thought you could use a friend. And a hug," Hester murmured into his shoulder.

He pulled away so he could look at her face. "You came all the way here to hug me?"

"I'll aways be here when you need me," she whispered. "Always."

Nora reached for McCabe's hand. Then she slipped her arm around June's waist and said, "Let's go home."

inside when a car squealed to a stop next to me. I saw the sheriff's department seal and got this sick feeling."

Estella's lip began to tremble.

"Take your time," McCabe said gently.

Jack offered Estella a cup of water, but she waved it away. "Hollowell put the window down and shouted my name. She said, 'There's been an accident at the bakery. You need to come with me.'"

June let out a cry of horror.

Estella nodded at her. "That's the noise I made. A thousand things were going through my head at once, so when Hollowell opened the back door for me, I got in. When I asked her what happened, she told me that my father needed me. She looked upset and scared, which made *me* upset and scared. As soon as she shut the door, I was trapped."

She was in a cruiser, Nora thought. *A wire mesh partition. No door handles. It was a mobile cage.*

This time, Estella accepted the water cup from Jack and took a drink. When she was done, she put a hand on his arm and went on with her story. "I thought there'd been a fire or something equally terrible. I thought my dad was seriously injured. Or worse. I begged Hollowell for information, but she said I'd find out soon enough."

"Did she drive straight out of town?" asked McCabe.

"Yes. And when she didn't drive past the bakery, I lost it. I started yelling and kicking the back of her seat. Told her I wouldn't stop until she answered me." Estella let out a puff of air. "She told me that my ex-con, bread-baking daddy was fine and to calm down or I might hurt my baby. When she looked at me in the rearview mirror, I knew I was in trouble. Her eyes were wild. And she was sweating. When we got on the highway, I asked her why she'd picked me up."

McCabe held very still. "What did she say?"

"That she'd waited too long to leave. That I could buy her some time. She said that all I had to do was listen to her and I wouldn't get hurt. She made me remove my SIM card and throw my phone and card out the window."

"But why you?" blurted Nora.

Estella let out a humorless laugh. "I wasn't her first choice. You were. But she didn't think she you'd fall for it, even if she faked a story about Hester being hurt. When I drove past her on my way to the salon, she decided I'd make a great hostage. A pregnant woman is the ideal human shield."

McCabe shot Nora a warning look before turning back to Estella. "Did Deputy Hollowell say anything else on the drive to the cabin?"

Estella stared into the middle distance. "She was muttering to herself, but I couldn't understand a word. At the cabin, she pulled her gun and pushed me inside. She let me use the bathroom while she watched and then handcuffed me to a chair in the kitchen. She left me there and did something in the bedroom. I couldn't see anything. I just heard her moving around. I tried talking to her, but she never responded."

Watching Estella, Nora knew that her friend was back in that kitchen, feeling the cold metal of the handcuffs biting into her wrists and her baby shifting in her belly.

Andrews spoke next. "Did she interact with you again before you got on the ATV?"

"She came to the kitchen and looked out the window. Then she *totally* freaked out. She started crying. One second she sounded heartbroken, and the next second she was furious. She yelled stuff like effing Fuentes and effing Andrews. Then she cried harder and said she was sorry over and over." She looked at McCabe. "I think she was talking to you."

"What makes you say that?"

"She was staring out the window when she said, 'you be-

Chapter 20

Sometimes the smallest things take up the most room in your heart.

—A. A. Milne

Downtown Miracle Springs was decked out in its holiday finest.

The streetlamps were festooned in tiny white lights and festive red bows. Wreaths hung from every door. The window displays shone with tinsel and candlelight. The living Christmas tree in the park was a beacon of color.

It was the second Sunday in December, and there was talk of snow, which only added to the frenetic energy pervading the town. Kids of all ages kept racing outside to stare at the sky. They put spoons under their pillows and flushed ice cubes down the toilet. They'd gone to sleep the night before with their pjs turned inside out.

There were only four schooldays until Winter Break, but that didn't matter to the kids. They still wanted a snow day.

Nora hoped their wish would come true. She was on her way to meet Sheldon and the rest of the Secret, Book, and Scone Society, and she wanted the whole town to feel the joy she felt.

Today was Estella's baby shower.

Ever since her release from the hospital, Estella had been on partial bed rest. She cancelled all of her December appointments and spent her time reading and binge-watching historical dramas.

On Friday, her obstetrician had informed her that she was two centimeters dilated and her baby's fetal weight was around seven pounds. Estella had immediately called her friends to share the good news.

"Jack should sleep better now, which means at least *one* of us will sleep. Our kid likes to practice their kickboxing moves between two and four in the morning. I never thought I'd be such a napper, but I'm really into them right now. I feel like our collective mental health would improve if we all curled up on a little mat and had quiet time every afternoon."

Nora had laughed and said, "I bet Sheldon would embrace that idea. I can totally see him having a siesta on the alphabet rug. He'd snore like a hibernating bear, and the kids could use him as a pillow while they looked at picture books."

"He's going to be the world's best uncle."

"The best," Nora had agreed.

In honor of the baby shower, Sheldon had purchased a sweatshirt embellished with a giant mustache and the words, NO NEED TO FEAR, THE COOL UNCLE IS HERE.

Nora, June, and Hester wore identical sweatshirts, but the text on theirs said, IN MY AUNTIE ERA.

"I'm sensing a theme here," Estella said when she arrived. June immediately handed her a gift box, and when she opened it and pulled out a breastfeeding sweatshirt with the logo, MAMA'S DINER on the front and EAT LOCAL on the back, she chortled with delight.

Nora placed a small stack of book-shaped packages on the coffee table. "I know you told us not to get you anything, but these aren't for you. They're for the baby."

Hester handed Estella the first gift-wrapped book. "We wanted to be sure your baby's library got off to a good start."

"All the books are inscribed," added Sheldon. "We each picked two of our faves and wrote notes to our littlest reader."

Estella opened Hester's books and read the titles out loud. "*Make Way for Ducklings* and *Goodnight Moon*. Two classics."

June's books were next. She'd chosen *Little Bear* and *The Snowy Day*.

"I hope it does snow, but later," said Sheldon. "After we've had our tea and cookies."

He passed Estella the books he'd selected, which were *Strega Nona* and *Harold and the Purple Crayon*. Finally, Estella opened Nora's books. It had taken Nora a long time to decide on just two, but in the end, she'd gone with *The Story of Ferdinand* and *Chicka Chicka Boom Boom*.

Over tea and Hester's homemade rolled oat cookies, the five friends talked about the possibility of snow. This led to a discussion about holiday plans, and when Hester announced that Andrews had invited her to Christmas dinner at his parents' house, June rubbed her hands together with undisguised elation.

Hester scowled at her. "I see the glint in your eyes, but it's not what you think. Jasper and I are friends. He's going through a rough time, and I want to be there for him. That's all."

"I didn't think he and Hollowell were that serious. Is he heartbroken?" asked Estella.

Hester dunked her cookie in her tea as she considered the question. "He's hurt, but his heart isn't broken. He feels betrayed, but also seriously embarrassed. No matter what anyone else says, he believes he should've known that Hollowell wasn't what she seemed."

"He'd get his equilibrium back faster if Hollowell would just confess." Nora sighed into her teacup. "Grant was right when he said that her word would carry more weight than Zeke's. There isn't enough concrete evidence to convict her."

June tapped the top of the table. "And too many unanswered

questions. If Lara was injected with the liquid version of Narcan, then where did the nasal spray Narcan come from?"

"Exactly," agreed Nora. "But there *have* been some promising developments this week. A woman who lived across the street from Lara and Enzo was interviewed by the Guilford County Sheriff's Department. This neighbor is an avid birder. Her whole front yard is full of feeders, and when she isn't watching birds, she likes to people watch."

Sheldon grinned. "My kind of girl."

"One day," Nora continued, "Lara came to this woman's house to deliver mail that ended up in Lara's mailbox. She and the woman were chatting when a jogger passed by with his dog. The dog saw a squirrel hanging from the neighbor's bird feeder and went ballistic. Lara got so scared that she hid behind the neighbor's porch swing. She said that she was terrified of dogs because she'd recently been chased by a police dog."

"When was this?" asked Hester.

"About a year after Hollowell moved from Michigan to Greensboro. Lara's description of the dog was an exact match to Hollowell's K9 partner, Warden. Lara told the neighbor that she'd bumped into the dog and his handler—a woman with long, dark hair who always wore mirrored sunglasses—several times before the dog chased her. Her intuition told her that the woman was dangerous, which is why she decided to avoid her instead of reporting her."

Nora's friends exchanged startled glances.

"I don't believe anyone can contact the dead, but I do think some folks have heightened intuition," said June. "Lara knew Hollowell was a threat, even if she didn't know why."

Nora shrugged. "I suppose so. Anyway, Hollowell was the only female K9 deputy in the department at the time, and the neighbor is willing to testify about the incident in court. That has to mean something."

Hester balled her fists. "I hate that this is going to trial. It's just like Hollowell to make this as miserable as possible."

"Considering she rejected the first plea bargain, she must feel pretty confident about her chances." A look of discomfort passed over Estella's face, and she put her teacup down. "Oh. Hello, heartburn."

June held up both hands. "Enough about Hollowell. Let's talk about something else. Like our next book club pick."

Estella said, "I'm vetoing any book that mentions childbirth. Fiction is not kind to women in labor. *The Handmaid's Tale, The Red Tent, Beloved.* See what I mean?"

"Let's read something set in Texas in honor of Nora's upcoming trip," suggested Hester.

Nora instantly warmed to the idea. "We could pick a Katherine Center book. She has a few with Texas settings, and she delivers all the feels."

When Sheldon offered to pull a few titles, Nora followed him. He was reaching for a copy of *The Bodyguard* when they heard a cry. Rushing back to the Readers' Circle, they saw Estella standing in the doorway to the ticket agent's booth, staring down at a puddle on the floor.

"Her water just broke," June said. "Everything's fine. Jack is on his way. He's totally calm."

"Well, *I'm* not!" shrieked Sheldon.

The women escorted Estella to the back door and bundled her into her coat. Nora slipped a knit hat on Estella's head and said, "You've got this."

"You're sure you don't want us to come?" Hester asked. "We're happy to hang out in the waiting room."

Estella said, "I'm sure. I can't take the pressure of knowing there's a room full of people waiting for me to deliver. Jack will call you as soon as the baby's born. Promise."

Nora opened the back door, and there was Jack, smiling like a fool as he held out an arm for his wife.

"Take care of our girl!" June pleaded.

The four friends stood in the parking lot and waved until Jack's car disappeared from sight. Instead of going back inside, where it was warm, they stayed rooted in place. No one spoke. No one moved. They stared at one another in a mix of wonder and fear.

Sheldon broke the spell by glancing at his watch. "It's been, like, a minute, and I'm already going crazy. How do we do this? The waiting?"

Nora smiled at him. "Let's lock up and go for a walk in the snow."

"What snow?" June asked as the first delicate flakes landed on her shoulder.

Hester held out her hand. "The first snow of the season, and look, it's so light. It's like tiny white flowers." She smiled. "Like baby's breath."

Jack called early the next morning to tell Nora that Estella had given birth to a beautiful, healthy baby girl. Nora and McCabe were in the living room, having coffee, when she took the call. She put the phone on speaker so that McCabe could hear the news too.

"I know this is a lot to ask, but can you wait until this evening to visit?" Jack said. "Estella was in labor for a long time and is completely wiped out. She wants to grab a few hours' sleep before the lactation consultant shows up."

Nora couldn't stop smiling. "I'm sure you're both exhausted. Oh, Jack. A little girl! What's her name?"

"Louisa May, but we're calling her Lulu."

"There are so many great children's books with characters named Lulu. Your sweet girl is in good company."

Jack mumbled something about having more phone calls to make, so Nora let him go.

"You're going to order all of those books as soon as you get to work, aren't you?" asked McCabe.

Nora laughed. "How can I not?" She shook her head with wonder. "Just imagine. A baby bookworm."

McCabe squeezed Nora's hand. "I hope Charlie can close tonight. If he can, I'll drive you to the hospital—unless my Hail Mary plan actually works."

"What's your Hail Mary plan?"

"I'm going to take Rambo to the jail this morning. Hollowell's been asking about him and her two pet dogs. She loves these dogs. I can't bring them all to the jail, but I can bring Rambo because he's a working dog and because seeing him will probably elicit a reaction from Hollowell. If it does, it might just be the opening I've been waiting for—the crack in her armor."

"Who's taking care of the other dogs?"

"Andrews. He didn't want them to go to a shelter."

Nora wasn't surprised. "He's one of the good ones."

"Unlike me. I'm going to try to manipulate Hollowell's emotions to get her to confess. The dogs are my biggest bargaining chip. Normally, I wouldn't barter with animals, but I don't want this case to go to trial."

"You're not a bad guy because you're bringing Rambo to her. You're doing whatever it takes to see that justice is done. I hope it works. I really do."

After McCabe left for work, Nora cleaned up the kitchen and played with the cats for a few minutes before heading out for the day.

Yesterday's snow was just a memory. The fragile flakes had melted the moment they'd hit the warm ground, forcing hundreds of disappointed children to shuffle off to their bus stops this morning.

For Nora, the magical feeling of that snowfall lingered. As she drove into town, she glanced at the blue mountains and felt a rush of happiness.

At a particularly long red light, she started a conference call with June and Hester. Her friends felt exactly as she did. Joyful, excited, and full of hope.

Pulling into the parking lot behind the bookstore, Nora saw several pickup trucks clustered around her tiny house.

"I almost forgot," she told her friends. "Reno on the Caboose Cottage starts today."

"Is it going to be weird? Watching your house transform into a meeting space?" asked Hester.

Nora gazed from the orange safety fencing surrounding her tiny house to the tarp draped over its ruined roof. "I don't think so. I just want it to be whole again."

"That's what I want for us too," said June. "After this mess with Hollowell. After the lives that were lost. We need to heal. We need to focus on what fills our cups. Like a new baby girl. Like spending the holidays with people we love. Or a gingerbread cookie that's crisp on the outside but super soft in the middle."

Hester let out a groan. "I'm baking them right now! You mentioned them at least four times yesterday, so I got the hint. This year's cookies are a tribute to Sheldon. They all have mustaches and Christmas sweater vests. I think he'll be tickled."

Sheldon was wild about the cookies. "We can't sell my mini-mes," he protested when Nora started loading the cookies into the display case. "I can't watch people bite off my arms and legs. It's ghoulish."

Nora promptly bit off a gingerbread man's head. "Hmm. Delicious."

Unable to stop himself, Sheldon reached for a cookie and nibbled off a hand. "I am *so* tasty."

"I have to put one aside for McCabe. No matter what kind of day he has, this will bring a smile to his face."

As it turned out, McCabe didn't need a cookie to make him smile. He entered Miracle Books with a bounce to his step and greeted Sheldon with a friendly slap on the back.

"My boss is making me leave early," Sheldon complained to McCabe.

Nora squeezed his hands. "You need to rest these delicate instruments. They'll be cradling a newborn soon."

Sheldon blanched. "I am *not* holding that baby until she's old enough to talk. I'm way too nervous."

"I am too, but we'll have to get over it," said Nora. "Lulu's part of the family. She's one of us. That means lots of cuddles and bear hugs from the world's coolest uncle."

"Fine, I'll ask June for pointers. Now get this man his coffee before the high school crowd shows up. *Hasta luego, mi corazón.*"

Sheldon wiggled his fingers in farewell and breezed out the back door. Nora told McCabe to have a seat while she poured him a decaf and brewed herself a cup of herbal tea.

"You have news," she said, joining McCabe in the Readers' Circle.

McCabe's expression was triumphant. "She confessed! She admitted to killing Lara and Enzo. We didn't get all the details, but she gave us enough. The DA's office is drafting a new plea bargain as we speak. Hollowell will take the deal. She has to."

Nora felt a wave of emotion crash over her. It was a confusing mixture of relief and sorrow. There would be justice for Lara and Enzo, but they were still gone. And Hollowell? She'd thrown away her future for nothing.

McCabe rested a hand on her shoulder. "I know. It's a lot to take in."

"A bunch of feelings just hit me at once." Nora blotted her eyes with her napkin. "My friend just became a mom. She now has a daughter to love with her whole heart. Lara had a daughter too, but she wasn't capable of loving her the way Allie needed. And Hollowell? Her mother was killed when she still had so much growing up to do, and her grandmother didn't put her first. She put her grief first. After she died, Hollowell ended up in a group home where no one chose her. No one invited her into their family. No one cherished her."

McCabe nodded. "I feel sorry for her, I do, but taking two lives only made that hole in her heart bigger. She was supposed to protect the people of this town. She was supposed to be on the right side of the law."

They sipped their drinks in silence for a moment. A customer said hello on his way to the cookbook section, and Nora told him to give a shout if he needed any help.

"She cried when she saw Rambo," McCabe said after the man moved deeper into the stacks. "I removed her restraints so she could pet him. He was wagging his tail like crazy and licking her face. It was hard to watch."

"I bet."

McCabe rubbed the stubble on his chin. "I felt like a heel, using the dog to get to her, but it worked. I told her she could have regular visits with her dogs for as long as Andrews was willing to bring them to the jail. *If* she agreed to cooperate."

"Can you make that kind of deal?"

"The DA was willing to go with it. Like I said, no one could get through to her. In every interview, she was stone-faced and tight-lipped. Without her badge and her partner, she couldn't see a future."

Nora frowned. "Wouldn't she rather go to trial in hopes of being acquitted? That's the only way she could reunite with her dogs."

"The whole process would take months. Her dogs would go to a shelter, and she'd never see them again. She couldn't stomach the thought. The dogs loved her unconditionally. She'd do anything for them."

"I know you don't have all the answers, but I'd like to know what made her decide to kill Lara the night of her event." Nora pointed at the purple chair. "Why here? Why not in Greensboro?"

McCabe's eyes also traveled to the chair. "She moved here to get away from Lara. She was trying to fight her demons by letting go of the past. Miracle Springs was her fresh start."

It was mine too, thought Nora.

"She had a wake-up call back in Greensboro," McCabe continued. "One of Lara's neighbors called the sheriff's department to ask why the deputy with the dog kept patrolling their residential street. When the sheriff questioned Hollowell about it, she made up some nonsense about suspicious activity, but that's when she realized that hurting Lara could ruin the life she was building. She liked being a K9 handler. She liked being a deputy. She liked her colleagues. Her male colleagues, anyway."

Nora grunted. "She does *not* like women. I guess there's a reason behind that. Were all of her grandmother's psychics women?"

McCabe nodded. "Yes. The hotline mediums were women, and when her grandmother visited psychics at county and state fairs, they were all female too. And then there was Lara."

"So Hollowell relocated to get away from Lara. She made the decision to focus on the future but couldn't stick to the plan. Why? Because Lara came to the bookstore?"

"Hollowell hated the idea of Lara profiting from her memoir. She read it, cover to cover, more than once. It reignited her desire for revenge. She decided to attend the event to see if Lara would be more honest or if she'd keep up the pretense that she could speak with the dead. Hollowell was prepared to kill Lara, but she didn't commit to the act until she saw her grandmother's ring on Lara's finger."

Nora gasped. "*No.*"

McCabe consulted his notebook. "It was an Edwardian ring with a Colombian emerald surrounded by cut diamonds in a platinum setting. The grandmother traded it for a cheap tourmaline necklace and a message from her deceased daughter. Not only did the ring have sentimental value because it was her grandmother's engagement ring, but Hollowell claims it's worth fifty grand."

When Nora thought back on that evening, she didn't remember seeing the ring. Even when Lara asked for Terry, Grace, and Hester to put their hands in hers, the ring hadn't caught Nora's eye.

"You can tell I'm not a jewelry person because I never noticed it."

"Lara was still wearing it when the EMTs loaded her into the ambulance. Hollowell knew Enzo would end up with the ring. She wasn't going to let him keep it. The idea of him selling it made her see red."

Such intense emotion had been roiling under Hollowell's surface during the entirety of the private reading, but she'd kept it well hidden. Nora had been suspicious of Hollowell's presence from the start, but she would never have thought that Hollowell had showed up at Miracle Books with murder on her mind.

"If Lara hadn't worn that ring, she might still be alive," McCabe mused aloud. "Hollowell almost didn't enter the bookstore at all. She sat in her car, trying to talk herself into making a different decision. That's why she was late."

Nora remembered seeing her arrive. "And Lara didn't recognize her?"

"Apparently not. Hollowell was out of uniform, and her hair's a different color and style. Lara probably thought she looked familiar but couldn't place her. In Greensboro, she'd only seen Hollowell wearing mirrored sunglasses, walking with a dog."

"How did she know about Lara's heart condition?"

McCabe didn't reply because the man returned from the cookbook section carrying a short stack of books. Nora headed to the front to ring him up.

When she was done, another customer needed help finding a hostess gift. Nora made a few suggestions before steering her over to the seasonal candle display. After that, she had to make a decaf latte for a woman who sat down in the Readers' Circle.

McCabe joined Nora in the ticket agent's booth. "You're

busy, and I need to get back to the station, but let me answer your last question before I go. Hollowell kept a close watch on Lara's Facebook feed, so she knew she was coming to Miracle Springs to promote her memoir. She became Lara's client because she wanted to see if Lara was still practicing the same bait-and-switch scam with the tourmaline necklace. Hollowell pretended to have a serious and inoperable heart condition. It was just a fluke, but it encouraged Lara to tell Hollowell about her enlarged heart."

"Do Hollowell's phone records prove that she made that call?"

"No, she probably used a burner. But after that conversation, Hollowell researched Lara's condition and knew she could kill her using Narcan, which, of course, we had in our evidence storage."

Nora selected a mug from the peg board. "Did she cause the power outage?"

"That was all Mother Nature. Hollowell didn't know when she'd inject the Narcan, but after the lights went out, and people started moving around, she saw her chance. Even though she went through the lifesaving motions, she knew she couldn't save Lara. At that moment, she was too angry to feel regret."

Nora put the latte on the pass-through window ledge. As she cleaned the milk frother wand, she said, "Did she bring a Narcan bottle too?"

"Yes. To throw suspicion on Enzo. If we looked closely at him, we'd discover how he and Lara worked together to scam Lara's clients. Lara would already be dead, leaving Enzo to face the music. She wrapped the bottle in a tissue, which was why her prints weren't on it. And the empty Narcan syringe? She tossed it in a trash can in the alley."

The sleigh bells jangled. A few seconds later, they rang again. Then again.

Nora smiled. "Sounds like school is out."

"Which means lots of Harry Potter Hot Chocolates, right?"

"Yep. Good thing I restocked the rainbow marshmallows."

McCabe opened a cupboard and pulled out a fresh bag. "Andrews loves rainbow marshmallows. He keeps a box of Lucky Charms in his desk drawer."

"Let me make him a hot chocolate. It's the least I can do after he took such great care of Estella."

McCabe watched her prepare the drink and pour it into a to-go cup. As she handed the cup to him, a group of teenagers swarmed the Readers' Circle. They dropped their backpacks on the floor and sprawled onto the chairs. The air crackled with animated chatter and barks of laughter.

Nora jerked a finger at the teens. "This is why the store doesn't feel haunted. For a while, I couldn't walk past that purple chair without seeing Lara. Since then, every customer who's sat in that chair has helped me recover from that awful night."

"That's good. The only ghosts you need around here should come from *A Christmas Carol*." He kissed her, told her to call him when she was ready to visit Estella, and left.

The sleigh bells rang again, and another teen joined his friends in the Readers' Circle. He plopped down on the floor, leaned his back against a chair, and showed the other kids a book he'd picked up from the front display table.

"You guys *need* to read this," he gushed. "Seriously. Just listen."

Then he cleared his throat, opened the book, and began to read the blurb printed on the dust jacket.

The boy's voice was strong and melodic. It rose and fell as he brought the story to life. Within minutes, his friends were spellbound. The more he read, the more it felt like the whole store had gone quiet. There was a magical hush—the kind of silence that happens when people listen not just with their ears but with their whole selves.

Nora gazed into the stacks and smiled. Tomorrow, she would have to order more copies of that book, as well as a dozen others. Just thinking about placing those orders filled her with contentment.

Her tomorrows were filled with books and readers. With strong coffee and soft chairs. With food and laughter and friendship.

She looked at the teens and knew that one day, she could entrust the future to them. They would take care of the world. And each other.

Of course, they will, she thought. *They're the best kind of people. They're readers.*

Epilogue

A book is a gift you can open again and again.
—Garrison Keillor

The members of the Secret, Book, and Scone Society were gathered in Estella's living room for a Christmas Eve brunch and book exchange. Having already opened their gift-wrapped books, they were preparing to enjoy a meal of fresh fruit, Nora's crustless breakfast quiche, and Hester's scones.

The room looked like the scene from a jigsaw puzzle. A fire crackled merrily in the hearth, candles glowed on the mantel, and a wide-hipped Christmas tree twinkled in the corner. Music played softly in the background. The air smelled of fresh pine and apple cider.

Hester passed around a basket of her Figgy Pudding scones, still warm from the oven, and hurried back to the kitchen for a bowl of clotted cream.

Lulu was asleep in a green Moses basket near Estella's chair, and Nora couldn't stop staring at her.

"She looks like a little pea in a pod," she said, keeping her voice low so as not to wake the baby.

Estella smiled. "The green bodysuit is from Auntie June. If you get close enough, you can see that the little clouds on it aren't clouds at all. They're sheep."

Hester whispered, "She's *so* cute."

"You can talk in your normal voice," Estella said. "Her tummy is full, her diaper is clean, and she's wrapped up like a burrito. She's like a library book—totally checked out."

"Are you getting any sleep?" June asked.

"Some." Estella broke off a piece of scone and added a dollop of clotted cream to it. "Jack's been a huge help, especially at night. And my dad's handling most of our meals and some of the housework. I really hit the jackpot with the men in my life." She turned to Nora. "Speaking of men, are you starting to feel like McCabe's house is your house too?"

Nora shrugged. "Not yet. I've only brought a few things over from my place—mostly kitchen stuff—but I haven't had time to do anything else. Between work and getting ready for our trip, I'm fried."

"I'm glad you're going to meet your man's family. It'll make him happy, and you need a change of scenery. This trip will give you a chance to hit the reset button. When you come back, you'll see everything with fresh eyes."

Nora looked at Hester. "I don't really need a reset. I'm okay. Honestly. Despite what happened there, the bookstore doesn't feel tainted. I know this sounds crazy, but it's like the books absorbed all the bad energy. Them, and the crush of customers we've had this month. They essentially cleansed the place with holiday cheer."

"Guess I'll return that smudge stick I got you for Christmas," June grumbled.

"Don't do that," Nora said. "I'll use it on Caboose Cottage before it opens to the public."

Their talk turned to the best furniture for meeting spaces, and then June asked if Sheldon was serious about buying a wine vending machine for his Blind Date Book Club.

"Oh, he's serious. It's a cool idea, but that machine isn't cheap," said Nora. "Luckily, he doesn't need any wine for next month's meeting. He's taking a page out of Allie Kennedy's mystery series and hosting a dry bar book club in January. They're reading *Colton Gentry's Third Act*."

Hester put a hand on her heart. "I *loved* that book! Colton Gentry is the ideal book boyfriend. A smoking-hot country singer with a troubled past who cooks like Gordon Ramsay and is still in love with his high-school sweetheart? Yes, please."

"What about your smoking-hot EMT? Can he cook?"

Hester frowned at Estella. "He's not *my* EMT, and I don't know if he's any good in the kitchen. We've had exactly two dates. Your wedding and a movie night. It's tough to start dating around the holidays. We'll get together again after they're over. I've also been hanging out with Jasper. And you're not going to believe me when I say this, but I've grown fond of Hollowell's dogs."

"Has she seen them since she was arrested?" asked June.

"Once," said Nora. "Before she was transferred to the women's prison."

Estella laid a hand on the side of the Moses basket and gazed down at her sleeping daughter. "I should hate her, for what she put me through. For possibly endangering my baby. And I don't know if it's lack of sleep or motherhood or what, but I wish her life had taken a different turn. I wish she hadn't lost her parents. Or that her grandmother hadn't spent all her money on psychics. I wish she'd never read Lara's memoir or seen her grandmother's ring on Lara's finger. She caused so much chaos. For other people and for herself."

June sucked her teeth. "Why *did* Lara wear that ring instead of selling it? It was such a dumb thing to do. Like she was flaunting her scam."

"She probably didn't see herself as a scammer. She probably thought she deserved those expensive trinkets. I don't know, but she obviously loved that ring. I went back and looked at all her social media posts. She's wearing the ring in every photo." Nora kept talking as she poured more cider into her glass. "I'm sure Hollowell saw the same images. It was an unusual piece, so she must've known it was her grandmother's ring."

"See where social media stalking gets you?" Hester smirked. "Hollowell saw the ring on social media. She saw the post with Lara setting up her meditation space in their new house in Greensboro. She saw the posts about her memoir and her event at Miracle Books. Social media sealed Lara's fate."

Estella pointed at her baby. "Lulu isn't going online until she's thirty."

"Technology will be a huge part of her life—that's just the reality of her generation—but she'll know how to handle herself because you'll teach her," said June.

The other women murmured their agreement.

As Hester spooned clotted cream onto her plate, she said, "We've got a pretty clear picture of Hollowell's future, but what's going on with Zeke?"

"I'm not sure. McCabe looked into the construction company he worked for, and it's almost impossible to determine if their trash went where it was supposed to go. After interviewing the Gonzalez brothers, he believes they told Zeke to dump debris all over town, but there's no proof of their involvement. McCabe doesn't think Zeke would do anything to risk his green card status unless he was forced to do so. Still, he's facing a steep fine."

"Better than going to prison for a murder you didn't commit," said Estella.

June shook her head. "I still don't understand how Hollowell executed Enzo's murder."

Nora glanced around her circle of friends. "Do you want to talk about this stuff now?"

"I feel like we have to get it out of our systems," said June. "It's like reading a mystery novel. You need that explanation chapter before you can finish. Everything needs to make sense, or you end up being dissatisfied."

Estella pulled a face. "I usually skim that part. I just want to see what happens to the characters at the end."

"But don't you want to see if you guessed the killer's identity?"

After considering this for a moment, Estella said, "I mean, I want everything to make sense, but sometimes the main point of the novel isn't the puzzle. It's the people. Take what happened to us, for example. Nora has known there was something off about Hollowell from Day One. She kept asking McCabe to look at her in a different light, but he couldn't see his coworker the way we saw her. If people were reading this in a book, they'd probably guess that Hollowell was the killer too. The real mystery is what made her act on her impulse. That's what I'd want to know."

Nora splayed her hands. "This is why there's no such thing as the perfect book. No two readers experience a book the same way. We all want something different from our books. Escape. Entertainment. Enlightenment. Or all three."

"I'm opting for enlightenment. Tell us about Enzo, and we'll be done with this chapter."

Seeing no point in arguing, Nora said, "Hollowell knew Enzo would eventually head back to Greensboro, and she wasn't going to let him leave with her grandmother's ring. She knew it was only a matter of time before McCabe tied her to Lara's murder, which meant she needed to run. But she also needed money. Starting a new life was going to be expensive. She needed cash, and she needed it fast. That ring would be a big help."

"I'm guessing he didn't give it to her," Estella murmured as she ran her fingertips over her wedding band.

"She pulled him over at a road with no shoulder. Then she told him it wasn't safe for her to stand out in the road and instructed him to follow her to the next driveway, which conveniently led to her house. Once there, she asked him to step out of his car. After he did as she asked, she told him that she needed to take Lara's personal effects into evidence. Unfortunately, Enzo refused to hand them over. He knew something was off about the scenario and threatened to call McCabe. That's when Hollowell tased him. When he was immobilized, she was so enraged that she ran him over with his own car."

Hester dropped her scone. It hit her plate with a thud. "That's messed up."

"It was," Nora quietly agreed.

"Doesn't her car have a dash cam? And what about her body cam?" asked Estella.

Nora shook her head. "She was in uniform, but she wasn't on duty. She slapped a light bar on her personal car and turned it on when she was ready to pull Enzo over. After killing him, she rolled his body in a tarp and put it in her garage. She parked Enzo's car in there too, which was why she couldn't allow Andrews to come over. That's why she cancelled their plans."

"I assume she drove Enzo's car to where it was later found and had to walk back to town using hiking trails afterward." Estella rubbed her temples. "She was a step ahead of her colleagues for a while, but it was never going to last. She made too many mistakes. Dragging Zeke into her mess was a huge risk. No wonder she ran."

June's eyes flashed. "She *almost* got away with two murders by pinning them on a man who was breaking the law out of desperation. A man who'd do anything to become a citizen of this country. Because of Hollowell, his life is ruined. He'll be sent back to a city run by killers and drug lords. He'll be separated from his family. He'd be better off in prison."

The women fell silent. As the instrumental holiday tunes filled the room, Nora stared at the Baby's First Christmas stocking hanging from the mantel and wondered how Zeke's family would manage.

"People talk about the ripple effect of murder, but it's not a ripple," she said in a hushed tone. "It's a series of earthquakes. Murder swallows people whole. It wipes out so many dreams. We can't help Zeke, but maybe we can do something for Zeke's family."

Hester tapped her watch face. "It's not even noon. We have time."

"They need more than fresh bread or one of my knit blankets," said June.

"We can't fix this for them," Estella argued gently. "All we can do is offer a little kindness. A little hope."

The four friends worked out the details of their donations while cleaning up the remnants of their brunch. Estella brewed a fresh pot of coffee, and they returned to the living room to savor a few more minutes together.

Their cups were nearly empty when Gus entered the house through the front door, inviting a swirl of cold December air into the living room. He greeted his daughter's friends before peering down into the Moses basket.

"Isn't she the most beautiful baby you've ever seen?" he whispered, laying a hand on Estella's arm.

"Your hand feels like ice!" she squeaked. "I just brewed coffee. Go get yourself a cup." She gave him an affectionate shove toward the kitchen.

"Cold hands, warm heart," he said.

"Tell that to the mayor," Estella teased.

Gus grinned. "I will. I asked if she'd accompany me to Sheldon's book club next month. It's for singles, after all, and we're both single. If she gets there a wee bit early, I can have her all to myself."

June beamed at him. "A new relationship for the new year? How exciting!"

"What about you, Ms. June? Any special Christmas Eve plans?"

"Jasmine and Tyson are coming over for dinner. After we

eat, we're going to play board games with Sheldon while *It's a Wonderful Life* plays in the background."

Gus smiled at Hester. "How about you, Boss?"

"Jasper's mom asked me to join the family for dinner followed by the candlelight service at their church, and I couldn't be happier. I love his folks and miss hanging out with them. Every year, they do this huge Santa's workshop puzzle. It's my job to put the toy train together."

"Are you bringing them a loaf of holiday bread?"

Hester held up two fingers. "One for dinner and one for Jasper's dad. He'll make French toast with it on Christmas morning."

Finally, Gus's cheerful gaze landed on Nora. "What about you, darlin'?"

"*Jolabokaflod*," Nora said with a straight face.

"God bless you," Gus replied.

Nora let out a laugh. "I've been practicing that pronunciation all week. *Jolabokaflod* is an Icelandic tradition where people give and receive new books. Then they sit around and read. McCabe and I have decided to adopt that tradition. I had a great time picking out a book for him, and I can't wait to see what he got for me."

After Gus headed to the kitchen for coffee, the four friends talked about how much they valued simplicity during the holiday season. Intimate get-togethers like theirs were exactly what they all wanted. Big meals, lavish gifts, and raucous parties belonged in the past.

"It won't always be quiet," Estella said, gesturing at her daughter.

"No," June agreed. "But every sound she makes will be part of the music of your life. From her first word to her first phone call from college, hers will be the most beautiful voice you've ever heard."

Hester gave June a shove. "Why do you always make me cry? Can you start telling Dad jokes instead?"

From the kitchen, Gus called out, "What do you call a snowman with a six-pack?"

"What?" the women shouted in unison.

"An abdominal snowman!"

Nora, Estella, and June let out matching groans, but Hester cackled like a cartoon witch.

Lulu began to stir, so the four friends carried their coffee cups to the kitchen and traded hugs.

Nora hopped in her Banana Van and drove to the grocery store to pick up a few last-minute items. After that, she and McCabe took a walk around the neighborhood. It got dark early, but they didn't hurry home. It was magical to watch the holiday lights come on, one after another, and to see all the silhouettes in the golden glow of their neighbors' windows.

By the time they returned home, Nora was ready for a glass of spiked eggnog. She and McCabe sat on the sofa with their drinks and their gift-wrapped books.

"You first," she said.

He unwrapped the book and snorted when he saw the title. It was *How to Tell if Your Cat Is Plotting to Kill You.* He flipped to a random page and burst out laughing. "This is totally Magnum."

Nora glanced over at the sleeping tabby. "He looks pretty sinister right now."

"He'll be sleeping off that Christmas catnip until Tuesday. Okay, your turn."

McCabe's face glowed with anticipation as Nora opened her gift. Her book was called *Bibliostyle: How We Live at Home with Books.*

"I thought this might give you some ideas. One of the libraries in here belongs to the woman with the famous bookstore in Paris." He knocked the side of his head. "What's it called. Oh, Shakespeare and Company. I figured she might inspire you, even though you're the best and most beautiful bookseller in the world."

My own library, Nora thought dreamily.

McCabe took her hand. "Come on. Let's look at the space."

Even though Nora had seen McCabe's office a hundred times, he was so excited that she readily agreed.

When he opened the door, she was shocked to find the room completely empty.

Watching her, McCabe grinned. "It's a blank canvas now, and I know you'll turn it into a work of art."

"When did you get this done?" she asked.

"While you were at brunch. I had some help. Andrews and Fuentes did lots of the heavy lifting. Sheldon was here too. He helped me organize my work stuff and relocate it to my office at the station. I owe him big-time. I'll have to bring him a cool souvenir from Texas."

Nora leaned against McCabe. Her heart was so full that she thought it might burst, sending rainbow-colored glitter and tiny iridescent bubbles of happiness into the air.

She put her arms around McCabe and drew him in for a long, lingering kiss. Then she rested her cheek against his and whispered, "Thank you. For the book and the room."

He pulled away so that she could catch the devilish look in his eyes. Pointing upward, he said, "I took the liberty of adding your first decoration."

Raising her gaze, Nora saw a sprig of mistletoe pinned to the top of the door frame.

"Kiss me again," McCabe murmured. "Then we can spend the rest of the night reading."

Nora didn't think she'd ever received a more alluring invitation.

Bibliotherapy & Book Lists from *The Tattered Cover*

Books for Kids Having Nightmares
Ken Baker, *Brave Little Monster*
Stan Berenstain and Jan Berenstain, *The Berenstain Bears and the Bad Dream*
Lindan Lee Johnson, *The Dream Jar*
John Rocco, *Moonpowder*
Emma Yarlett, *Orion and the Dark*

Fiction with Travel Themes — Adult
Ben Aaronovitch, *The Rivers of London*
Penny Haw, *The Woman at the Wheel*
Michael V. Ivanov, *The Cabin at the End of the Train*
Sidney Karger, *The Bump*
Beth O'Leary, *The Road Trip*

Fiction with Travel Themes — Middle Grade/Young Adult
Danielle Binks, *The Year the Maps Changed*
John Green, *Paper Towns*
Morgan Matson, *Amy & Roger's Epic Detour*
Angie Stanton, *Royally Lost*
Karina Yan Glaser, *The Vanderbeekers on the Road*

Dystopian Climate Fiction
Octavia E. Butler, *Parable of the Sower*
Lilly Brooks-Dalton, *The Light Pirate*
Charlotte McConaghy, *Migrations*
Fernanda Trias, *Pink Slime*
Jeff VanderMeer, *Annihilation*

Classic Picture Books
Margaret Wise Brown, *Goodnight Moon*
Tomie dePaola, *Strega Nona*

Munro Leaf, *The Story of Ferdinand*
Crockett Johnson, *Harold and the Purple Crayon*
Ezra Jack Keats, *The Snowy Day*
Bill Martin Jr. and John Archambault, *Chicka Chicka Boom Boom*
Robert McCloskey, *Make Way for Ducklings*
Else Holmelund Minarik, *Little Bear*

Other Books Mentioned
Margaret Atwood, *The Handmaid's Tale*
Katherine Center, *The Bodyguard*
Zanna Davidson, *Table Manners for Tigers*
Anita Diamant, *The Red Tent*
Nina Freudenberger and Sadie Stein, *Bibliostyle: How We Live at Home with Books*
Toni Morrison, *Beloved*
Bob Raczka, *You Are a Story*
Elva Ramirez, *Zero Proof: 90 Non-Alcoholic Recipes for Mindful Drinking*
Kennedy Ryan, *This Could Be Us*
Lyla Sage, *Swift and Saddled*
The Oatmeal, *How to Tell if Your Cat Is Plotting to Kill You*
Jeff Zentner, *Colton Gentry's Third Act*